Vlada

Jacob Russell Dring

www.jrdwriter.com

KEIGN, ILLINOIS

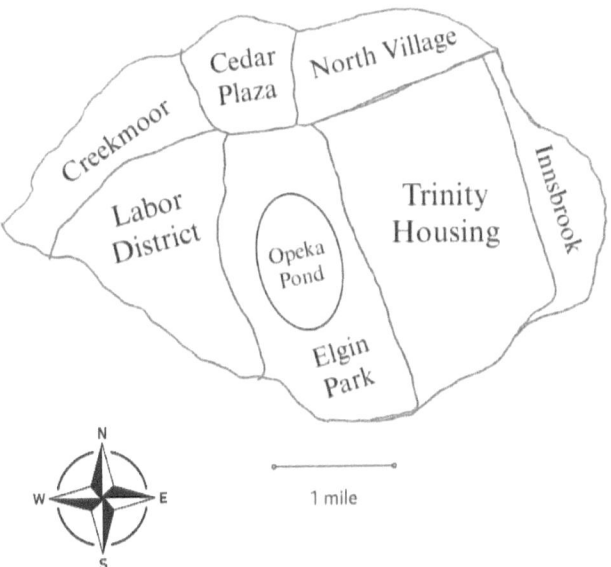

Creekmoor

Cedar Plaza

North Village

Innsbrook

Labor District

Opeka Pond

Trinity Housing

Elgin Park

N
W E
S

1 mile

"There are wounds…deeper and more hurtful than anything that bleeds."

Laurell K. Hamilton

1

Cradled by darkness and stars, she floated through the void. Pressure previously unknown, only read about, devoured every square nanometer of her body. The milliliters in her blood seemed to tighten, as if her veins were trying to break free of their imprisonment. She awaited the threat of freezing temperatures known to accompany the vacuum of space. In her subconscious, a prisoner herself, Vlada didn't understand—

How was she not dead yet?

Still, she floated. Adrift in emptiness. The kind that only existed after death, if that. But there was something different about this. It wasn't outer space. The presence of stars, somehow visible to her naked eye, in the darkness where they had no atmosphere for light to reflect off of, suddenly fizzled out. Leaving her all alone.

A new physical pressure introduced itself.

Isolation.

Complete and utter loneliness.

It was carnivorous, even predatorial, this solitude. Not the peaceful kind that philosophers wrote of. Not the serenity that Vlada had sought all her life.

She was alone, until she wasn't.

And then, she wished she was.

They began with a cut on her arm. A pre-existing slit across each wrist. The left was bigger than the right. Because, when she had made it, she had all the strength and vigor of her

1

right hand. But after sundering the tendons in her left wrist, she was unable to cut deep enough in the right. If memory served her right, and at this point memory was but a relic of her fading humanity, it was only because of this that she hadn't bled out.

Paramedics arrived.

The goddamn guard wasn't sleeping on his ass that night. Any other time, he'd be drowning in a mug of whiskey that he had smuggled through the checkpoint. Not that night. He was awake, and relatively attentive.

What Vlada had been preparing to be her last night on that godforsaken cot in a rank cell, was suddenly no more than a prelude.

Why she was there, she couldn't begin to fathom.

Because they were crawling now.

Like a thousand arachnids, but the likes of which Earth didn't know, teeming out of the darkness and pouring over her limbs. Seas of these insectoid creatures skittered across her pale skin, crawling through the scarlet slits in her wrists, widening the wounds just enough to invade. They trespassed her bloodstream, engorging the vessels with a steadfast hunger only known to the mindless.

Vlada's head whipped back, a cry of voiceless pain caught in her throat. An unseen vice grip not unlike a hand of gaunt bone snatched her long, black hair. It coiled the fibers over its skeletal knuckles and pulled. She could feel her scalp ripple as the roots were plucked from her skull.

Inside, the arachnids formed schools.

Like fish.

They no longer crawled, but *swam*.

Inside of her.

Their voracity knew no measure. They began consuming everything they could. From her blood cells to her nerves. A pain previously undocumented now propagated inside of

Vlada's body. But not just her physical form. This was the fallacy of pain. That it existed purely on the tangible realm.

Her mental state, where thoughts were processed and given meaning, now squirmed in agony. A searing, chittering pain. She could hear a thousand tiny legs scurrying across her skull, not beneath her scalp, but inside her cranium. She could hear them, feel them, eating away at her brain.

The void was not emptiness.

It was everythingness.

Everything that hungered, and ate.

Vlada wasn't just food, but a corpse within which an infestation could begin. For larvae. A utopia of maggots.

It wasn't a scream that woke her. Not her own, nor anyone else's. It was a hollow, hoarse croak of a cry. Parched, incapable of forming syllables or even a sound worth hearing outside this room, Vlada Stoia sat up as if resurrected from the dead. The second it dawned on her that she was awake, and the night terror had died away, she began coughing.

Part of her brain insisted she keep coughing, in an attempt to vomit out the infestation.

And then she swung for it.

The bottle by her bed. She knocked it over in the process. It hit the floor but didn't bust open. There was something to be said about those metallic bottles. She knew that most of the crew on deck envied them, over their comparably inferior plastic containers.

What else did they envy?

The immense strength, unmatched dexterity, enhanced metabolism, and virtually unlimited stamina.

Everything else, she doubted.

Vlada essentially threw herself out of bed, and snatched up the bottle. She uncapped it with such ease that she nearly decapitated the container. As she raised it to her mouth, it dawned on her. She had no hands—not really. Her limbs were as she remembered: not hers. Not anymore. Not for sixteen months. From shoulders to fingertip, they were biologically extraterrestrial. Almost insectoid in nature, but not like any insect on this planet.

Her bottle seemed to be empty.

More than that, she struggled to hold it now.

She didn't have any fingers to do so. Instead of hands, her arms ended in scythe-like points.

No. I have *hands. Not these.*

At least her mind worked.

And then her bottle wasn't empty.

Spiders the color of bone poured out. Into her parched throat, onto her face. They covered her, no longer teeming inside her veins, but *inside*—

Vlada woke coughing. Wet, phlegmy coughs that would be deemed fruitful if she was sick. Unconsciously, she reached for her bottle. She grabbed it successfully, now sitting at the edge of her bed, and coughed up spit and smidgens of bile onto the concrete floor between her feet. She could feel the veins and tendons in her neck strain, could feel her eyes bug and her skull seem as if it wanted to escape her skin.

Finally, after what felt like minutes, Vlada caught her breath. She upended the bottle and *drank*.

Proper fluids.

It wasn't water, though.

She didn't need water anymore, even at thirty-eight. Her impeccable bill of health couldn't be compared to other humans, though. Nor her needs. The modified fluid an amalgamation of electrolytes, cockroach milk, and synthesized genetic crystals from the same DNA that now coexisted in her body.

It wasn't the most flavor-rich substance to drink, but a

decent swig hydrated her twice as efficiently as twenty ounces of Gatorade would an adult man. Besides, Vlada's tastebuds weren't as operable as they were before the bonding process. For over a year, she had not experienced food the same way she once had.

One of many concessions.

As if having her entire arms replaced by alien organic matter wasn't flabbergasting enough, Vlada had very humanly resisted drinking 'cockroach milk.' But the company's lead xenobiologist responsible for Project Outreach had reassured her.

Or believed he had.

"As early as 2016, studies proved that milk derived from the reproductive protein crystals of the cockroach species *Diploptera functata* yield a higher nutritional potential than conventional mammalian milk."

Dr. Ginley almost laughed as he explained.

It was a scientist's mania of hope and innovation.

"I mean, the applications, if rendered properly, are immense. These protein crystals contain rich stores of essential nutrients such as oleic acid, conjugated linoleic acid, omega-3, short-chain and medium-chain fatty acids, vitamins and minerals, not only comparable to mammalian milk but leagues beyond."

On top of this, the fact was, Ginley's modified fluid, which he stamped as Apofuel, was the only thing that effectively hydrated Vlada post-procedure.

To boot, she simply didn't require food the way humans did. Not anymore. The MRE's developed by Ginley were a fraction the size of combat rations carried and consumed by present day troops, while utilizing the same ingredients in her Apofuel.

Dr. Michael C. Ginley was renowned for his work in in robotics, despite a greater passion for xenobiology. Both contributed to his selection by CyTech, the world's leading research and development company in the realm of biological enhancements. An offspring of DARPA and NASA, CyTech received additional funding from IBM upon its launch nine years ago.

Ginley had a kind face, including a zealous grin that never seemed to fade, except when the Apophid Landfall occurred eight days ago, within Keign's city limits. A year and a half after the alien genome was extracted from meteor fragments a quarter mile outside of Keign.

Designated the Keign Fragments by CyTech, the astrological debris contained active extraterrestrial DNA that would eventually form a symbiotic bond with Vlada's genes.

Even then, as grateful for his work as she was, Vlada feared Dr. Ginley's smile hadn't taken a very long hiatus. Hundreds of civilians perished when the meteor shower volleyed Keign last week, most of the casualties occurring in the Labor District. Entire office complexes were battered and the neighboring hospital was incapable of doing much good before the first hostile life forms were reported. Vlada wouldn't put it past Ginley for being excited that "they" had returned to the planet— only now in physical form—regardless of their belligerence.

She couldn't share this hype.

Since the Apophids' return, for lack of a better word, Vlada's nightmares had increased in frequency, intensity, and realism.

As if they were calling to her.

This notion was anything but encouraging. It spurred her to her feet, eagerly preparing to leave the confines of her private quarters. Positioned outside the main barracks, it was still in the same quadrant of the FOB. Erected and staffed two days after the Landfall in Keign, the Forward Operating Base was four miles east of the city. Eleven miles southwest was the Pegasus Facility, CyTech's home away from home. Their headquarters was based in Nevada, but Pegasus was both a lab complex and a campus for on-site personnel, spanning twenty-two acres.

Vlada's lodging at Pegasus made this banal ten-by-twelve room look, and feel, like a prison cell.

Despite inactive sweat glands thanks to the alien DNA, her tear ducts still functioned. Every time she slept, and dreamt, Vlada was reminded of this. So she went to the sink in the corner and washed her face with cold water, avoiding the tarnished mirror above it.

Not that Vlada's face, or even eyes, had been affected by the procedure. Only her arms, visibly. Everything else was at a cellular level.

Still, the war waged on. In her head, in her heart.

Too often she felt on the verge of defeat. A battle to convince herself that she remained human at her core.

Meanwhile, CyTech seemed dead-set on prioritizing the 'replacement.' After all, her arms had not been infused with alien genetics, but broken down and completely restructured by them. The fact didn't terrify Vlada any less, no matter how much stronger and faster she became as a result, in the months of testing and training that followed.

"Sometimes to create, one must first destroy."

Although she knew it wasn't his own to credit, hearing that quote from Dr. Ginley had not been comforting. She knew he was trying to console her, and instill hope, but it didn't work.

Ironic, considering this was Illinois.

Since the Great Chicago Fire of 1871, the city's ambitious reconstruction paved way for the state's rapid industrialization and modernized infrastructure. But never could anyone have predicted that the first undeniable extraterrestrial contact would be made in a small Illinois city.

Keign covered an area just under two-million square feet, or about forty-thousand acres. It was primarily composed of luxury apartments, exurbs, an extensive arts district, and dense office complexes. As of last year's consensus, Keign's population was 9,142. Although the bulk of its denizens worked within city limits, many commuted to jobs in neighboring towns, such as Virgil to the west and Campton Hills to the east. Others traveled *to* Keign to experience its offerings, and there were still shy of a dozen properties up for sale. Since its completion in 2025, the city's slogan was "the Reign of Keign," given the ambitious nature of its architects and investors.

Eight days ago, that era ended.

Replaced by the United States' swiftest, securest, and vastest quarantining in American history. The Q-Wall itself was a steel frame with tungsten joints and concrete filling, standing eighty feet at any given point. Had the Apophids not been so fixated on Keign's denizens, the containment might not have worked. It also helped that CyTech had already been contributing to a project called Wall-In, founded by FEMA and Homeland Security, for the last three and a half years.

It was commitments like that which made a difference.

Vlada felt she could relate, but wasn't necessarily thrilled about it. Since her procedure sixteen months ago, she often wished she had not been the patriot she was at heart. Volunteering to fight for her country and contribute in ways that no other could, or would be able to say they did. Of course, she wasn't CyTech's first choice. Or second. Or twentieth. But, to most of the personnel at Pegasus, and even a lot of the soldiers on base, she was nothing but "21X."

CyTech's twenty-first attempt to bond the Keign Fragments' alien DNA with human tissue.

None of her predecessors survived.

It wasn't until two months ago that she was given full disclosure on what entailed those procedures. Most of the subjects suffered asphyxiation, as the alien genetic material clogged their tracheas. Others died far more violently, including cranial combustion and arteriovenous hemorrhaging.

Remembering the latter made Vlada want to scratch an itch that had no specific location.

The night terror had not helped.

It wasn't even night out.

Nine-forty in the morning. Nearly two and a half hours from her scheduled deployment.

She slept in spells, never longer than four to five hours at a time. According to Dr. Ginley, she simply didn't need to. She didn't fatigue like a normal human, no matter how much she exerted. The thing was, no scientist or physician would be able to convince her that she wasn't *tired*; psychological exhaustion wasn't a myth.

Vlada was both mentally and emotionally drained.

Despite her prowess and acquired strengths, she still felt fear. It all but ate away at her. Now, for the last eight days, more than ever. For over a year, the alien DNA was just that—a genetic code to be studied in a lab, under microscopes and computer-assisted analysis. Even when the human trials began, the failures offered no elaborate insight.

It wasn't until 21X that CyTech's perception of the alien genome exploded. Although Vlada had little memory of the procedure itself, it was purportedly an extremely painful process, but ultimately successful in a manner that nobody on-site, Dr. Ginley included, could have predicted.

When Vlada regained consciousness—two days after the DNA bonded with her on a cellular level and refabricated her arms in sarcous alien matter—she spoke of vivid visions. And a knowledge that almost seemed implausible.

Ginley, being "a man of infinite acceptance," documented her statements as if they were the Word of God.

Vlada claimed to have seen "fragments of their past," including the race's presence through galaxies, but not the specifics of how they traveled or propagated. She could barely even describe their physical forms, except that their scale was "terrifying" and their bodies were "vaguely arachnid." She also mentioned a feeling of "psychological presence," marred by a lack of clarity, insinuating that they communicated via telepathy. The most coherent information she was able to relay regarded "conquered civilizations" and the word "Apophids" uttered by those that fell in their wake.

A linguist present had shown a pang of both disbelief and intrigue.

"As in, perhaps, *Apophis*, also known as Apep," Dr. Janice Wanngård had posited. Her eyes darted between the four individuals present in the lab that day. Vlada, occupying an examination slab in a sleeveless patient's gown; Ginley, opposite Wanngård and left of Vlada; two CyTech assistants assigned to Project Outreach, their nametags reading Kerry and Miguel. Then Wanngård cleared her throat and explained. "The ancient Egyptian deity of the Underworld, an embodiment of darkness and disorder, Apophis is often deemed the God of Chaos in Egyptian mythology."

"Fitting," Vlada had said, her voice a dry croak at the time, and her plump lips barely moving.

Reading a bleakness to her otherwise expressive green eyes, Ginley swiftly tried to assuage any mental discomfort that Vlada was feeling. He chuckled his way through a poor attempt of a segue, only to be cut off by the linguist. Much to his chagrin, Wanngård insisted on making her point, even if it fell on deaf ears.

"If what she says is true, then these *people* who have been conquered by this alien race speak, or have spoken, a language known here on Earth. Even if it is an extinct dialect from a hieroglyphic script, this alone suggests that humans, or dare I posit our ancestors, exist elsewhere in the observable universe."

Wanngård then chuckled herself, albeit nervously.

"Which, I mean, is just as great a discovery, if not greater, than this biological matter."

She proceeded to ogle the chitinous, dark purple and

bone-gray arms protruding from Vlada's shoulders. As if countering herself in the moment, Wanngård was held captive of her own awe. She marveled at the limbs' humanoid replication, despite the absence of regular skin or the presence of traditional bones after X-rays were performed. Right down to the imposing hands, both sleek and vaguely feminine while still immensely capable. Five digits each, opposable thumb included, but without nails, nor any need for them; the fingers ended in sharp tips of flesh-infused keratin.

"Perhaps, indeed," Ginley had said, clearing his throat.

Wanngård had begun to look away.

And then Vlada, lying there on the slab, nonchalantly flexed her right hand. Her digits curled inward, before spreading out, appearing to have no distinct joints.

Wanngård flinched, and clutched her chest.

As if she had forgotten that the arms were attached, molecularly, to a living human host. Directly before her.

Theories would always exist.

But now physical evidence was given the spotlight, and suddenly Wanngård had to submit to the unprecedented possibilities. Discerning that humanity still existed in Vlada's eyes, facial features, and seemingly the rest of her body, sans her arms, disturbed Wanngård. It both gave her a lick of hope, and instilled a fear she couldn't place.

Making others uncomfortable was the last thing Vlada Stoia wanted to do. But as she tore out of the room, devoid of a jacket or vest, it wouldn't occur to her until minutes later that she would be doing just that. At this point, it was unavoidable. She was still human, to whatever extent others would argue or deny, and she had to cope with the burden she had accepted.

A gift and a curse, if ever there was one.

Vlada would spend the next half-hour jogging around base. The 5.6-acre property had a perimeter consisting of Hesco bastions, each five feet tall. Given the uneven terrain outside the

11

FOB, and inconsistent visibility, most Marines avoided this route. Those that had tackled it made a competition for lap records during their limited downtime.

Master Sergeant Cris Gaspar had managed a minute and eighteen seconds, without any gear.

Vlada rarely ran full-speed, except during tests or training at Pegasus. The first time she did here, Gaspar curiously timed her. Although she had no interest in the number, her superior hearing caught it in passing.

Forty-three seconds.

The Marines stopped doing laps after that.

Right now, though, Vlada just wanted to jog. To feign humanity again, to remind her body and mind that a hint of relaxation was still possible, even in exercise.

Exercise she simply didn't need, physically speaking.

At first glance, if it weren't for her Apophid enhancements, Vlada wasn't an athletic specimen. At 5'8" she was taller than the average woman, but lean. Before the procedure, she had some fat distribution and even muscle definition in her limbs and stomach. The bonding process proved that the alien DNA required a lot of nutrients to manipulate her flesh and fabricate her new arms. This, paired with Vlada's new minimal diet, reduced her frame.

As if her Romanian name, which meant "to rule"—her last name, "to stand"—wasn't enough, now her appearance and physical prowess helped the "vamp" nickname stick. She wasn't fond of being compared to a vampire; maybe once upon a time, when she was younger. Her black hair, slightly sunken cheeks, distinct facial structure, large eyes, plump lips, and all-black attire didn't keep the moniker at bay.

Her arms, though…

Fused to her very human skeletal structure at the shoulders, albeit infesting her joints with an almost impervious genetic matter, the Apophid flesh provided her with superior melee weapons. Nobody on base, neither here nor at Pegasus, let alone the off-site training facilities she had visited over the last sixteen months, ever chanced a physical altercation.

Anyone with the right security clearance, or who had witnessed it themselves, could see the damage she was capable of during tests. She could pull the doors off a Humvee with ease, and hoist the engine out of its compartment. The latter took actual exertion, as a diesel V8 weighed around nine-hundred pounds, but her ability to do it at all, without additional equipment, was both astounding and terrifying. Against dense meat, such as a frozen slab of beef, her digits—claws—could maul it to shreds.

Despite the absence of a fifth finger, she wasn't hurting for it. Her dexterity tests and weapons handling were off the charts.

Before the procedure, Vlada wasn't the best shot, but she wasn't terrible, either. Although her memory was fuzzy, she had been told that she used to be an excellent archer. Going that route with her weapons training had yet aligned, however. The priority was firearms and melee.

Especially now that they had an urgent objective.

With seven whole days down the drain, Keign wasn't faring well, given their new residents. The Apophids were laying waste, but showed strange signs of reservation. Which wasn't to say they weren't extremely hostile, and beyond any form of communication.

The first force to be boots-on-the-ground in Keign was put together under the name Operation Downpour. The idea was to "put the fire out," so to speak, via two SFODs. One twelve-man team—Army Rangers, Marine Raiders, and SEALs among them—composed each Special Forces Operational Detachment.

They were given call-signs Ferret-One and Ferret-Two, ultimately deployed by helicopter at two separate infils. The helipad on the roof of Celestine Hospital, and an open space in Elgin Park. Heavily armed and capable of thorough cross-communication, the operators were also equipped with video feeds courtesy of CyTech, to record their experiences.

Then, strategically, they disseminated into Keign.

After occupying the city for forty-five hours straight, the SFODs were extracted. In a single helicopter. They had suffered eight casualties, and reported an estimated six kills. Six, among an indiscernible quantity of enemies. The intel they provided during their urgent debriefing, however, would help immensely. The video feeds recovered were equally beneficial, and those that survived were grateful.

"The footage made us feel less crazy," Gaspar had admitted post-debriefing.

Given, much of it was low-framerate and shaky, but something at ground-level was better than just the word of soldiers.

For starters, the Apophids were as Vlada had described, however obscurely. Her arms were "disturbingly similar"—one of the survivors had put it—to the enemy's flesh. Their exact physical structures varied, but a bone-white exoskeleton and dark purple scale-like formations were common, including glimpses of burgundy muscle. Although less dense than their exoskeletons, the purple scales covering skulls, shoulders, legs, and spines were believed to be a chitinous form of armor.

As such, this aspect of the Apophid anatomy was termed "panoply," after ancient Greek armor.

Appropriate, given its high density and resilience to most calibers, especially the high-velocity hollow-points operators were equipped with. This was swiftly amended, at least when looking into the near future.

The most immediate reaction involved an aerial advantage.

With no air force, the Apophids could be sniped from

sharpshooters in helos passing over the city, albeit to minimal effect. The smaller Apophids had less panoply, but kept to building interiors, whereas the larger ones roamed streets and open spaces, but were virtually impossible to kill. High-caliber rounds were effective, but the second an Apophid was injured, it retreated too swiftly for any number of snipers to finish the job.

Two days ago, three kills were achieved by helicopter.

The mid-sized Apophids had been deemed *Warriors* by Ferret-Two, given their array of appendages used as melee weapons. About the size of two up-armored Humvees—one vertical, on top of one horizontal—they were nearly impervious to rifles. That day, a pair of Warriors roaming the top of an allegedly empty parking garage were targeted by a patrolling AH-64 Apache. The pilot was cleared for engagement, and deployed a single Hydra 70 rocket that ultimately decimated the two Warriors, resulting in minimal damage to the structure itself.

That evening, the largest creature in the Apophid rank had wandered into an open area. *The* open area in the city, rivaling Manhattan's Central Park. An imperfectly rectangular 7,200-acre expanse, Elgin Park had scarce tree coverage and a pond that occupied nearly a third of its surface area.

It was here that the immense Apophid had roamed, and not to take a drink. Its true intentions were a mystery, and as easy as it was to label the Apophids "mindless beasts," there was enough evidence to suggest the opposite.

Given the call-sign *Behemoths* by Ferret-One, this rank of creature was almost the exact size of two M1 Abrams tanks, double-stacked. Arguably just as armored, with a violet crablike carapace covering the bulk of its body, including its joints, but not the raptorial scythes. A single four-foot horn protruded from the top of the skull, almost like a rhinoceros's. The arachnid arrangement of its four spiked legs provided it with a level of maneuverability that a creature that size should not possess.

An unmanned AH-6 Little Bird was in the quadrant at the time. On patrol, the armed drone was operated by a pair of controllers at a base outside Great Lakes, fifty-two miles from Keign. Utilizing its GAU-19 rotary cannon, the helo was able to kill the Behemoth in less than ten seconds, before it could evade. The GAU-19's armor-piercing .50 BMG rounds had a muzzle velocity of three-thousand feet-per-second, and a fire rate of 1,300 rounds-per-minute from its three barrels.

It was possible the Apophid hadn't been expecting that level of firepower, much less from the sky. Unless, of course, it was "taking one for the team," so to speak, as a further test to measure their enemy's capabilities.

During the Little Bird's withdrawal from the area, video feed from its surveillance mount relayed something unsettling.

Yet when Vlada watched the footage, she felt an odd pang of discomfort that she couldn't put her finger on, at first.

The slain Behemoth had been reached by two Warriors, its corpse then savagely dragged back into the city before the Little Bird could return.

This raised a plethora of questions, but they all boiled down to two possibilities. Either the Apophids shared a camaraderie not unlike men, or they ate their dead. Necrophagy wasn't rare among insects, so for humans, the latter theory was oddly more acceptable.

However, when Vlada suggested a third theory, it didn't sit well with anyone.

"They could use their dead as larviposition."

Her Romanian accent was an Americanized tinge that might've confused some people, but those in the room heard her fine. It was the word itself that threw them.

Except for Dr. Ginley, whose eyebrows immediately raised. To the other blank stares, Vlada would feel compelled to elaborate. And it became clear to them that she was more than just a weaponized test subject, but an educated person of high intellect. However, it wasn't always that way.

An orphan adopted by Ukrainian parents that lived in Romania, Vlada grew up with her natural dialect, and at a rough time for the country. But eight years after the Revolutionary victory of 1989, when she was thirteen, her foster parents were killed in a traffic collision. Her childhood memories existed with little clouding, including her relocation to the states, and application to the Army. From there, memories blurred.

Intelligent as she had always been, her exemplary knowledge about many subjects didn't exist before the procedure. At least, not explicitly. Ginley had proposed a radical theory, despite inconclusive neuro-scans. That the Apophid bonding altered her cognitive abilities, "unearthing knowledge inherent to all life on Earth."

Whatever the reason, Vlada didn't dissect the how or why. She just spoke her mind, in hopes of contributing something useful.

"The act of reproduction using dead tissue," she explained. "Common in flesh flies, which are oviviparous. Meaning they deposit their hatched larvae, or maggots, directly into dead tissue, which then act as a food source, providing nutrition for the young."

Although the others were disgusted or horrorstruck by the concept, much less when applied to malevolent alien species now inhabiting an American city, Ginley was fascinated.

"Of *course*! Yes. It's brilliant, really. They're entirely self-reliant. They eat and reproduce, but only perform the latter when they die, thus, when their existence is threatened."

The Doctor's exaggerated hand gestures when he spoke passionately about something often caused his glasses to slide down his nose. He adjusted them, and chuckled a bit awkwardly.

"Really, it's quite the perfect cycle of life. Simple, and spectacularly efficient."

Not even Vlada was thrilled about that.

It was one more tally of faults she saw in Ginley, although she still trusted him more than anyone else at Pegasus. Even the on-site psychologist, Dr. Vera Ankany, who was part of Vlada's assigned weekly routine, she trusted less. Ankany seemed genuinely interested in how her psyche was processing this whole process, but there was something very clinical and almost robotic about her interest that put Vlada off.

What didn't help that relationship was Vlada feeling the whole routine was fruitless.

Meanwhile, the Apophids in Keign were quite possibly using their very few casualties as cradles for more creatures. Which put a severe dent in humanity's attempt to rid the city of the infestation.

Although the U.S. government was dispatching its own military resources, their cooperation with CyTech had reached its peak yesterday. Operation Malathion was green-lit, named after the popular insecticide. It involved the deployment of an MSOT, composed of two five-man tactical squads—Raven-One and Raven-Two—into Keign. Apart from the voluntary inclusion of two MARSOC Raiders who survived Operation Downpour, the biggest element of Malathion was 21X herself.

Vlada would be attached to Raven-One, led by Master Sergeant Gaspar. She was to follow orders like the rest of the squad, but any insight to possible locations or maneuvers by the Apophids would be considered.

Over the last five and a half days, they spent most of their time going over the SFOD intel, theories posed by Ginley *and* Vlada, revising their gear, and conducting exercises in an urban training facility twelve miles away.

It was a lot to do in less than a week.

The bulk of the MSOT's work was performed without Vlada. Their few interactions with her were in a briefing room, where she would speak no more than three to five lines in the

18

span of an hour.

As she jogged around the FOB, she passed a few of these men with each lap, albeit over the five-foot barriers surrounding the base. Eventually she would see more, and less of the others. The ten Marines, as she had been assured, were "overqualified" for this op. Given the unprecedented nature of the op, she didn't believe that word was accurate.

However, part of her felt vaguely consoled that the two highest-ranked men in the MSOT were the Downpour survivors. Their firsthand experience had high potential, and seemed to have injected renewed confidence in the others.

Unfortunately, their faith in *her* seemed questionable at best.

Meanwhile, she had easily memorized their names, ranks, and faces, despite a clouded memory of her own past.

"This is to be expected," Dr. Ankany said, during Vlada's appointment two days ago. "According to Dr. Ginley, your abilities extend beyond the physical realm. Your perceptiveness, and memory—"

"It's just weird," Vlada had interrupted.

Although a soldier at heart, she believed she was still more human than anything. While this conviction remained a struggle, sometimes her impulsive mannerisms and reactions were evidence enough.

When Vlada's casual statement, which could have been interpreted as adolescent or unprofessional, clearly shook Dr. Ankany, she took a moment to respond.

"Right, well, be that as it may, it's still…for lack of a better word, *normal*." Ankany paused again, and then shrugged. "Given your circumstances."

She proceeded to write something down in her tablet.

On occasion, Vlada would repeat those words in her head. They irked her.

Given your circumstances.

She also didn't like that Ankany seemed to have weaponized her tablet, a better-funded replacement of a clipboard or notebook. The doctor, while highly educated and qualified in her field, was not terribly unlike the soldiers inhabiting the FOB. Vlada was sure to avoid eye contact as much as she could. She didn't want to elicit any misinterpretations.

Be they hostile or sexual.

Especially the latter.

It wasn't rare for a random soldier to whistle when she jogged past. And she wasn't deaf to chitchat, the sort of gossip that still existed in grown men defending their country. While not the only woman on base, she never wore a uniform, and was the only active-duty female—although many of the staff present didn't even consider her that.

"Part alien is all alien, far as I'm concerned," she had heard a Marine say.

Sergeant Jayson Roback.

Easily her biggest critic. And, coincidentally, one of the bigger troops on base. Large shoulders, robust arms, wide chest. But to her, a bigger head. He emanated egotism in a manner she found vile, but didn't dwell on it. If it wasn't for his persistent verbal disapproval of her, she wouldn't be so swift to judge a book by its cover. Especially in her situation.

Physically, and with a belligerent look to his eyes not present in the others, he might have scared her. Once upon a time.

Now, his likes were only an annoyance.

The criticisms and doubts among the soldiers on base weren't unbeknownst to her. Nor did Vlada not understand them. She wasn't dumb. But given the active threat four miles away, to American citizens trapped in Keign, she figured it would be smarter to focus on saving their lives than anything else.

"And you think you'll have no qualms with killing your own kind?"

She loathed the question, and that it was clearly an attempt to rile her. Much less yesterday, less than twenty-four hours from their deployment.

It came from one of three operators that clearly disapproved of her the most. There was Roback, who unfortunately belonged to Raven-One, as well as Corporal Anthony Wilson. But the Ranger that had hit her with that question was Corporal Dylan Fuller, on Raven-Two. He was like a slightly younger, smoother-faced version of Roback, although the choleric look in his eyes was no different.

"I have severe qualms with killing my own kind," Vlada had replied, staring the man in the eyes, from about ten feet away. A pause. And then: "Lucky for you."

Some of the others present had to hide their smirks and save their jesting until they were in private. Among them, Gaspar seemed the most amused, yet professionally reserved.

Vlada's defense of her humanity tallied a small win.

"That's enough, Corporal, sit down," Captain Samir Aleem demanded. Such a deep voice from such a small-statured man, his eyes not quite darker than his skin. To the particularly perceptive Vlada, he was more than just a decorated uniform and commissioned officer. There was respect in his gaze, voice, and demeanor, but at the same time he had his own doubts about her, they just weren't vocal.

Aleem was Malathion's tactical commander. He was staying here, along with Chief Warrant Officer Rose Barley, the MSOT's headquarters element. Together they would oversee real-time footage from remote-piloted aerial drones, specifically the RQ-8 Shadow, during Malathion. CWO Barley would relay intel to the MSOT when necessary, such as enemy concentration and movement.

The only uniformed woman attached to the op, and yet Barley's faith in Vlada seemed even less resolute than Aleem's.

She knew not to dwell on others' perception too much. It

was one of the all too few topics discussed with Ankany that Vlada actually agreed with. And more important now than before, with hardly an hour to go before she and the MSOT were wheels-up.

As she began her eleventh lap around the base, she noted the time. A large digital clock on the security gate booth at the front entrance indicated that it was 1100 hours.

Come noon, they would be in the air.

Out of the beating Illinois sun, at least temporarily. It was mid-April, and looking to be a warm spring for the region; warm, wet, and arguably fruitful. Just not for Keign. Something she hoped to help change, but wasn't wholeheartedly confident in her ability to singlehandedly make such momentous waves.

As she jogged, Vlada could feel the heat against her pale skin, which no longer faced the threat of a tan. Despite the detection of warmth, there was no burn, nor sweat. Her airways didn't tighten at all, she neither wheezed nor panted, and her body showed no hint of soreness.

Eyes from staff around the FOB remained a variable.

Some stuck, others were fleeting.

The uneven terrain, Vlada's height, and the scattered higher platforms throughout the base almost nullified the perimeter barriers. This was the last shred of downtime the MSOT had before deployment, so anyone that wanted to ogle her didn't hesitate.

Vlada was relatively flat-chested. There was a notable shape to her hips and backside, but she wasn't curvaceous by any means. The little muscle tone in her thighs and stomach were but faint relics of her former self.

Her long, straight, jet black hair swayed behind her without any restraint. When training, she would fasten it into a ponytail. In the past, for some exercises, she had it double Dutch-braided, so as to reduce potential snagging. Each braid reached her shoulders, but was close to the skull, and snug, unlike a ponytail. She anticipated doing this today, upon returning to her room.

Presently, Vlada wore apparel most would accompany exercise with. A snug crop-top and a pair of fitted pants, both black, except the latter rode her hips. Flat black boots in women's size nine were the only exception, and that she could run in them without a hitch was further proof of her motility. Head to toe, it was the same attire she would wear on the op. This raised criticism among the troops during yesterday's briefing, after Vlada's departure.

"This isn't exactly a day at the gym," Sergeant Marco Arrington had said, with no intention of being funny. His concerns about Vlada's combat competence were sincere, but basing them solely off her garb was what irked Ginley.

Before he could pose a retort, however, another operator from Raven-Two voiced his own skepticism. It just so happened to be Arrington's childhood friend and fellow Ranger, Corporal John Graves.

"We know she's great with a rifle, and she's got Superman arms, but is the rest of her bullet-proof, too?"

"Stab-proof," another operator scoffed. Caught in a web of correcting Graves while not necessarily disagreeing with the sentiment. Gunnery Sergeant Evan Lloyd had been assigned to Raven-One and as such would be fighting directly alongside Vlada herself. As the second highest rank in the MSOT, Lloyd felt a burden of both maintaining morale but also addressing issues.

Finally, it seemed like Dr. Ginley was given a chance to actually respond. And he did so with both passion and confidence.

"With maneuverability like hers—the marriage of gymnastics with martial arts—she proved most effective with less restraint around the midsection and, for obvious reasons, shoulders. I must remind you, although her arms are the only physically visible alterations, her entire physique, even her brain and other organs, have been affected by the bonding process. So, Vlada showing midriff is not an act of *sex appeal* or *vanity*—it is pure function."

Ginley was among the very few Pegasus staff members that referred to, and addressed, Vlada by her name. The majority, even in direct contact, used 21X. Vlada never refuted these instances, nor bickered. But she felt more seen, and understood, even if it was all a façade, when her real name was used.

It was the only information provided to the orphanage.

According to Ginley, and memories from her foster parents, Vlada's single mother had given her away before her death of trichinellosis.

All the more reason to cling, and give honor to, that name. Its own meaning was motivation enough. Vlada just had to be sure she was ruling the right cause.

"I'm more comfortable in my skivvies," one of the operators had retorted. It was half a jab at Vlada, and half an ingredient to his own personality. Gunnery Sergeant Sebastian Lebeau was a large man with an acne-scarred face, a husky voice, and a frequent smirk. Despite the latter, he didn't seem thrilled about Vlada's participation, apart from a silent gratitude that it wasn't Raven-Two she would be a part of.

Ginley had begun to respond, but Aleem verbally stepped on his toes for that opportunity.

"Then by all means, Gunny, wear your kit *over* your skivvies when you deploy in Keign tomorrow. Just keep in mind that you are not as aerobatic or agile as 21X, you carry more weight, more munitions, and you likely cannot engage an Apophid with, pardon the term, your *bare hands*."

To which Lebeau's sardonic smirk faded, he crossed his big arms, and diverted his gaze.

No other complaints were voiced.

Ginley had not informed Vlada of this exchange, but she assembled a similar scenario in her head after she left the briefing room. The operators were, by and large, predictable. She had seen them work as two separate units, communicating and engaging targets with impressive results. How that would translate in the frenzy of combat against a large, armored, non-human enemy force, in an urban environment occupied by civilians, she didn't know.

Vlada only had so much confidence in herself for that matter. Training and exercises went a long way, but nothing compared to actually being *in it*.

The Downpour survivors' debriefing said this much, and then some. Even Vlada had taken that to heart, although she doubted any of them were experiencing the level of nightmares she'd been having.

The longer she jogged, the less frequently she saw members of the MSOT. Which was a good sign—they were inside, focusing on various levels of prep for Malathion. From saying their prayers and sending messages to loved ones, to doing gear maintenance.

A final lap around the seemingly empty FOB—save from sentries and front entrance security—helped clear her head. Then she reentered the base, leaping clear over the boom gate without a hiccup in her speed, not to boast but just because it felt natural. She made a beeline around barriers, sandbags, and parked vehicles, including a single M1 Abrams tank left of the front entrance, past barracks buildings, and eventually to her own room.

A repurposed maintenance shed.

It served its role, and was the only private room on base. She couldn't fathom the level of envy from some of the soldiers, although not everyone stationed here was part of Operation Malathion.

After all, there were two tanks on base. That only one was parked in its spot when she returned meant the other must be out on sentry duty. A roaming patrol this side of Keign, to ensure that the Q-Wall was still effective. Helicopter flybys and frequent UAV surveillance provided additional lookout.

A slightly confusing and troubling speculation, as made by the SFODs during their time in Keign, and by recent radar imagery, was that the Apophids didn't seem to have any interest in escaping. No attempts at testing the Wall's integrity, trying to scale or bypass it in any way.

Their focus on staying in Keign was, while good for the rest of the world, baffling and disconcerting otherwise.

Vlada was not without her own intrigue.

Unfortunately, she had no answers or theories for that one. Which nobody was thrilled about, of course.

Despite her own version of nervousness, Vlada didn't have an uneasy stomach or the need to purge herself. Feeling sick upon waking up from a nightmare was one thing, but apart from that, she had not vomited once in the last sixteen months. According to Ginley, among the other changes to her body, she now processed waste in a far more effective and resourceful way, needing to expel it less often.

Malpighian tubules, which only exist in some arthropods and crustaceans, had formed profusely along her intestine, assisting the kidneys in removing nitrogenous waste and facilitating osmosis.

In the meantime, Vlada used neither mirror nor additional tool to rearrange and fasten her hair in double Dutch braids. She had begun this practice eight months ago, and it only took her a few weeks to do perfect it without a mirror, in the span of four minutes.

Most would take a single glance at her arms and fingers, the latter often regarded as no more than flexible claws, and assume that she wasn't capable of meticulous acts. Much less braiding her own hair. But of course, with her increased fortification of keratin, Vlada's own hair had become immeasurably strengthened itself.

"So many improvements, most of which would spell envy or even reverence from humans everywhere," Dr. Ankany had said during an early session of theirs. "Not all, of course, but so many."

Both her outright statement and the honesty that followed it, Vlada saw the validity in. However, it warranted a single response, one that she imagined could be reiterated in a different tone and interpreted comically.

It was, of course, no laughing matter for her.

"But," Vlada had responded, "at what cost?"

This was a notion that had plagued her for over a year. During her extraordinary feats while training and testing, Vlada wasn't devoid of her own awe. She felt invigorated, alive, and in ways unstoppable. This was almost never an anxiety-inducing experience, but the opposite. Her unease didn't develop until well after she had performed so remarkably.

A liberty she didn't have with Malathion.

2

Featuring a capacity of fourteen troops, plus four crew, the tiltrotor MV-75 from Bell was the perfect delivery system of both MSOT squads. A prototype that reached mass development in 2032, its capabilities were ideal for urgent long-range transport of armed forces, but would serve just as well today. With Keign only a four-mile drive from the FOB, their flight was expected to take seventy seconds, if that. Whereas by Humvees they would reach the city's southeast vector within eight minutes, although the Q-Wall offered no inlet.

No access points of any kind, to ensure its fortification.

As such, their infils had been assigned well off the ground. Raven-One was set to deploy on the Celestine Hospital helipad, and Raven-Two would disembark on the roof of the MOCA. Since the Museum of Cultural Arts had no helipad or flat enough space for the large MV-75 to land, the squad would have to fast-rope down.

While the op did prioritize threat elimination, the extraction of civilians was a secondary objective—under the right conditions. Squads were encouraged to direct civvies to Elgin Park for safe exfil, but only if the circumstances were right.

No immediate threat, to the theoretical LZ or the civvies making that move.

In a perfect scenario, the squads would escort gathered civvies to Elgin for extraction, just as they planned to themselves. Eventually. The op had no proposed duration, only an estimated window of "ten to forty hours," which was quite a gap. With Vlada in tow, that window could be halved, but nobody expressed this degree of confidence in her, apart from Dr. Ginley of course.

Despite being an active member of the U.S. Army prior to the procedure, Vlada's proficiency in live combat was a skeptical topic among the seasoned operators around her. Regardless of her extensive training, with flying colors, over the last fourteen months.

Nonetheless, a microcosm of comfort assuaged her as she and the others finalized their selections at the FOB armory.

For starters, nobody shoulder-checked her in the process, gave her a push or an elbow, or even made a snide remark. She still got the stink-eye from a few of the men—particularly Roback, Wilson, and Fuller—but it was already a massive improvement.

She suspected that, with the op officially in motion, a sense of professionalism and focus couldn't be ignored. It was just as dutiful as it was required, to maximize their own efficacy.

Of course, Vlada wasn't expecting to have drinks with the men at a bar outside of Pegasus when this was all said and done. Besides, with her enhanced metabolism and improved stamina, intoxication was impossible. No matter how hard she tried.

She couldn't fathom any man *envying* that.

Another sign of comfort in the armory was witnessing a hint of revitalization to the operators' faces. Most were bearded, but even the smallest tics of confidence, Vlada could read.

She imagined it had to do with their gear.

Everyone was armed to the teeth, but it was more than just that. Thanks to Operation Downpour intel, their arsenal had undergone major revisions. Gone were smaller calibers and hollow-points in favor of larger rounds, full-jacketed and steel-cored for maximum penetration against barriers. Or, in this case, the natural panoply of an Apophid. This extended to everyone's handgun, a non-negotiable selection.

Most of the operators didn't like going into a fight, however unorthodox the circumstances were, with a *revolver*. Even if it was considered among the three most powerful handguns available, much less with a five-inch barrel. Only Roback seemed unfazed, seeing the option as a privilege.

"I don't like it any more than you do," Gaspar had stated. He personally advised the revisions. "But fact is, nothing else compares. Nine-mil is useless against 'em, especially from a pistol. Ten-mil is a tad better, forty-cal and forty-five ACP are step-ups, but when it boils down to it, if you're breaking out a sidearm against an *Apophid*—you're already near-SOL. So might as well make it count."

Everyone stowed their gripes after that.

The Taurus Raging Hunter was a two-tone black and stainless, robust revolver with a five-round cylinder and a heavy-duty ten-pound trigger pull. Chambered in .454 Casull, the revolver could topple a charging rhinoceros—if within range. The outrageous recoil made it an unavoidable two-hander if any hint of accuracy was desired, something that the operators could all manage without much issue.

If Vlada wasn't the hybrid she had become, there simply would've been no way. The smallest among them was easily Fuller, and he himself wasn't thrilled about the mandatory change of sidearm.

Almost every one of them carried a CTA G6 as their primary weapon. Only Roback, Lebeau, and Arrington toted belt-fed machine guns, the True Velocity RM338 to be specific. A 22-pound suppressed LMG chambered in .338 Norma Magnum, giving these men and their peers more confidence in panoply penetration.

The G6, however, was in the running to be the U.S. military's newest rifle. It was no replacement of 5.56 platforms, but conquered the AK-74's efficacy on all fronts. Manufactured by CyTech Arms, the G6 was named after the Grendel 6.5mm cartridge, providing superior penetration and ranged ballistics compared to sleeker projectiles.

While none of the men enjoyed the weapon more than their favorite AR-15s, nobody denied its capabilities. Vlada had more experience with the G6 than anyone else present, and despite her lean frame, the Apophid appendages provided unmatched recoil control.

If the seasoned special operators insisted that they harbored no jealousy in that regard, they would be lying. Outright.

They might also be envious of Vlada's hearing capabilities. She could intuitively filter out high frequencies such as gunfire, muffling them while focusing on voices and quieter sounds to heighten her environmental awareness. All without the use of inner-ear protection, the likes of which anyone downrange used. The CyTech plugs sported eighteen hours of battery life and mobile charging cases. Their functionality was unmatched, except by Vlada.

She wasn't exempt from comms, though.

It helped tie her to the other men more, reminding everyone on the op that she was in fact part of the team.

Communication equipment went hand-in-hand with their CyTech ear-pro, the plugs featuring a wireless connection to a three-inch transmitter affixed to a strap on their vests. In Vlada's case, the left shoulder strap of her sports bra. It was a push-to-talk setup, a button to depress whenever someone wanted to speak. Having the transmitter at chest-height was better than the plug itself, or on a belt, as it reduced the distance a hand needed to move while holding a weapon.

Opposite the transmitter on the men's vests, and Vlada's strap, was a CyTech tactical video recorder. The same configuration used in Operation Downpour.

Their comms were specific to an encrypted frequency

privy to Operation Malathion. It could be piggybacked by both Raven squads based on proximity—a range of a hundred yards—as well as air support.

This was about as far as Vlada got to relating to the operators, apart from carrying the G6 and Taurus.

As if to reinforce this, one of her very few "supporters" spoke to her while the operators were slowly filing out of the armory. Fact was, Vlada would be going into combat with significantly less on her person than the rest of the MSOT. A belt of magazine pouches was affixed to the base of her waist, securer than others', in anticipation of her acrobatic capabilities. The Taurus occupied a drop-leg holster strapped to her right thigh, and the G6 stayed on her torso when she wasn't carrying it via a proper sling.

Apart from these items, she was comparably 'bare.'

"No Rattler?" Corporal Chuck Russo asked, pointing at the vertical rack of compact rifles left of where they stood. His expression, eyes, and body language were all much slacker than the rest of the team. Black scruff on his face, a well-groomed but dense head of hair and a healthily robust frame all indicated he belonged here. While not nearly as bulky as Roback or Arrington, Vlada had seen him in training over the last few days; she had no doubts about his capabilities downrange.

Regardless of how they perceived her, she didn't lack any faith in the others, either. They were where they were for good reason.

Russo's casual air had simply taken her off-guard a little. She tracked what he said, and shook her head.

"Unnecessary. You?"

Vlada noticed that, despite being fully kitted like the other operators, Russo was only carrying the G6 and Taurus. Not unlike herself.

"Ehhh," he skeptically exhaled, turning to size up the rack of short-barreled rifles.

32

To battle the middle-ground between a high-caliber primary and a higher-caliber handgun, the SIG Sauer MCX Rattler was offered as a secondary option. With only a six-inch barrel and a retractable stock, the compact automatic weapon could theoretically be fired with one hand. Which wasn't to negate the power of the supersonic .300 Blackout rounds, either; with the Rattler attachable to vest bands, it could be carried worry-free and accessible in emergency situations with ease.

Whether mid-reloading another weapon, or forced into close-quarters and hoping to avoid the hand-cannon.

"Tempting, for sure," Russo said. His head tilted. "But I'd rather sustain as much mobility as possible, with what we're going into. If it's even half as bad as Gaspar puts it…"

Russo clicked his tongue before shaking his head.

"Yeah, I wanna *kill* what I *shoot*. But I also wanna be able to *move*. Ya know?"

Russo looked at her arms and sort of grimaced.

"I mean, of course *you* know."

Then he bared his teeth as if to say he regretted saying so much, and walked away with the last few operators before Vlada could formulate a response.

She didn't know how she felt about that, except that she more or less agreed with what Russo had said about prioritizing movement.

Before leaving the armory, she took one last look-over at what all had been prepped and provided.

More on impulse than need. Sometimes she found herself mulling over all forms of intel and information just because she could, without mental fatigue or confusion. Her attention to detail, both in real-time and recollection, was arguably unparalleled. Months ago, Ginley had claimed she had the mental acuity of an AMD Ryzen chipset, or an IBM z16 microprocessor. Although unfamiliar, Vlada understood.

When compared to the experienced men she was joining

on this op, however, she couldn't see herself as Ginley did. And not once, even with Roback, Fuller, or Wilson, had she theorized her mind, let alone combat awareness, superior.

"Fact is, Vlada, you *are* superior," Ginley had insisted, not two days ago. "That's just...undeniable. Like, uh. Do...Do you know what color the sky is?"

"Depends on the...time of day," she had responded.

Ginley's smirk came through.

"Blue, more often than not. It's...just as undeniable as your superiority."

"I feel like...if I truly was 'superior'...I wouldn't have the nightmares that I do. The gaps of memory. The..."

Ginley had watched her form fists and grind her teeth, audibly, before she relaxed and completed her sentence. With borderline nonchalance.

"Crushing burden of an unknown pain."

This was, unfortunately, something that Dr. Ginley, in all his scientific wisdom, could not touch upon. And it was a psychological obstacle that Dr. Ankany had consistently failed to dissect.

Unless they simply weren't divulging something with her. A notion that *had* occurred to Vlada, but usually dissipated shortly after its manifestation.

Now, as the MSOT boarded the MV-75, Vlada's troubled mind compartmentalized to focus on everything immediately pertinent to Operation Malathion. From the provided demographics of Keign to better understand possible civilian presence, to the detailed map of the city and its many districts in case she got separated from the team, or to better understand their strategy altogether. Every little detail helped, and knowing she was surrounded by upper-echelon fighters, regardless of their perception of her, was comforting.

It also helped that the operators around her remained focused on the mission, instead of giving her shit. Their silence wasn't devoured by fear, at least not visibly; it was readiness, and hardened poise.

Vlada had gotten good at convincing herself of dubious concepts.

At least the starboard gunner in the helo seemed in good spirits when she boarded, behind the others. Though he remained sitting, harnessed to a rotating seat behind the six-barrel M134 minigun, the uniformed Marine was vocal.

Everyone had put on wireless headgear that dangled from the ceiling of the helo's interior, complete with a connected mic. Vlada was no exception, for communication's sake, especially as the aircraft came to life. From the six 17-foot-long rotor blades to its twin T64 turboshaft engines.

"Corporal Oscar De Hortas, at your service," the gunner announced. Most of the operators were relatively stone-faced in return, not sharing his enthusiasm. The man was in his mid-thirties, curly black hair and early gray scruff on his face. A blue and gray yin-yang patch on his right bicep indicated that he was part of the 29th Infantry Division out of Fort Belvoir, Virginia.

The man was no novice, but also not nearly on par with the operators aboard.

This wasn't something that made Vlada any less appreciative of his contribution.

After the helo had ascended, its dual-wing rotors advanced to the forward position, allowing it to fly significantly faster than other helicopters. Inside its sleek fuselage, everyone stayed seated. A row of back-to-back, suspended, modular, polymer seats on steel frames accompanied the eleven troops. Vlada included, who could've stood without holding onto anything and remained stable mid-flight. Naturally, she didn't want to draw any more attention or criticism her way than she already had, just by existing.

On that note, she looked around.

Almost unnoticeably. She didn't blatantly stare at anyone, and size them up. Her eyes, while distinct features to her face, were capable of so much with such little motion.

Considering the absence of enemy gunfire awaiting them—a parameter no modern soldier on this planet was used to—helmets were omitted. Most of the operators confessed that they felt 'naked' venturing into combat without one, but the survivors of Downpour had been thorough in their statements. Ditching their helmets provided increased situational awareness, desperately needed in Keign.

Apart from that, it wasn't like the troops were going without vests and plate carriers. Vlada being the odd one out, again.

According to Gaspar and Lebeau, during their first day in Keign, many of their men, including Gaspar himself, had been saved by their plates. Another contribution from CyTech, the military's go-to body armor since 2027—a Level IV ballistic steel plate infused with a patented layer of graphene and coated in ceramic tiling. Each plate was ten-by-eight inches, ideal for chest and back coverage, at "only" eight pounds.

The stabbing motion of a Drone's scythe-like arm would indubitably penetrate the second time, but that some operators survived a first strike was nothing shy of miracle fashion.

"Did I bruise like a banana? Sure. But no broken bones, somehow, and with some brotherly assistance we made sure there wasn't a second time. Not from *that* Drone, anyway."

Master Sergeant Gaspar had been convincing.

Besides, it wasn't like they weren't used to the additional weight. Which included loaded magazines, ammunition belts for the gunners, medical supplies, and provisions, in case they were in Keign for more than four to six hours.

As expected.

Their flight was brisk in every fashion. A linear route at an elevation of barely two-hundred feet. Merlin-Three was the helo's call-sign, its crew fully aware of the MSOT's infil strategy and their hopeful exfil.

De Horta became attentive as they approached the easternmost district of Keign. Innsbrook was a community of mid-income exurbs populated by sixty homes and an estimated 250 residents. Properties were scarce, no home on any more than half an acre. The exurbs on the other side of the city, Creekmoor, featured larger homes of greater quality, but less connected to the surrounding nature.

"Movement, I'm tracking something," De Horta said, his voice in everyone's ear. Vlada impulsively stood, pausing six feet to his right. He became rigid and attentive behind the minigun, its pivot-mount just as flexible as his seat.

The helo decelerated and began to bank, but slowly.

"Five o'clock, your five o'clock," he stated.

With the metal panel doors shut, there were three sizable windows on both sides for passengers to look out. Vlada peered through the nearest and scanned the exurbs below. From an aerial view, Innsbrook consisted of three rows of houses with very little color or style variance, but heavily populated by lush green trees. She almost immediately spotted what De Horta had seen—a single green canopy of leaves and branches shuddering in the wake of something moving beneath it.

Her eyes darted slightly, tracking the next sign of movement, now two houses farther.

Vlada's vision was crisp and clear; at the sign of motion, no matter how small and how far, she developed binocular capabilities otherwise implausible to the human eye.

"Raven, please advise, should we investigate?" one of the pilots asked.

"De Horta, clarify," Gaspar requested, from where he sat. Among the operators, only Russo and Graves had gotten up to visit the other two windows right of Vlada.

"I, I don't know, but the *trees* are moving," De Horta replied. He glanced back at the seated operators. "And I don't think a civvy is doing that."

"Sherlock over here," Wilson said, shaking his head.

De Horta returned his attention through the elevated reflex sight of the 32-inch-long minigun. The three-by-two-inch Trijicon optic provided a clear 2x magnification downrange. He began to stammer something else, but couldn't get it out before Vlada spoke.

"Drones, two of 'em, navigating around the houses, using trees for cover. They know we're up here."

Had it not been for the mic and headphones, her Eastern European accent and faintly raspy voice would've been lost to the sound of the helo.

Wilson scoffed. "How could they *know* we're—"

"It isn't exactly a paper airplane," Lloyd said.

Wilson's tongue clicked. "You know what I meant. I doubt some *creature* knows what's making so much noise."

Vlada shot him a stern look.

"Two days ago. The Behemoth neutralized in Elgin Park. *It* had an idea. The Apache taking out the two Warriors earlier that day. These things learn quick. Not quick enough for that Behemoth, but quick."

She spoke fast and to the point. No syllable wasted.

"Merlin," Gaspar said, without taking his eyes off Vlada, "take us down, sixty feet. Track the movement."

"Copy," the pilot replied. The MV-75's rotors returned to their vertical state, like a traditional helicopter, allowing it to hover. "De Horta, advise location of bogey."

De Horta tracked shaking trees and glimpses of movement. The Drone was a minivan-sized Apophid with four pointed legs and two scythe-like forelimbs capable of impaling prey. Vlada got closer to De Horta's gunner seat to peer over his right shoulder. She could see clear glimpses of the Drone's bone-white exoskeleton and purple plating, which included sharp spines protruding from its back, and a serpentine tail.

"Come around, uh, on your three now."

Vlada detected a sense of unease, even irresolution, to De Horta's voice. She noticed that the red cap over the arming toggle had been raised, but per SOP the green bulb was *not* illuminated. The minigun was still disarmed, although De Horta's profuse sweating and both thumbs hovering over the firing buttons—an M134 didn't have triggers—was still a little disconcerting.

It was one thing to hear about the Apophids, it was another to see them for yourself. Much less in a civilian environment.

Vlada glanced back, making swift eye contact with Gaspar. With the slightest head movement, she relayed her thoughts. A bit to her surprise, Gaspar seemed to read it to a T.

"Do not engage, Corporal," he said, and then stood from his seat. Half of the MSOT stood in tandem. Gaspar pushed the mic bulb closer to his mouth. "I repeat, *do not* engage, De Horta."

"C-Copy, standing by," De Horta said, easing his breath. Vlada looked back down at him; he capped the arming toggle and his thumbs retracted to where his hands held the vertical grips on the minigun. Then she stared past them, and down the linked barrels.

"Merlin, drop to forty feet and hover for five seconds," she said into her mic. "Announce when elevation is reached."

Gaspar strode forward. Lebeau stood up behind him.

"Negative, Merlin," Gaspar said, while glaring at Vlada. "Hold sixty."

"Copy."

Gaspar wrapped a fist around his mic, standing three feet from Vlada. He spoke just below normal small-room volume, knowing full-well she could hear him.

"You are *not* to deviate. You wanna contribute? *Share*."

"Let me deploy," she said, bluntly. "We cannot risk an entire squad down there, and we need to make it to our infils. This I understand. But the threats are undeniable."

Gaspar ground his teeth and shook his head. He looked back, for Lebeau, just as De Horta exclaimed.

"Four, I've got *four* targets, two more converging from the west, bearing nine o'clock! Civvies in the open, on the road, stalled vehicle. Red pickup. How copy?"

Gaspar cursed under his breath and found Lebeau.

"She wants to commit hara-kiri? Let her."

He wasn't of much help.

"We were given *one condition* with her," Gaspar said. "That she *can* branch off, but never alone."

Lebeau exhaled, angrily.

Without taking his eyes off Gaspar, despite Vlada standing right there as well, Lebeau spoke.

"I need two volunteers to join 21X on the ground."

Vlada turned away, to stare back down the path of the minigun. Before the MV-75 departed from Base, a helo retrofitted with 1600-watt loudspeakers delivered a public announcement during a Keign flyover. They declared that a military operation was underway, to eliminate the threats within the city, and advised that civilians remain sheltered, hidden, and quiet.

Anyone outside was defying this request and putting themselves at risk. Their reasons were one of three: either they were trying to reach loved ones, they were seeking supplies, or they were on "vigilante missions," trying to eliminate Apophids themselves. All possibilities were bad, but the latter was the worst, given their insufficient firepower and resources.

"Forty yards. Thirty." She sucked her teeth. "Don't have time for this."

"Fuck it," Russo said, turning away from a window to

40

stand near Vlada.

"Ditto," came a voice that made her turn her head without fully rotating. It was a Slavic accent. She remembered him, as she did everyone else. Sergeant Nikolai Popov, the rare silent storm, socially reserved but nothing shy of flying colors in performance, which eventually led him to MARSOC. He only stood out to her because he was Ukrainian, and didn't seem to wholeheartedly despise her. There remained an itch of distrust in his eyes and demeanor, but it was on a level she believed she understood.

Gaspar nodded. "Merlin, take us—"

"Permission to engage," De Horta said.

"Oh, shit, civvies are armed," Graves blurted, staring out a window behind Russo.

Below, muzzle flashes and tracers barely indistinguishable from daylight indicated gunfire along a residential road. Two men surrounding a stalled red pickup truck were engaging the approaching Drones from both directions. They were armed with semi-auto AR-15s. Their marksmanship was surprisingly good, but their firepower was simply inadequate.

Vlada jerked the heavy steel door open, which slid wide on its rails. Air whipped into the passenger hold. Unlike the others, she didn't so much as squint against the turmoil of wind, and it helped to have her hair braided.

"I see only two in the open, only two Drones in the open," Vlada said. She looked back at Gaspar, baring her teeth as she spoke. "Where are the other two?"

Gaspar finally nodded. He looked at Russo and Popov.

"Merlin, this is Raven-One, descend to forty feet. We need to deploy one rope, starboard."

"Copy."

"De Horta," Gaspar snapped. "How good is your aim?"

"I'm *set*, Master Sergeant," the gunner replied, with reinforced conviction.

Gaspar nodded. "Clear to engage. Watch your fire."

Vlada glimpsed De Horta comply. He uncapped the arming toggle, flipped it, and the second the bulb lit up green, his thumbs jabbed forward. The linked barrels spun, sounding like a chainsaw in twelve-round bursts, each dozen spitting out a fraction of a second. Her gaze returned below. De Horta was true to his word, pleasantly surprising her. He took a moment before connecting with the first Drone, westbound. But the 7.62mm armor-piercing rounds cut into the creature with great effect, significantly stalling it from colliding with the nearest civilian. The third burst cut it in half, leaving only a few stray rounds to pepper a nearby lawn.

"One target down," De Horta declared. "Tracking another in from the north, uh, eleven o'clock. No clear shot. Garnet, take us around, crescent."

"Copy," the pilot replied. He swung the helo around in a semicircle fashion, providing De Horta with a more direct view of the eastbound road.

The other Drone was now taking both civilians' gunfire, appearing to annoy it. The creature had slowed down to a near-stop about thirty feet away, if that. It used part of an abandoned SUV as cover, although its higher parts protruded above the vehicle's roof.

Meanwhile, Lebeau helped Popov and Russo deploy a weighted-core Kevlar rope tied off to a steel ring on the floor. Sixty feet of it fell below, into someone's backyard. Popov and Russo had pulled heat-resistant gloves on, and were ready to descend moments later.

"Our infils are multiple klicks west of here," Gaspar informed Vlada, while Popov and Russo listened in.

Behind them, De Horta occasionally spit out a burst from the minigun, keeping the other Drone at bay. A third civilian was inside the red pickup, attempting to get it to start.

"I know," Vlada responded. "Celestine and MOCA."

"Right. But do not try to rally with either of those. As soon as Innsbrook is clear, I want you three to take Route 80, *bypass* Trinity Housing, along the southeast Q-Wall. Base should provide UAV updates within the hour. When you reach Elgin Park, cut north, west of Opeka Pond."

Gaspar paused.

"Getting all this?"

"Crystal."

Gaspar smirked briefly; he had a photographic memory, but suspected Vlada's was tenfold as accurate. Then his face returned to pure solemnity.

"There, try to reach Raven-Two by comms. If you can't, take a vote—proceed to the Labor District to rally with Raven-Two, or north, to the Village, for us. Got it?"

Vlada nodded, backpedaling without looking. The open door to the helo within arm's reach behind her.

"We'll make it," she said, utterly devoid of doubt.

Gaspar opened his mouth to say something. Russo was standing to Vlada's left, and Popov was kneeling to her right, ensuring the rope was secure. And then Vlada's heels cleared the edge of the platform, and she plummeted toward the ground below. All three men piled near the open space to gawk down. Forty feet below the hovering craft, Vlada was crossing the backyard. She put her back to a four-foot wrought-iron fence, neighboring the next yard, and put the G6 in her hands.

"Well, fuck me," Gaspar mumbled.

"What's that, Raven?" the pilot asked.

"Uh, just maintain a hover. Ten seconds." Gaspar cleared his throat and stared at his two men. "Good luck."

"Likewise," Russo said, before sitting at the edge and scooting off, fast-roping down.

Popov simply nodded, and then followed suit.

From the ground, Vlada could see the civilians in contact, through a narrow gap between houses, about fifty feet away.

Although she couldn't physically see the Drone approaching from down the road, to her right, she could *feel* it. All of her senses indicated its proximity: smell, sound, even touch and taste. The hairs on her nape and arms bristled, and a bitterness offended her tastebuds.

These grew stronger as the Drone neared.

Behind her, Russo landed. Two seconds later, Popov joined. Together they advanced to the fence where Vlada *had* been. After a brief pause, they followed her path, walking in Vlada's same footsteps—more or less. She had longer strides, and was lighter-footed. She nearly leapt with each step, illustrating her urgency. By the time they reached the front lawn, Vlada had enthusiastically joined the nearest civilian's attempts to deter the Drone. It had crawled over the SUV, crushing it in its wake.

Vlada's G6 was remarkably more effective against the already bullet-battered creature than the civvy's AR-15. Her shots were gravely more accurate, too. Apophids had very small eyes, horizontally teardrop-shaped orbs on the side of each skull, directly adjacent their cranial panoply. Unlike the dull yellow of Warriors' and Behemoths', Drones' eyes were a milky white. They were far from easy targets, but Vlada had already shot out both of the Drones', reducing it to a wandering vehicle of pain and anger.

The civvy had already backpedaled to join his cohorts in repelling a third Drone. It had come from the north, navigating houses and yards, while trying to evade De Horta's minigun. Even sixty to seventy feet below the helo, its sound was distinct. De Horta's bursts sustained accuracy and lethality, but only when his target was in the open. He wouldn't risk firing upon a house, for fear of civilians being inside.

To this effect, Merlin-Three repositioned the MV-75 above the area in hopes of its gunner providing better support.

Behind Popov, Russo squeezed his left shoulder.

Popov advanced into the open, firing his G6. In semi-auto, the rifle spat a round with every trigger squeeze. Bullets punched into the Drone's bone-white limbs, forming chips and shallow holes. It would take much more to cripple the creature. But once Russo moved into the open, too, and began firing upon the Drone, their combined efforts made a difference.

Vlada darted toward a parked car on the left side of the road, barely twenty feet from the annoyed Apophid. The operators watched her effortlessly mount the car's roof, lowering her weapon to do so for only half a second. Then the G6 was shouldered again, and in two-round bursts pummeled the front of the Drone's skull.

Her recoil mitigation with the high-caliber assault rifle was alone enough for the men to envy.

Shaking their surprise, Russo and Popov resumed their engagement of the Drone. Four seconds later it was on the asphalt, unmoving and bleeding. Before they realized it, Vlada had dismounted the car and headed in the opposite direction, toward the red pickup.

Its engine was running, and the civvies piled into the bed, while their driver shut his door.

Vlada paused left of the truck and jerked her G6 up to aim over the hood. Without flinching, only the felt recoil of the rifle moving parts of her body—not her arms or shoulders—she fired toward a house across the street. Ejected casings clinked against the windshield, and the other operators playing catch-up were flabbergasted at her actions. Firing in the direction of a house, unable to see any sign of a threat—

The Drone suddenly emerged, leaping away from the cover that a stout oak had been providing. The canopy more than just shuddered, several low-hanging branches breaking off and leaves frenzying into the air. Vlada toggled full-auto with a finger and unloaded into the inbound creature. It emitted a high-pitched warble as it pounced in her direction, armor-piercing bullets battering at its chest and skull.

In what everyone else processed as maybe two seconds, Vlada transferred the G6 into her left hand, stepped in front of the truck, lowered her right shoulder, and pushed it against the grille. The truck's tires skidded across asphalt as it slid backwards.

The Drone landed, missing the front of the pickup by maybe ten inches. Its right foreleg collided with Vlada, and together they tumbled across a sidewalk, then someone's lawn. The creature righted itself with only a minor display of clumsiness, but Vlada sprang into the air, nimbly landing on the awning of a veranda.

Russo and Popov exchanged bewildered looks.

Then they darted forward, urging the men inside the pickup to return to their homes. Without properly responding, the driver tore off down the road.

Vlada let the sling of her rifle carry it while she drew her Taurus. The revolver blasted down at the hissing Drone, which had not attacked her as quickly as the operators suspected it would. As if it was studying her, and waiting for something.

Even as it took one round after another.

The imposing .454 Casull bullets collided with great effect. Vlada didn't just handle the immense recoil, her hands and arms dispersed it. Every shot hit its mark, although the Drone wasn't trying its hardest to evade.

Picking their shots, mindful of the house on the other side, Russo and Popov began putting G6 rounds into the creature's backside. Finally, it collapsed in a riddled heap, violet blood irrigating the grass.

"Fourth hostile at your five o'clock," De Horta said.

His voice in her ear.

The other operators turned to scan the row of Innsbrook houses behind them. The dull gray quarantine wall itself was visible beyond, clearing the tops of houses by nearly seventy feet. Initially, they had zero point of reference for this alleged enemy. And then…a tree shook. A wooden fence rattled. And, somewhere terribly close, a distinct warbling announced the alien's approach.

Vlada had long since holstered her Taurus in exchange for the G6. Russo and Popov were maybe a second or two from engaging the creature when Vlada's rifle echoed faintly eighty feet behind them. Faint only because of their ear-pro. The minivan-sized Apophid emerged from shadows provided by surrounding trees and houses, only to repeatedly flinch and recoil from multiple bullseye hits. Vlada had cut back to semi-auto, utilizing the rifle like a nail-driver.

Finally the Drone shrieked, shook its nasty head, blood and pulp gushing from an eye wound, then darted down the road. Toward the meat of Keign—Trinity Housing. The outer layer of apartments was owned by Vista Residential, easily the cheapest and most highly populated homes in the city. Rows of buildings which were three stories tall and a hundred rooms each.

If the Drone reached them, supposing the Apophids had not already raided that sector, its residents would be hopeless.

"Merlin-Three, you need to…" Vlada began, but her voice fell. She amended it, quickly—and spoke just as fast. "Master Sergeant. Target is en route to Vista. It will stay on the main road for as long as possible, as it is the quickest route. Recommend Merlin-Three take advantage and gun it down ASAP."

Russo and Popov exchanged looks again, behind her. They were equally, but quietly, surprised at how efficient she was not only in combat but comms, too. It seemed like everyone had good reason already to put a foot in their mouths and provide due credit.

"Copy. Continue on mission. Great work." Gaspar cleared his throat, and likely hand-signaled the pilot to comply.

The last thing he said before their connection dropped was: "Happy hunting, Raven-Three."

Her blood pumping and adrenaline placating, Vlada told herself to catch her breath before realizing she didn't need to. Then she turned to see Russo and Popov jog up to her, their weapons lowered and trigger fingers taking some time off.

She didn't need to look over her shoulder or up to know that the helo had already banked in the opposite direction. Russo, however, did look up—he saw the rope withdraw toward the MV-75 before the starboard minigun zipped out one burst after another, tracers cutting down toward the fleeing Drone.

"We did good, no?" Vlada asked, glancing at Popov but then staring at Russo.

"Corporal," Popov said, firmly.

Russo lowered his eyes. They fell to Vlada's briefly, before he redirected them at her arms. The violet flesh and bone-white tendons were a jarring sight each time. Only a little less now that he had encountered the far worse version.

"Sorry. Yes, right. I'd argue that much." Russo cleared his throat and looked over at Popov. "Sergeant?"

Popov nodded once. He looked around, noticing a few curtains move by windows, those that were intact, anyway. Many of the homes surrounding them appeared to have been broken into, and not by men. It wasn't that whole doors were missing, but some of the houses had been bereaved of their entire verandas, and chunks of their structures. Drones, after all, were the size of a large vehicle.

"Yes," Popov finally said. "I believe Innsbrook was already hit, but…the Drones revisited it for some reason."

"Us," Vlada said, and then gestured with her head in the direction of Vista. Popov followed tacitly, and Russo sighed before taking his six.

Half a mile away, in the air space bound to be above Vista, Merlin-Three circled as if a vulture. The starboard

48

minigun ripped out a few curt bursts, each maybe ten rounds, before the helo banked west. Its departure suggested that the Drone had been dealt with, although this didn't mean much.

It was more than likely that other Apophids existed between Innsbrook and Elgin Park.

In passing the Drone previously cut in half by De Horta's minigun, Vlada paused. She turned only her head to the left, looking at the two chunks of alien corpse in the middle of the road. Each nearly the size of a hay bale, connected only by a trail of viscous blood and gore, about seven feet long and eight across. Fragments of whitish exoskeleton and strips of dense muscle made the smear pulpy. The odor it exuded had the two operators wrinkling their noses, but Vlada appeared unaffected.

At first.

A pulsing tension flowered behind her eyes, rising into her skull. Initially standing there looking not unlike a statue, Vlada's legs suddenly wobbled and she staggered forward. Her left arm reached out and the hand clutched one of the Drone's raised, spidery, bone-white legs. It kept her from collapsing, while she caught her breath.

Behind her, the operators looked at each other before jogging to catch up. Russo reached out to touch her back but then stayed his hand.

He mustered the first syllable of her name before her sudden motion silenced the second. She turned toward the Apophid half and extended her right leg, the sole of her boot pressing into the burgundy mass between what should be its ribs. She exerted, a fraction of her voice straining out of her throat as she pushed. The lump of alien meat and bones rolled twelve feet away, bumping into an abandoned vehicle partially parked on the sidewalk.

She grunted, steadied her breath, and continued walking down the road. She had to refocus all of her senses and thoughts on the mission at hand, to mitigate the inexplicable stress in her body. The itch in her scalp, as if she could feel every neuron firing, and the odd *pull* to her blood, the cells in her veins reacting to some sort of magnetism.

Or a calling.

Not just from within her body, but fathoms deeper than any measurement was capable; than any electron microscope could observe. And yet, somehow, directly beneath the surface.

She had to resist scratching the itch.

Lest she rip herself apart.

A few tics passed across her face before she stopped twitching. Both her gait and posture became as it had been. Composed, vigilant, and determined.

Ten seconds later she stopped at a three-way intersection. The road continued onward toward the Vista complex, but it also branched right, a throughway leading around Innsbrook. Skid marks were lost on the black asphalt, but noticeable on the curb and sidewalk, where the pickup had hung a right.

From where they stood—Russo and Popov having caught up with her—the road appeared undisturbed.

"Sergeant?" Vlada said.

"We continue toward Vista, hang a left of 80, and reach the Park as Gaspar instructed," Popov said.

"Once Innsbrook is clear, were his exact words," she lackadaisically rebutted.

"Right. So we knock on every door, spend the next, what, *hour*—clearing Innsbrook? Supposing we survive to even make it to Route 80, let alone Elgin."

"I would suggest we split up, but we are only three," Vlada said. There was no attitude or heightened emotion to her voice, nor her body language. She was only stating facts. "Innsbrook needs to be secured, though. We won't make exfil in less than a day. Time is irrelevant. The safety and security of civilians is."

Popov had gotten little annoyed for a moment, but then

he just sighed and looked over at Russo. Who just shrugged.

"Your orders, Sarge," he said.

"I apologize if I have spoken out of rank," Vlada said, bluntly. "I am only prioritizing Gaspar's last order. It...seemed an absolute, but I understand that things change in the field."

"Jesus Christ," Popov said, shaking his head. He looked around. Merlin-Three was no longer visible, or audible. When he looked back at Vlada, he spoke like a rusted knife. Sharp enough to cut, but too dull to do any immediate damage. "Sometimes you speak like a fucking robot, 21X."

Russo opened his mouth to retort, in defense of Vlada. Who herself appeared only slightly offended, but not retaliatory. And then Popov shrugged and spoke again.

"But most COs do, anyway. And they're usually far less *intuitive* than you are. So, fine. We follow Gaspar's order to a T, and guarantee Innsbrook's safety. The only trouble is, even if we leave it *cleansed*, doesn't mean it'll stay that way."

"A natural risk," she said.

Popov shouldered his weapon. "Fair. Mind leading the way? *Vlada*?"

His Ukrainian accent put a twang on her name that she had not heard in a very long time. If ever, it felt like, considering this new *version* of her existence.

"My pleasure," she said, taking point.

The others followed at her five and seven o'clock, although down this road houses only lined the right side. The left was a narrow greenbelt situated between Innsbrook and Route 39. The rural highway ran parallel to Vista for about two miles, reaching the industrial district of the North Village. Or Novi, as many called it.

Vlada's nose hairs bristled and her nostrils flared at a new scent. Ignoring a fleeting flash of pain behind her forehead, Vlada's pace quickened. The operators broke into a light jog, attentive. They had quickly developed a renewed confidence in their guest's capabilities, but were still not devoid of fear.

3

Streets were dead, ostensibly lifeless. It was difficult to imagine that, just last week, Keign was a busy city of labor and culture. If the MV-75 wasn't thumping across the sky, one would suspect the buildings to creak emptily, like the strain of old trees in a winter wind—except it was April. And when the helo cut across the airspace above Elgin Park, evidence of the contrary was supplied: clusters of Apophids were strewn across the 7,200-acre green space, primarily Drones but some Warriors and a single Behemoth noticed farther away. To avoid drawing even more attention to themselves, Gaspar had instructed De Horta *not* to engage the creatures during their flyover.

Upon reaching the Labor District of Keign, populated by large and richly constructed office complexes, that "ghost town feeling" returned. Despite many of the structures still standing, others had been outright demolished by the meteor shower day one. Per the Downpour debriefings, many civilians remained trapped inside the buildings, or in hiding. The road separating the office complexes and the hospital from Elgin Park was mostly devoid of vehicles or bodies, exacerbating the ghost town vibes.

The men aboard the helo weren't blind to the fact that the city was still very much alive. It was half the reason they were going in, the way they were. Tactical teams instead of whole waves of soldiers, with explosives and the like. Urban warfare where the enemy didn't shoot from windows and rooftops but instead dismembered and devoured was unprecedented any-where on Earth.

Operation Downpour had made history in breaking that ground for the first time in human existence.

Now, it was Operation Malathion's chance to make an even greater mark: victory. Even a semblance of one could turn the tides.

The operators aboard Merlin-Three weren't pressured by the public eye or what millions of Americans, let alone billions worldwide, were expecting. Doubting. Hoping. Fearing. They had their own maelstrom of emotions and thoughts to worry about, except they didn't. They bottled those, stowed them away. Fear would be the hardest to combat.

But it could be suppressed.

Not unlike the RM338 machine gun carried by Roback as he disembarked the helo on the hospital's rooftop. Only he, Ar-rington, and Lebeau could carry the 22-pound LMG with a hint of ease. The padded buttstock pressed firmly into his burly shoulder, Roback surveyed the roof, periodically sweeping his aim in every direction. The weapon's affixed suppressor was more for gas and muzzle flash reduction than quiet, although the latter helped to make it a little less rattling for potential ci-vilians.

It wasn't like any civvies in the area would be oblivious to the military presence in their city.

The MV-75's tiltrotors had upended to provide a stable hover before it descended to the helipad below. With landing gear deployed, the engines and rotors nonetheless remained alive, in anticipation of an eager ascent.

The instant all of Raven-One was deployed.

The second squad still needed to infil on the museum's rooftop, just under two miles northeast of the hospital.

Minus Russo and Vlada, Raven-One was now a four-man squad, the same as Raven-Two, sans Popov. Their equality made the operators feel a little more at-home so far as the op was concerned, although the knowledge that three of their people—*21X* included—were already in the thick of it, miles away, wasn't necessarily comforting.

Nobody would admit it, but if anyone was going to lead a three-member unit in a hostile alien-infected residential district, they were glad it was 21X.

Gaspar was last out of the helo. He didn't leave as swiftly as the others before him only because he was exchanging brotherly words with Lebeau and the others.

"Contact, ten o'clock!" Roback all but shouted.

Having knelt twenty feet away from the octagonal helipad, Roback had his back to the nearest edge of the roof, a drop-off point that led straight down to the pavement below. It was where ambulances drove in to load or unload, as this was the ER wing of the two-story building. However, Roback spotted movement ahead of him, over a nine-foot emergency supply shed and the attached ventilation housing. The latter was half the size of the MV-75, supplying air-conditioning to the whole hospital. It was over this nine-foot structure that a Drone had climbed, hissing malevolently.

Roback's weapon fired in tight bursts.

The other operators fanned out to hit the creature from different angles, focusing on the eyes and soft spots where the exoskeleton didn't cover.

A moment after Roback indicated this new threat, two more Drones manifested at other sides of the roof. One directly behind the helipad, less than thirty feet from the MV-75's tail. The other portside, about forty feet from the helo. With scarce space between the helo's nose and the supply shed on the roof, the operators' aim had to be precise.

While Roback engaged the Drone coming over the top of the massive A/C housing, its progression stubborn despite the wounds slowing it, Lloyd fired at the other, and Wilson targeted the one behind the helo. With their luck, De Horta's gun was mounted starboard, incapable of helping in the situation.

"Get this bird in the air, Merlin!" Gaspar shouted, just as he disembarked.

The pilot lifted off as soon as Gaspar was clear of the starboard rotor. By his lonesome, Roback was able to cut down the Drone he had been targeting just as it dismounted the A/C structure. A forelimb dismembered by large-caliber bullets fell off its body, before its entire mass tumbled onto the roof in a tremulous heap.

The Drone left of the helo had to be abandoned by Lloyd so that he could assist Wilson in repelling the third creature behind it. The damn thing had come within arm's reach of swiping the helo's V-shaped tail when it finally ascended. It took both men's G6s to push it off the edge of the roof; the crashing sound it made when it landed below suggested it had fallen on a vehicle, possibly an ambulance.

"Coming to you, De Horta," the pilot declared, as he swung the helo around. His voice was in Raven-One's ears, too, suggesting they clear the helipad's proximity.

The helo was barely thirty feet off the roof when De Horta was able to line up his minigun. The linked barrels spun with a metallic whir, followed by the distinct chainsaw sound as he let it rip. Armor-piercing rounds capable of chewing through a tank tore the shrieking Drone right down the center.

"All clear, great work," Gaspar said, his chest heaving with relieved breaths. He gave Roback a firm slap on the left shoulder, and congratulatorily nodded at Lloyd. Wilson's back was turned, as he approached the parapet lining the edge of the roof, where the other Drone had fallen.

"Raven-Two, inbound to infil," the pilot said, his craft's rotors tilting forward to propel it across the sky. *"Happy hunting, Raven-One."*

"Appreciate it, Merlin-Three," Gaspar responded, and

then took his hand off the transmitter. The MV-75 became a gnat in the sky within seconds. Gaspar gestured at his team, rallying Lloyd and Roback, but Wilson's back was still turned. He called out. "Wilson, sitrep."

"Got an injured Drone, but it's still kickin'."

"Execute, then stack up."

"Wilco." Wilson adjusted his aim, training the red-dot optic mounted to his G6 on the wounded Drone below. It had crushed the ambulance it fell on, which was just a sight smaller than itself. One of its limbs had gone through the chassis in a way that seemed to momentarily immobilize it. This aided Wilson, as it was otherwise virtually impossible to deliver a kill-shot to one of its eyes.

Three squeezes of the trigger later and a divot of flesh and pulp shot out of its left eye. The creature went limp and Wilson could've sworn the stench reached him. Two stories up.

He promptly rallied with his squad.

Gaspar led them past the Drone slain by Roback, its odor almost dizzying. They circumvented the A/C housing, Gaspar recalling a stairwell on the other side of it that led down to the second story. The only other access stairwell was on the other side of the roof; straight across, it was about sixty or seventy feet, but the catwalk bridging the two sections of rooftop had been damaged in the wake of the Drone. Going the long way around wouldn't be hard, but the more time they spent on the roof, the more time they were left exposed to more attacks like the last—easily flanked.

Originally, with Vlada and Russo in their squad, the plan was to split up. Now, down to four, minus their "star quarterback," they couldn't chance it.

"On me," Gaspar said, under his breath.

He led his men into the tight stairwell, down to the landing, and then the next flight. No incident. Nor any sign of life. The base of the stairs was another story. The door was propped open by the body of a nurse. Her scrubs were pattered red. Gaspar walked past her arms to clear the open doorway, and ensure nothing was lying in wait on the other side.

"Clear," he said, although he didn't sound thrilled.

Lloyd transferred the G6 to his left shoulder and lowered his right to check the woman's pulse. But Gaspar grunted and drew his attention.

"Don't bother," he said.

Lloyd's brow shifted. "Why?"

Gaspar tilted his head. Beckoning Lloyd. With a sigh, Lloyd stood and stepped forward, peering through the open door. In addition to the hospital halls littered with dead bodies, many of which appeared partially eaten or radically dismembered, the woman in the doorway wasn't whole. Sundered at the base of her waist, and not evenly. Part of her pelvis had been ripped out, the bone and organs splayed on the gray tile floor. A lot of the gore from the wound had puddled into a jagged crater in the tile, about five inches in diameter.

The tip of a Drone's forelimb. Informally called scythes, for their shape. Although used to impale prey, not traditionally cut them, as one would use a scythe.

The woman had likely been tripped, or fell, and then crawled toward the door, but before she could get up, the Drone pinned her to the floor. And pulled away the rest.

Lloyd's chiseled, handsome face soured and turned away. The words "for fuck's sake" shaped his lips but not his voice. He looked up from the poor nurse and made grim eye contact with Wilson. Then he shook his head. Wilson's bowed briefly.

"I'm hearing some shit up here," Roback said, quietly, via comms. He was poised on the middle landing in the stairwell, his LMG pointing up. "Echoes, faint, could be more bogeys making the roof. Hunting us."

"Let 'em come," Gaspar said. "We're moving. Come to, Roback."

"On you," he replied, and held the LMG close to his body as he descended the steps.

"Take point, brother," Gaspar said, once Roback was close. He hoisted the machine gun so the suppressed barrel pointed at the ceiling; it was the only way he could wield it and comfortably clear the doorway. Once out in the hall, Roback shouldered the machine gun and knelt in the middle, fixating on one end, while his teammates funneled out of the stairwell. Gaspar went last, but the second Lloyd had joined Roback, he turned to face the opposite end of the hall, G6 shouldered.

Gaspar wasn't happy about leaving the nurse's corpse as a doorstop, but it worked.

Most of the bodies down the hall appeared to be hospital employees. Nurses, assistants, doctors. A few bodies with patient gowns on could be seen, too. Some were difficult to distinguish, given the heavy mutilations. Occasional spots of tile were caved in and parts of walls had been crushed or gouged.

A Drone could fit down these halls. Not pleasantly, by any means. But one could. And some had.

"On me," Gaspar said, and everyone but Roback, whose head became a swivel, rallied where Gaspar stood. He indicated a map mounted to the wall. It was, by no small miracle, still intact. But not untarnished—a pulpy brushstroke of blood obscured one corner.

The men parted like a small sea so Roback could periodically glance and follow. Gaspar dragged a finger across the length of the longest hallway on this floor.

"This is us. We're gonna cut right, forty feet down, check the employee area on the left, cross the hall, bypass this stairwell, and clear the patient rooms…here. Then we double back, and repeat down…there. Twice as many patient rooms, though. No Drones are gonna be hiding in a room, so we're just looking for signs of life. Attend any wounded, try to rally them in the breakroom, where there's food and water."

Gaspar thought he heard a sound down the hall, in the opposite direction they were planning on heading. He paused to press-check his G6, confirming a round was chambered.

"That said, they can clearly cram themselves down these halls. Which is why I need Roback to stand guard. Keep that pretty head on a swivel, brother. Cover our six."

"You got it."

"We're gonna make this quick. One more floor below us, including the ER. Then we head northeast, one block at a time; Base should be chiming in with a UAV update shortly. Regardless, we rally with Raven-Two at the Sheriff's Office."

No objections.

But when they assembled on Roback, Lloyd posed the one question nobody else seemed keen to ask.

"What about the others? Russo, Popov." Lloyd paused, glancing at everyone else. "21X?"

"They'll rally with either us or Raven-Two. They know the way. And I trust that *Vlada* has a better mental picture of the Keign map than myself." Gaspar looked around, believing he heard something down a hall nearby. Then he nodded at the others. "We'll see our brothers again, I assure you. On me."

Roback remained.

His knee became a pivot-point, which he used every ten seconds to cover both directions of the hall. Once stark-white and sanitized, a passageway for men and women who had dedicated their lives to helping and saving others'. Now a cesspool of spilt blood, viscera, and the lingering bacteria of despair.

Nonetheless, Raven-One advanced, unflinchingly.

For now.

4

Against the foreground of destruction that had ravaged Innsbrook over the last eight days, there were iotas of hope that only a trained eye could notice. This wasn't exclusive to Vlada's paramount vision, either. Popov and Russo realized it just the same, as they had earlier. The occasional curtain movement in windows that had not been shattered or demolished. Silhouettes, single or clustered, cowering behind them. The sort of cowardice that could not be criticized or condemned, but commiserated, given the circumstances. It also made their job easier, although they had to resist any human urge to knock on every door—those still on their hinges or in one piece—and convince the survivors inside that they were doing the right thing. A certain string of words came to mind.

"Stay here, stay quiet, stay alive."

On occasion, Russo and Popov would make eye contact with a resident through a window and simply nod once. Or show a palm, then lower it.

Keep hiding. Stay low.

Vlada, on the other hand, couldn't imagine what these people were feeling or thinking, much less when they saw her. Ambling down the street with two seemingly human soldiers in tactical gear. Vlada, a woman that by most merits had no place in combat, much less this sort of situation. But her *arms*. No attempt to hide them, and oh how disturbingly similar they were to those creatures that had sacked this city eight days ago.

Down the residential roads that the squad—designated on the fly by Gaspar as Raven-Three—walked, there was an abundance of obstacles. Navigated easily on foot, but not without a pang to the conscience. Vehicles either abandoned, stalled, or charred by fire. Many of which weren't in one piece anymore, thanks to Apophid interference. Human corpses were common, but just the same rarely intact.

After traversing a single three-hundred-foot backroad with no encounter, Raven-Three had made a few deductions. One, it seemed more obvious now than before that the Apophids were, in fact, eating much of what they killed.

Or at least they *had*.

Most of the Innsbrook mayhem they witnessed was pure aftermath. And by no means recent. Likely day-of quarantining, or the very next. It raised a curious, dreadful question—whether or not the Apophids had returned to the community 'for seconds.' Be it attacking again, routing out survivors, or just feasting on remains that scattered the roads and lawns.

As Vlada had suggested and suspected, it seemed likely that the Drones they encountered upon flying by had come because of her. She was airborne at the time, but as Vlada had come to *feel*, these creatures didn't measure distance the way humans did.

It was something incorporeal to them.

This plagued her more than any potential confrontation that awaited her and the operators. The notion that her mere presence spelled a greater doom to the residents of Keign. Could they be better off just storming the city with larger waves of trained manpower? Perhaps her being here wasn't in Keign's best interest.

Just CyTech's.

The bizarre and unnerving sensation she had felt twenty minutes ago when they decided to focus on Innsbrook suddenly returned to her. They had just reached the end of this road, which curved back east, and would circle the northern corner of the tight-knit residential sprawl. The greenbelt was now at their backs, which didn't thrill her. A cynicism about that narrow verdant metropolis nibbled at her subconscious. On their approach of the next intersection, a curved T, Vlada stopped midstride and turned her head to the left. Popov and Russo looked in that direction, not realizing she was really thinking about the greenbelt behind them.

Left of where they stood was the Innsbrook community center. A pavilion covering picnic tables and public restrooms, next to an outdoor pool, across from a parking strip and rows of mailboxes under lock and key.

If any survivors were in the area, they would have to be held up in the restrooms. Not the ideal hiding place, but considering they were brick structures with decent ventilation and city plumbing, there were worse choices.

No Apophids could be lurking anywhere, though.

Behind the community center were a row of trees acting as a sort of natural barrier between Innsbrook and the surrounding Illinois fields. Except now a greater barrier existed, the gargantuan Q-Wall. The closer they were to it, the less apprehensive they were about an Apophid encounter. Unless a theory shared by Captain Aleem was proven true—that Drones were regularly scouting the interior Wall, searching for weaknesses.

"Should we investigate the pool, restrooms?" Russo asked, at normal volume.

Vlada thought she heard something. As if her hearing had muted Russo altogether, she suddenly turned on her heel and nearly jostled him aside. He and Popov stepped away to avoid such an incident. She strode up the curb and onto the grass that eventually dove into a run-off ditch before meeting the greenbelt. From their perspective, about forty yards away, the deciduous treeline was unmoving and inactive. In the stillness that would be pocked by traffic sounds, barking dogs, and playing children on any other day, there was the faint chirp of insects and birds in the air.

Comforting, in a bucolic way, if nothing else.

"What is it?" Popov asked, quietly.

Vlada's left eye twitched as she stared at the greenbelt. One corner of her mouth flinched in the articulation of a word, although nothing came out at first.

"Fall back," she finally said, initially a whisper.

"Say again," Popov asked, taking a step toward her.

"The pavilion," she said, louder. The G6 snapped up to her shoulder. "Fall back to the pavilion. Two warriors, inbound. Eleven o'clock."

The men raised their weapons and each took a step in the opposite direction, but remained behind her.

"Go!" Vlada shouted.

Russo flinched. Popov whistled under his breath, and then turned. Russo reluctantly followed. They sprinted toward the community center, the pavilion itself equal distance to the greenbelt. They would reach it in eight seconds, but a glance behind them showed Vlada still in the same spot.

As they caught their breath under the pavilion's roof, movement snagged their attention. In two separate directions. One, fifty yards from where they stood, by the row of trees on the other side of the fenced-in pool area, nigh the Q-Wall. Low branches bent or broke around the driving force of a Warrior, leaves fluttering into the air around its imposing figure. The pale exoskeleton and purple panoply were immediately noticeable in broad daylight, even backdropped by the green and brown of foliage.

Everything else in the area offered no semblance of camouflage for an Apophid; a hint of relief for any human on the lookout. In this case, the upright Warrior was simply too big to go unnoticed, compared to the Drone. At first glance a Warrior

might be perceived as bipedal, and although its torso was elevated in an upright posture at all times, its legs were crablike.
Four pointed limbs supported its massive body, connected via
the petiole, a dense hub of muscle and sinew. From each robust,
exoskeletal shoulder emerged a *pair* of equally terrifying appendages. The lower arms ended in serrated, machete-like
limbs, composed of pure bone. The upper arms were larger ver-
sions of a Drone's scythes, more akin to a Behemoth's. Only at
a much higher elevation, and reach.

An oval skull beneath a purple carapace ended in jaws
that were undeniably carnivorous.

There wasn't a single Apophid that appeared capable of
physical manipulation of tools or the like, only barbarism.
There was a reason they had arrived via astrological debris and
not a ship or other technology.

This, of course, didn't nullify the threat they posed.

If anything, it made them more terrifying.

"Warrior inbound, from the Q-Wall," Popov announced,
transmitting it so that Vlada would know, too.

As if she needed the earplug to hear him.

Her weapon began firing at the two Warriors that had broken through the greenbelt's treeline forty yards ahead of her.
Every shot was one after the other, never full-auto. Which was
reserved for medium- to close-quarters engagements only, for
accuracy's sake. Her aim fixated on the narrow gaps in the
Apophids' exoskeletons. The 6.5mm Grendel rounds punched
mushrooming cavities into their abdominal muscles, delaying a
step here or there, but far from crippling them.

Slowly, she began to backpedal.

The charging duo of Warriors had caught Russo and Popov's attention as well. The latter had spun to use a pavilion
column as stability while firing his G6 at the Warrior approaching the pool area. One of its pointed legs snared the wrought

iron fence surrounding it, ripping the section right out of concrete and not appearing to impede the creature at all. A brief entanglement delayed it seconds later, agitating the Warrior in addition to Popov's bullets.

Russo fired a few rounds in Vlada's direction, having clear shots over her at the approaching Warriors.

"Focus on the other Warrior, Russo," Vlada demanded. There was very little emotional sway to her voice, even when she added: "Thank you."

"Right," Russo nodded, taking a deep breath. He swung around to face the more impending threat. Navigating around a picnic table, he knelt by it and deployed the G6 in a more stable state. With his assistance, they were able to injure and irritate the Warrior by the pool enough to deviate it.

This was bittersweet, as it meant they lost visual.

It seemed to be moving behind the restrooms to their right, perhaps to circumvent the community center as a whole and flank them roadside.

Meanwhile, Vlada had backed into the intersection.

The two Warriors before her had sustained some major injuries but were still steadfast. She was six rounds from requiring a reload, her mental account of what she had already fired keeping her on track. Just as they ascended the grassy slope, their forelegs leaving holes in the sidewalk, Vlada felt a jarring pain in her skull.

She cried out and dropped to a knee.

At the pavilion, Popov and Russo had changed position. Russo remained where he was to ensure the Warrior didn't fake-flank them and cut back toward the pool; Popov had advanced to the main entrance to the pavilion, an open space and concrete path leading to the road. Anticipating the Warrior's route to actually flank them.

Popov's gaze cut right, and an unusual fear filled him. Possibly their greatest tool or weapon in this fight was now down on one knee, clutching her head. The G6 was barrel-down on the asphalt, its buttstock crammed into her left armpit; the sling it was attached to had drooped off of her. Vlada's mouth was open, saliva spilling onto the pavement, but no sound came out. She was neither screaming or communicating with them, but was clearly in pain.

"Russo, Vlada is down," he transmitted. "Rally on her."

"No," she croaked.

The two Warriors had paused at the top of the slope, on the sidewalk, within twenty feet of her. They exchanged looks, chittering at each other. The creatures began to fan out, circling and very slowly approaching Vlada, whose neck muscles were beyond strain.

"Stay," she added, conviction returning to her voice.

Russo had rallied on Popov, and although he tried to keep an eye on their six, Vlada suddenly stole both of their attention.

She jerked the G6 up with her left arm, wielding it singlehandedly. In this same blink of an eye, she had meticulously thumbed the fire selector to *auto*. The assault rifle went off, blasting the nearest Warrior in the face with a burst of rounds within a ten-foot range. It trilled and recoiled. The gun went empty. The other Warrior took a swing at her, but she raised her right forearm; the serrated exoskeletal limb collided with her arm, producing a loud *thwack* sound that didn't seem to faze her. The Warrior wasn't injured, only angered. Its jaws lashed down at her, salivating and ravenous. She released the G6 and shoved her hand into its mouth, gripping something before withdrawing.

The Warrior's tongue, all two feet of it, exited with her hand. Blood and pus gushed from the creature's jaws as it backpedaled, hacking.

Vlada sank where she stood, knees bent, as the other Warrior stabbed both of its upper scythes down at her. She then sprang up, launching herself airborne. Both legs extended in either direction, essentially performing the splits midair, but her right boot connected with one Warrior's shoulder, from which she pushed off. Her left landed on the other's nose, at the edge of its panoply. It jerked its head up, like a dog catching a treat, and she rolled down its armored spine, her body unscathed from its protrusions.

Her arms extended before she completely cleared its torso, both hands gripping the base of the Warrior's right shoulder. She interlocked her digits and swung her body forward, producing momentum. As she launched herself away from its body, her hands successfully wrenched the Warrior's right scythe out of its shoulder socket. There was a sickening, wet *crunch* sound and the Apophid howled a jarring cry of pain.

The likes of which neither operator had ever heard, across hours of footage from Operation Downpour.

Despite its excavated tongue, the other Warrior suddenly charged her, scythes stabbing down in a frenzy. The one she had just wounded swung its serrated limb at her, spiked feet scurrying about the asphalt. She ducked, evading it by inches. Down on a knee, Vlada spotted her G6 and kicked it; the weapon skidded across the street, beneath the creature, and into the clear. Reducing the risk of it being trampled.

When she returned to her feet, she had brought the severed scythe around to wield like a knight's lance. Tucked under her right arm, she gave it a thrust, just as the Warrior neared. Its brethren's detached limb speared it in the chest, between two ribs. The exit wound was gruesome, as part of its exoskeleton tore away from the impact, and the force she was able to deliver. The Warrior warbled in pain and collapsed onto its side, legs twitching.

Vlada's earplug spouted activity.

She jerked around to see a third Warrior skittering around the side of the pavilion. A half-second later, Russo and Popov were retreating under its awning, firing their rifles. Vlada instinctively ducked without actually seeing her enemy swing its serrated arm, and heard the velocity of it cut the air above her. Then she kicked off the asphalt, a single backflip to evade the stabbing motion of its *other* scythe. The one still attached to its shoulder.

After landing, Vlada was essentially defenseless.

It wouldn't occur to her until later, that whatever footage might be extracted from her video recorder would likely be nauseous to study.

But, for Ginley anyway, highly satisfying.

Evidence of her abilities.

To further this proof, albeit without a shred of egotism or self-awareness, instead of continuing to evade the charging Warrior, she launched herself at it. A fraction of a war-cry broke from her throat as she reached the creature, her alien hands and sharp digits clamping onto the lip of its cranial panoply. Her boots landed on its shoulders, anchoring between the base of each limb, including the bloody stub from the one she had torn off. Once more screaming with strain, both arms flexing, she slowly tore the carapace of purple armor off the Warrior's skull. It came away in halves, leaving behind a slop of pus and blood that dripped around its bone-white skull.

Vlada landed twelve feet behind it, brandishing part of the panoply—about four feet long—like a weapon. The slime dripping from its soggy underside rolled over her hands and might've made anyone else recoil in disgust or even vomit, but Vlada was unaffected. Her gaze itself was weaponized, and her stance unyielding.

Even as the Warrior turned to face her, snarling.

The remaining scythe jabbed down at her but she sidestepped it with acrobatic grace, simultaneously flinging the chunk of panoply up at the creature. As if a chakram of irregular shape. The sharpest end of it, where it had broken away from the rest still on the creature's skull, lodged into a sliver of an exposed abdominal muscle. The Warrior shrieked in pain and madly swung both of its serrated arms at her, in a move that would've cut anyone else into thirds. But Vlada sprang into the air, *using* the flat surfaces of each appendage like steps. She dove over its snapping jaws, and landed on the asphalt behind it. Once again.

Except this time she drew the Taurus from its holster strapped to her thigh. The heavy revolver barely bucked in her hand as she fired it, a superficial betrayal of physics. The massive .454 Casull slug caught the Warrior in the petiole, blasting a nasty hole in the band of muscle. A quavering cry uttered from its jaws as it spun around, but not before Vlada put two more jarring holes in the petiole.

Back at the pavilion, Russo and Popov were shrinking back toward the pool. Their attacker had been joined by a pair of Drones that were in the process of flanking them. The Warrior, heavily wounded by their rifles, was trying to demolish the columns of the pavilion; if it could not physically reach them, it would crush them.

One of the two Drones deviated from the parking lot to instead focus on Vlada. It paused briefly to lift its drooling snout, at the faint thump of helicopter rotors. Vlada assumed it was Merlin-Three returning to base.

Then the Drone charged her from behind.

Meanwhile, the Warrior before her, exhibited a steadfastness she found less admirable and more annoying. The second it showed its face, she fired again. Emptying the cylinder of its last two rounds, she blew out one of the Warrior's eyes before the second 22-gram copper slug followed its exact path. Inside its skull, the elliptical Apophid brain was chewed through by the reverberating bullet. Its body collapsed in a heap and without thinking twice, Vlada holstered the empty revolver, spun on her heel, and faced the approaching Drone. It was already essentially upon her. She began to leap over its rapidly advancing head, but the brunt end of its skull clipped her shins. She tumbled in the air, landing awkwardly in a manner that would've broken multiple bones had she been completely human. Instead she righted herself, and could hear a myriad of sounds thirty yards away.

From the gunshots of her comrades' weapons to their back-and-forth shouting—not on comms—to the gnashing jaws of the Warrior, its grunting breaths and the occasional collision of its body against the pavilion.

Behind her, the Drone made a brisk U-turn, simultaneously crushing the hood of a parked vehicle and shattering its side windows. Vlada looked around for a weapon, realizing her G6 was too far away to reach in the time that the Drone would be upon her again, much less also reload it.

A glance over her shoulder revealed that in two whole seconds, the Drone would close the distance. No time to reload her revolver. No weapons.

"Unlike most operators, even those of the upper echelon," Dr. Ginley's voice occurred in her head, "when disarmed, Vlada still operates at peak functionality."

She felt the Drone's hot, rank, moist breath on her nape. A nanosecond later and its teeth might have sunk into her shoulders. But suddenly she tumbled left, missing its jaws by inches. The creature corrected its path without losing much time or space, thanks to the four multijointed legs. But as soon as it had her in its white-eyed sights again, Vlada was poised. Both of the Drone's scythes stabbed down at her. She caught each in her alien hands, the arms flexing and easily dispelling the creature's strength. Her thumbs dug into crevices of the limb's exoskeleton before her wrists exerted a level of vigor that trumped the Drone's own.

From the pavilion, Russo bore witness during a simple

glance her way. He nearly dropped his magazine mid-reload, while Popov emptied his own into the obstinate Warrior.

Vlada tore the four-foot-long sharp ends of the Drone's forelimbs off at the joints, hosing the asphalt with blood. She spun them around her knuckles in the manner that one would expect a ninja to, with much smaller bladed weapons, and then plunged each tip into the Drone's cataract-like eyes. Impaled and fatally lobotomized, the head dropped before the rest of its body went limp.

Without taking a breath, or looking over her 'work,' Vlada ran over to where her G6 was. She picked it up, resecuring the sling around her torso, and reloading on the run. Each bounding stride driving her closer to the pavilion at a rate that would mortify Usain Bolt.

"Changing," Popov announced, retreating to behind a pillar nearest the pool area. As he reloaded his weapon, Russo refocused and racked the firing lever on his own G6. He started pumping rounds into the wounded, bleeding, yet unrelenting Warrior. It had already demolished one corner pillar, but the sagging awning didn't assist its progression. It could only duck so much.

It began to navigate to the parking lot side of the pavilion, but paused to look in Vlada's direction. A serrated limb swung at her and, while still running, she leaned left, bent at the waist in a manner that didn't seem humanly possible. When she was upright again, she leapt onto two of the Warrior's insectoid legs, her own parted to a near-horizontal split. She jammed the muzzle of the G6 into the gap between the Warrior's ribs, and with the rifle toggled to full-auto, squeezed the trigger. The large-caliber, steel-core bullets pulverized the Apophid's muscle mass before chewing up its viscera.

The operators watched the creature begin to topple, only to crawl over two parked cars, the shattering glass and mangled steel appearing to disorient Vlada.

Instead of flinging herself off the creature, she *climbed* it. The G6 dangled close to her body, on its strap. The Warrior snapped its salivating jaws at her, but almost like a lizard she crawled around its torso, from its chest to its back. She used both the gaps in its exoskeleton and the gunshot wounds inflicted by her comrades as placements for her feet. As the Warrior spun around—shrieking, biting at air, and swinging its limbs, all futilely—Vlada formed two fists and screamed. She swung them down, inward, and both fists plunged into the Warrior's bright yellow eyeballs, pulverizing the vitreous tissue. Divots of pus and optical fluid dripped from the sockets, coating her hands up to each wrist.

The Warrior's legs sprawled out and its body sank to the asphalt. Vlada excavated her fists and dismounted in two steps. She flung chunks of Apophid eyeball tissue from her hands, partially grateful she had no fingernails to dig gunk out from under.

Leaving the pavilion, the front of which could collapse at any moment, the men rallied with Vlada.

"That was...fucking insane," Russo panted.

"I second that," Popov said, unsure where to look.

But a mere twelve feet behind Vlada, the Warrior began to regain its stance. A long tongue flicked out of its jaws to lap at the dripping wounds of its eyes, likely trying to clean itself. What good this could do, none of them understood.

"As if you need eyes to see," Vlada snarled back at it.

Russo and Popov exchanged uneasy looks.

She then unholstered her revolver, ejected the cylinder with one hand, and reloaded it via a moon-clip in the blink of an eye, all while looking back at the Warrior.

"How are you on ammo?" Popov asked.

"Quite fine. Yourselves?"

"Manageable, but that goddamn thing sponged a lot of

rounds. Even now, it's still breathing. How do you propose killing it?"

"A Casull to the eye socket, scramble the brains," she said simply, brandishing the Taurus.

But then, to their puzzlement, she holstered the revolver. Popov opened his mouth to speak, to address this, but she was quick to explain herself.

"When the time is right," she said, approaching the creature as it turned toward them. "But first, we take a shortcut."

"A shortcut to what?"

Vlada paused, within arm's reach of the towering Warrior. She glanced back at the men, who intelligently kept their distance.

"Ensuring Innsbrook is clear of Apophids," she said, the simplicity of the statement confusing them further. Upon reaching the Warrior, she shouted: "Keep an eye and ear out!"

Part of Vlada wanted to smirk at saying 'eye.' She doubted the operators would find much humor in it. And then she leapt onto the creature, just before it began swinging its arms at her. The scythes were useless now; she was just too close. Evading its jaws, she flung herself onto the creature's head, and punched both fists into its devastated eye sockets.

The Apophid let out a warbling shriek of pain, one that likely echoed for miles. It was a sound that reached Russo and Popov through their ear-pro, filtered like white noise, muffled but not devoid of power.

They didn't have to interrogate her to deduce her intentions. She was torturing the creature, knowing—or justifiably believing—that the Apophids cared about their dead, for whatever reason. And if not that, maybe they would rush to one's aid. The men's faith in this strategy began to wane, and they wondered if maybe Vlada just wanted to make the beast suffer.

And then they emerged from the woodwork.

Two Drones skittered into view from across the way. One

crawling over the roof of a house with startling nimbleness, its spiked feet leaving gouging holes in its wake. The other crashed through someone's fence, shrieking as it reached the intersection left of the pavilion.

Vlada heard her comrades engage the creatures with their weapons, and a glance back their way revealed another threat: a Warrior, beelining down the main road, about a hundred yards and closing. She jerkily removed one fist from the creature's eye socket, but only so she could plunge her entire arm into the other. Down to the elbow, anyway; her clawed digits manually scrambled the Apophid's brain, and could feel its composure melt beneath her. As the Warrior crumbled lifelessly, she dismounted and landed twelve feet away.

The G6 returned to her hands and she shouldered it, tracking the Warrior through her optic.

Sixty yards out.

She began firing, semi-auto, planting rounds in the area of its face. Incapable of landing a surefire eye-shot from this range, with its nonlinear movements, didn't keep her from trying. A Drone kept at bay by Russo's gunfire suddenly crossed the Warrior's path. It paused for half a breath to literally kick the smaller Apophid away from it, with an arachnid leg, and the Drone rolled once before righting itself. It snarled at the passing Warrior, then returned its focus to Russo.

Vlada was three-quarters through her magazine when the Warrior closed the distance. She released it, sling keeping the rifle close to her, and drew the Taurus. The Warrior's left scythe dropped, but she side-stepped it with what anyone else would have called shocking ease. Then she raised the revolver and it roared with a bright muzzle flash. The heavy bullet scored off a chunk of the Warrior's skull, missing the eye by a few inches. The creature nonetheless recoiled, and began to turn, but still brought its other scythe down.

Evading this one seemed to have been anticipated by the

Warrior, because it simultaneously brought its serrated limb around as a counter. Vlada raised her left forearm in the literal last split-second; the contact was jarring for her, but her alien flesh held, visibly unscathed.

Irate, the Apophid roared down at her before cocking both scythes up for a final attempt to impale its enemy. To any human, this would not have been perceived as taking several seconds. But Vlada's superior speed and acuity allowed her to discern every small movement, before making her own.

She righted the revolver and fired, a round catching the Warrior's left eyeball. Its scythes dropped anyway, but with dampened strength and momentum. She spun out of the way, revolver still raised at the end of her straightened arms, and she fired again, up at the Warrior's throat. Although not completely exposed, the jugular featured gaps in the exoskeleton for muscle flexibility, providing the Warrior with limber head movement.

Another trigger squeeze punched a second .454 Casull round into the creature's throat. Its head drooped on its neck and blood gurgled out of its jaws. Vlada ducked under an arching leg, reached the nearest curb, turned, and fired again. This time the bullet hit its eye socket at an angle that instantly pulverized the brain.

The operators watched the Warrior drop like a sack of bones and meat.

They had slain the two Drones at a rate that surprised even themselves, especially after the whole pavilion ordeal. When Vlada met up with them by the intersection, the men ensured their rifles were fully loaded and clear of jams. Partially depleted magazines were stowed for last-resort use.

Popov began to speak but Vlada said "wait."

He didn't object.

Ten seconds passed. No sounds.

"Permission to make a suggestion," she said, looking at Popov. Respecting ranks.

"Fuckin' hell, speak freely."

Russo smirked.

"Proceed to Route 80, per Gaspar's instructions. I have it on…good faith…that Innsbrook is safe. For how long, I can't say. Possibly less and less, the longer we stay here."

Popov nodded. He looked at Russo, who just shrugged. Popov sighed, shaking his head. When he looked back at Vlada, his eyes scaled her, head to toe and up again. He wasn't ogling her; he was in silent awe. Everything she had performed, the acrobatic feats and close-quarters combat with creatures eight times her size, and she looked virtually untouched. Even her double Dutch braids appeared as if they had not moved an inch during all of that.

"On one condition," Popov finally said.

"I'm all ears."

"*You* take point."

A corner of Vlada's mouth twitched into a minuscule smile.

5

An undeniable absence of hostile activity, or any indication of Apophid presence, should come as a relief. But it didn't. As Raven-Three took the sinuous Route 80 away from the exurbs of Innsbrook and around one end of Trinity Housing, it occurred to them why. The cheaper Vista Apartments to their right were densely populated, capping around four-thousand residents across twelve buildings. Or, once upon a time. It was quite viable that the Apophids had already razed the structures and reduced their population to half.

Vlada feared this much.

It was all too quiet as they trekked Route 80, a four-lane highway that would take them all the way around Trinity Housing, and then Elgin Park.

She hated to admit it, and as such avoided voicing her thoughts, but this terrible deduction made sense. Eight whole days in Keign gave the Apophids, especially the more meticulous Drones, an abundance of time to wreak their havoc.

To hunt, to feed.

And, however they were doing it, to reproduce.

If Vlada's theory about larviposition had any reality here, the true number of Apophids in Keign could be nauseating.

Still leading the three of them down the center of the road, Vlada paused less than they did. Every fifty or sixty steps, either Popov or Russo would slow, sometimes even stop midstride, to study the apartments to their right. Interspersed trees, never taller than ten feet, lined the edge of the outer property, permitting scattered visibility. The nearest building was about three-hundred feet from the highway; a noise barrier didn't begin until the Prosperity development, which was about that same distance from Vista.

Far edgier than Vlada, given their imperfect awareness, Popov and Russo would occasionally think they spotted movement in the direction of the apartments. Or heard a sound worth scrutinizing. After the first of these 'mistakes,' despite continuing to make them solely out of human reflex, Vlada assured them there was nothing worth their time. Nine times out of ten, whatever they had seen or heard, was a survivor blundering as they scurried from one building to another, or to a car, be it for supplies or simply to relocate.

Deciding to trust her heightened senses, and their own reluctance to investigate Vista Apartments, the men conceded.

As they neared the Prosperity development, a greater sense of dread entered them. While still not nearly as upscale as Optima Suites, the Prosperity Townhouses were a major step above Vista, in terms of quality living. Four fifty-room buildings surrounded an outdoor recreation center complete with a pool, basketball and tennis courts, a dog park, and a cyclist trail.

With a rough population of six-hundred people, it was less daunting from a crisis management perspective than Vista, but still disconcerting. More so given the noise barrier, which disrupted their view of the housing. Even if Vlada's hearing was leagues superior than Popov and Russo's, she didn't have X-ray vision.

Vlada implicitly acknowledged this by stopping once they reached the beginning of the barrier. A hundred feet ahead was a bridge that passed over Route 80, with two exit ramps on either side of the road.

She looked at her comrades, and when gestured solely with her head in the direction of the apartments. Still respecting rank, she would defer major decisions to Sergeant Popov.

"Look, I don't know if you share a telepathic link with the Apophids," Popov said, "but Russo and I aren't psychic. Use your words."

Though meant more as a wry jest, Vlada seemed to have taken offense. She abruptly stepped into Popov's personal space, herself an inch taller than him, although Russo had three inches above both.

"The last thing I want in my mind is an Apophid," she sneered. "I deal with them enough every time I shut my eyes."

Russo stepped forward, brandishing a palm.

"I don't think he meant anything by it," he said, in defense of an unexpectedly shaken Popov. "We just, we should communicate with our words more. Be clear."

Vlada pulled away with a scoff. She stared forward, her eyes scanning the small bridge and its uneventful, but lightly shaded underpass. Few vehicles occupied Route 80, but those that did showed signs of severe damage, were overturned, or were simply empty. Bodies were scant; those left behind had been severely mutilated, and likely eaten pieces at a time.

"I'd sooner let Roback set up camp in there," she said, referring to her mind, "than an Apophid."

Russo gave Popov a firm squeeze on the shoulder. They exchanged nods before Popov advanced to stand to Vlada's right.

"I apologize for offending you," he said. "Frankly, I cannot fathom the effects that Outreach has had on you. But…after twenty failed subjects, you pulled through. So…clearly, you are special. I don't think anyone can deny this. Even Roback or Fuller. Fuller, I know, is just jealous. Hell, I think most of us are. But…"

"But whatever burdens you're dealing with," Russo butted in, joining them, "we can hardly imagine, and we don't want to. That said, you're all we got right now, so we really need to be as direct with each other as possible."

Vlada sniffled once and nodded.

She finally faced them.

"Yes. Absolutely. I appreciate your...attempt to understand. I admit, I do feel like I don't belong here. But fighting amongst you has made me feel less of an outsider."

"*Amongst* us?" Russo said, scoffing but smirking. "Lady, you're *well above* us. Roback can eat shit, if he saw what we did back there, he'd be kissing your feet."

Popov smiled blandly and shook his head.

"Maybe there *is* something to be said about...a *little* discretion."

He walked past them, toward the bridge.

While Vlada in part agreed with Popov, she also cherished Russo's transparency. She didn't wholeheartedly agree she was *above* any of them, but understood his perspective.

"Hold up," she said, calling to Popov, who stopped and turned to look back. She extended her right arm, behind Russo's head, a single long, tapered alien finger pointing at the noise barrier. The vinyl-shingled gable rooftops of the Prosperity Townhouses could barely be seen over the top of the barrier. "I think we should consider continuing along the inside of the soundwall. If a civilian is in danger, scaling or circumventing it won't be efficient from this side."

A great point, one that had occurred to the others but they were too apprehensive to bring it up. And for practical reasons.

"Gaspar instructed we *bypass* Trinity, sticking to Route 80 instead," Popov said. A pause. "But I do agree with your sentiment."

"I understand. I just thought it should be addressed."

"Corporal, care to weigh-in?" Popov asked.

"Uh, not really. *Sergeant*. See, that's the thing. This is uncharted territory for most of us. But not for Lebeau and Gaspar. Seeing as how they're also the tip of the command chain, at least during our stay in lovely Keign, I say we respect Master Sarge's input to a T."

There was no denying that Vlada's point was sound.

Still, orders were orders and Russo had an even more convincing case: that Gaspar had been here before, maybe not in this region, none of them knew this much, but he had experience in Keign where they had zero. This counted heaps on top of his already superior rank.

Vlada respected this. Even if she didn't agree with the instruction.

"Then it's settled," she said. "We keep along Route 80, bypassing Trinity altogether. Recommend we take a brief hiatus to the top of the bridge, though, just to put eyes on Prosperity. For a moment."

Popov nodded, considering this.

"Alternatively," Vlada offered, "I can zip up there to have a look, and report back."

"Option two, if you make it quick," Popov said.

"Want to time me?" she asked, already stepping away. A tiny smirk graced her otherwise stern face, a subtle reminder that, despite her circumstances, she was still human. Where it mattered.

Then the smile vanished. She turned and sprinted toward the off-ramp. The men watched in awe of her speed. The world record 100-meter dash was just over nine seconds. Vlada made ninety in seven. Uphill, too. And with gear.

Popov and Russo exchanged bewildered glances.

Vlada's stomach undulated with intense breaths, instead of her chest—evidence of superior diaphragm control. That said, her posture remained perfectly erect; she wasn't tired or short of breath.

She looked in both directions. Down the road, leading into the Trinity Housing development, which composed nearly a third of Keign's surface area. Prosperity covered less acreage than Vista, but a narrow greenbelt converted into a forest park divided it from Optima. Designated the Emerald Ribbon, this small park featured a sinuous footpath and scattered benches but was much less marked by civilization than Elgin Park.

From where she stood, Vlada could see the treeline between a gas station and McDonald's, left of the road. To the right were the townhouses themselves, mostly blue and white clapboard siding.

The road between Prosperity and the amenities this side of the Emerald Ribbon appeared lifeless. Fewer vehicles burdened the path than Route 80, or those that wound through Innsbrook. Suggesting, to Vlada anyway, that most of the residents had stayed home during Downpour, and since. Whether this meant that the majority of Prosperity's population had been killed within the community, or that the Apophids had not gone on a thorough hunting spree, was up for debate.

Not every square foot of Keign had been traversed and surveyed by the SFODs. Aerial surveillance over the last week helped fill in some gaps, but not all.

"You have eyes-on?" Popov asked, in her ear.

Vlada pressed her transmitter, but took a second longer to gather her response.

"Affirmative. Very still. Recommend we continue. Will rally at the underpass."

"Copy. Advancing."

Popov and Russo jogged toward the bridge.

Ten seconds later, Vlada decided her report had not changed. She turned away from Prosperity, only glancing in the direction of the Emerald Ribbon in the process. For a split-second, she thought she saw movement. She paused midstride, and found herself returning to the road. She went so far as approaching the gas station, and then stopping within ten feet of the curb. She slowed her pulse and breathing, narrowing her perception to sight and hearing alone. But fixated on the treeline of the park, about two-hundred yards away. Squinting, she could see the subtle sway of underbrush, likely against the wind and nothing else.

The longer she stared, the more Vlada felt as though she was being stared *into*.

An unnerving sensation, as if an overpowered magnet was attracting the iron in her blood, calling her to the trees. She even took an additional two steps, before the toe of her boot collided with the curb and she freed herself from the hold. When she staggered back, Vlada silently acknowledged this lapse of self-control. It was immensely demoralizing, but she wouldn't dare share it with anyone else.

Maybe only Dr. Ginley—supposing she made it out of Keign alive.

Preferably no later than tomorrow.

"We've reached the underpass," Popov radioed. "Where are you?"

Vlada shook her head. She pulled away, and returned to the off-ramps. Her hand raised to press the transmitter.

"En route. Proceed. Will—"

A Drone shrieked as it cleared the noise barrier to her right. From fifteen feet off the ground, it leapt. Vlada shouldered her G6 and spun to face the barrier, backpedaling at the same time. She managed only two shots before the Drone landed. The asphalt beneath it was torn up in the process, and the Drone exerted a shocking display of maneuverability after an initial tumble. Vlada pumped out four more rounds into the creature's head and chest before her back collided with the bridge's parapet. She rebounded off it, but not toward the road; she ducked into a controlled tumble, down a grassy hill adjacent to the exit.

Skittering into the parapet itself, the Drone was less nimble in its own reorientation. Below, the two men witnessed the end of this: the creature landed on the road before them, not twenty feet away, with a loud and uneasy sound. Two of its legs compound-fractured, momentarily crippling it. Chunks of asphalt sprayed out on impact, but the men were unhurt.

Immediately they began firing at it, while Vlada righted herself at the base of the hill. Upon springing to her feet, Vlada radioed them.

"Cease fire, cease fire."

Reluctantly, Popov complied. He and Russo nonetheless backed up. Vlada approached from behind the wounded, somewhat immobilized Drone, but at an angle. She walked along the Jersey barrier to her right, G6 shouldered and Taurus in one hand.

"It's wounded, and we have it dead-to-rights," Popov radioed. "Care to explain why we're not—"

"Same reason as before," Vlada said, just shy of shouting it. Without comms.

"Fuck's sake," Russo said, not thrilled by her blatant dismissal of sound containment. Given their gunfire, and the noise made by the Drone, it didn't really matter. But having creatures like these roaming around, potentially hunting them, made him a little jittery.

Once Vlada was within normal-volume earshot, Popov's rifle still trained on the Drone, he addressed her without comms.

"You want to see if others are in the area, lurking about. By torturing this one, no?"

"Essentially," she admitted.

Though wounded, with two opposing legs severely broken, the Apophid was still ambulatory. Even if it didn't seem intent on proving this. Why it didn't try to relocate or defend itself was anyone's guess. The milky white eyes appeared to fixate on Vlada as she neared, tracking her movements.

"Russo," she said, without looking at him. She had slowed her pace, but still approached the others, maintaining a ten-foot berth from the Drone. "Without raising your rifle, do you think you can hit its left eye in a single shot?"

"Uh…copy."

"I am a better marksman," Popov boldly said. "I can."

"Negative," Vlada said. "It knows you're in charge. The smallest movement from you will trigger it into action."

Russo scoffed, more offended by Popov's statement than Vlada's.

"It can't *know* he's in—"

"But it does," she said simply. "Now when I say 'fire,' take out that eye, and both of you clear the underpass. Together."

"Our side or yours?"

"Yours," she said, and stopped walking. The Drone began to produce a low hissing sound, and excess drool poured out of its ghastly jaws. "Fire."

Russo's G6 snapped up. He fired three-quarters of a second later. Just at the fringe of the Drone appearing, in Vlada's eyes, to acknowledge his movement. The shot rang true. They all watched as a divot of blood and pus spit out of the Drone's left eye socket. It let out a shriek of pain and spite. Vlada holstered her Taurus and leapt onto the creature's elongated skull, its spiked panoply making her footwork precise.

Popov and Russo backpedaled clear of the underpass. They trained their weapons on the exit ramp leading up to the road where Vlada had been. Waiting; anticipating what they hoped would be nothing. The last time Vlada pulled this strategy on a whim, it had worked spectacularly.

Not that they enjoyed the experience.

While she sank her fist, just past the wrist, inside the Drone's socket, it let out a series of trilling cries.

Time passed.

By the eleventh second, Vlada was done playing rodeo. She drew her Taurus with her free hand, and dismounted the bucking Drone. The instant she landed, she fired a round into

86

its socket, and its brain turned to mush inside the skull. Its body went limp. She holstered the revolver and fingerless-whistled; the men assembled.

"I guess we can rest easy, then," Russo said. "On not taking the inside of the wall."

"Mostly," Vlada said. A fragment of her childhood memories still floating around her subconscious couldn't resist the *Aliens* reference. One that neither of the men seemed to grasp, although she didn't let it linger for long. "Either there aren't any other Apophids in the area…and this Drone was just a straggler, if not a sentry…*or*—they've wised up."

"Already," Russo said, half question and half statement. "From Innsbrook to here."

Vlada shrugged. "They're smarter than everyone seems to be giving them credit for. And I don't say that admirably."

"One might argue," Popov said, "that because everyone seems to have underestimated *you*, there's a relation."

"Right," Vlada scoffed. She looked Popov dead in the eye, resisting the urge to once more step up to him. At first, there was a sense of frustrated humor in her voice and disposition. As she spoke, though, these dissolved in exchange for self-resentment. "The thing is, unlike the Apophids, I *do* have something to prove. Everyone wants to insist they don't, because the second you have something to prove, it eradicates one's sense of self. Takes away autonomy, introduces puppet strings."

The men could perceive a very human anger rising in her voice and eyes. Not toward them, but herself. It was a quiet pyre in her dark green eyes.

"Unfortunately, *I* have the burden of being CyTech's marionette. I might function independently, but the reputation of the company, and possibly the lives of this MSOT, rely on *me*. I have more faith in men like Roback, Wilson, and Fuller than I do my own heroism."

She uttered the last word as if it was painful.

Then she turned away from the operators and reached out with her right arm. She singlehandedly clutched one of the dead Drone's intact legs, and slowly dragged it behind her. She hauled it up the exit ramp, while Popov and Russo followed in silence. Then they watched her manually wrench its broken limbs off its thorax, tossing one onto the bridge like a discarded, useless car part. She used the other to impale the creature through its mouth—something that could not have been done in a fall, or by any human.

Afterward, she shook her arms and with surprising ease flung Apophid blood completely off them.

"A warning, of sorts," Vlada said, banally, as she passed the bewildered men.

"I think I like her more now," Russo whispered to Popov, who recoiled.

Naturally, Vlada had heard him. Not that she showed any indication of this.

"Perhaps not the wisest idea," Popov suggested, catching up to her as they proceeded down the ramp and along Route 80. "Wouldn't want to provoke these things any more than they already are."

"Case in point," she said, cradling the G6. "They're inherently provoked. Just by being on Earth, let alone surrounded by humans. Imagine you've crash-landed on an alien world, in a city of strange structures and scurrying insects the size of cats. Relatively speaking, that's what it's like for them. Except of course, Apophids are innately hostile. They eat, reproduce—likely asexually—conquer, and spread."

"You're charming," Popov said.

"I'd like to believe I once was," Vlada said, without looking at him. Her eyes briefly climbed into the sky, leaping from one uneven stratus cloud to another. "But then I thought I could make a change, and become something *more*, for the betterment of this country. For people."

88

"You regret volunteering," Russo said, on her other side. His voice was sapped of excitement, like he spoke reluctantly.

"At times. Especially when I sleep." She cleared her throat, and her eyes focused on the road ahead. It gradually curved around the now-visible towering glass and steel constructs that were the Optima Suite luxury apartments. "But no, I am not an Apophid puppet. Or shell. I have some memories, before Outreach. And I still have wit, to some degree. A personality that isn't allowed the spotlight at all, so I keep it under wraps."

She tapped the camera lens affixed to her right shoulder strap, lightly with the tip of a finger.

"Good thing this has no volume, huh?"

The men exchanged looks before speaking, and had to talk over each other before one took the lead.

"Having run combat exercises with you at Pegasus, if only for a few hours total," Russo said, "I knew you were more than a husk. So much more."

"Easy, Romeo," Popov said.

Russo scoffed.

"I appreciate that, I do," Vlada said, though not smiling. She even made brief eye contact with Russo before looking over at Popov, and then forward again. "I apologize for oversharing. Anyone else, barring maybe Gaspar, would tell me to zip it. But I'm not an Apophid; I'm not the enemy. And I'm done feeling like an alien, despite these." She raised her arms.

"I don't ask for pity, and I can't expect the rest of Raven-One or -Two to perceive me the way you now do, or have. I only hope we can make a difference this time around."

Some time passed before a response.

"We will," Popov said, sounding uncharacteristically optimistic. "If nothing else, we'll ensure the Apophids know they can't—"

Vlada sibilated, sharply. Popov's brow furrowed and he

clammed up. She stopped walking, midstride in the road, and looked around. The men exchanged glances, then shrugs. Russo asked "what is it" in just above a whisper.

"That sound," she said. "Like a whir. But faint."

"We don't hear anything," Popov said.

Then their earplugs bristled with activity. A two-tone chirp preceded a feminine voice.

"Barley here. An RQ-8 Shadow is at three-hundred feet. Innsbrook and Vista have been mapped, showing no signs of Apophid activity. We've got you on Route 80, south of Optima. How copy?"

Popov looked at Vlada, awe on his face. It occurred to him and he seemed just as shaken as Russo had been when they watched Vlada rip the panoply off a Warrior's skull with her hands.

"Three-hundred feet," he said, quite plainly. Without transmitting. "The RQ-8 is near-silent at a hundred. How could you *possibly* hear that?"

Vlada didn't respond. Not verbally. She just shrugged— her very non-human shoulders.

"How copy, Raven-Three?" Barley repeated.

Popov straightened. He pressed his transmitter, bypassing the order to satisfy his own, and likely the others' as well, curiosity.

"You've spoken with Raven-One?"

He could imagine Barley sighing and rolling her eyes before Captain Aleem greenlit her answer.

"Affirmative. Raven-One has cleared Celestine. No casualties. Minimal contact. Raven-Two is still at MOCA, encountering heavy resistance but no casualties to date."

A pause, while the two operators exchanged hopeful nods, and a small sense of reassurance manifested on Vlada's own face. One that both men seemed to acknowledge, too.

"Raven-One has updated us with your orders. Sitrep?"

"Good progress, ma'am," Popov replied. "Major resistance in Innsbrook, but all threats eliminated. No casualties. Should reach Elgin in the next ten minutes."

"Copy. Advise you expedite. Merlin-Three reported Apophid activity around Opeka, albeit forty mikes ago, during RTB. They're hip to your presence."

Popov shook his head.

"Requesting alternate routes," Vlada transmitted.

A long pause followed, while the men looked at Vlada. Hand off her transmitter, she acknowledged them.

"If we take the Diamondback Trail, we may be able to reach Raven-Two sooner than if we try to rally with One on the other side of the pond."

Very slowly, Russo nodded.

"Suggest you take Sycamore Boulevard, between Optima and Elgin. Head north, toward Novi. Hang a left on Mayfield Drive, MOCA is your third right. By then, Raven-Two should be clear of the area and heading west, to the Sheriff's Office, at the end of Mayfield."

A moment.

"Another option is taking the Diamondback Trail in Elgin, which runs parallel to Sycamore. After passing the pond, hang a left, and then take your first right. That footpath leads directly onto Mayfield."

"Solid copy, ma'am," Popov said, while looking at Vlada with a very, very small smile of confidence.

"Will relay an update on Elgin in five to ten minutes. Over and out."

That distinct two-tone chirp punctuated Barley's transmission.

"How should we proceed?" Popov asked.

"You're asking *me*?" Vlada said, touching her chest.

"You can't be surprised by that."

Vlada shook her head once. She then turned it, staring

down the road. The curve ahead triggered her detailed memory of the road map of Keign, shown during their briefing. The southeast corner of Elgin Park, adjacent Sycamore Blvd, was hardly five-hundred feet away.

"I say we take Barley's first rec," she said. A moment later she nodded, as if indicating that she had mulled it over too quickly, and then confirmed the choice. When she explained, for once, she made consistent eye contact with the two men. "The Diamondback Trail would put us *in* the Park, which doesn't offer much cover. If a Behemoth, or even two, caught us in the open, there's no telling what could happen."

"Wait, you're telling me you can't just snap your fingers and make that fucker disintegrate?" Russo asked, brow furrowed.

Vlada let a little smirk slip.

"Afraid not, Corporal."

"A damn shame."

"Quite," Popov said. Then he cleared his throat, gestured forward, and the three continued their trek down Route 80. "So we take Sycamore, which I believe has a soundwall between it and Elgin."

"Copy," Vlada said. "We should book it, though. Barley pressed urgency."

"I imagine you could make it to the museum in the time it'd take us to reach Sycamore," Popov said. "Barring any interference."

"Possibly, but this isn't a race."

"Naturally, I don't mean that you should leave us in the dust. But perhaps you taking lead, as a forward sentry, might be helpful."

"I'd rather not chance the Apophids flanking me to ambush you two. This isn't a bad horror movie. We won't split up, unless a CO demands it."

Russo side-eyed Popov as if to say "I'm falling in love"

but stowed any word of it.

"In that case," Popov said, and began to break into a jog. "You'll just have to deal with a light run. Like your casual laps around the FOB."

On her other side, Russo picked up speed as well. He could easily outrun Popov, but like Vlada said, this wasn't a race. They might subtly challenge each other's speed so as to preserve urgency, and discourage shirking. But there would be no sprinting ahead, or at all.

"But feel free to lead by a few strides," Russo suggested. "Help us maintain pace."

"Wilco," Vlada said, as if taking orders from the Corporal. She had no rank herself, and although some of the operators in the MSOT regarded her as less than a Private, let alone a Corporal, Popov and Russo now perceived her as something flexibly higher. More akin to a Master Sergeant or Lieutenant, but under certain conditions.

Once they were, optimistically speaking, within the presence of Gaspar again, his orders took precedence. But until then, they qualified her input just as highly as his.

After breaking the bend, Raven-Three found themselves hanging a smooth right onto Sycamore Blvd. Named after the canopies of large sycamores visible over the top of the noise barrier to their left, along the east edge of Elgin Park. Though narrower than Route 80, which continued across the south end of the Park, Sycamore was still a spacious three-lane road. Two lanes flush with Trinity Housing, northbound, and one lane oncoming, toward Route 80.

Increased traffic could be expected on this road, especially farther north, but their initial perspective yielded an easy walk. No abandoned vehicles or indications of catastrophe. Unfortunately, the first few hundred feet of Sycamore were on a slight incline. Once they summited, they would be able to see the latter stretch of the 2.5-mile road, and whatever awaited them. Their fingers were crossed, so to speak.

Hardly a minute after walking down Sycamore, Vlada whistled quietly and pointed up. The three of them stopped jogging, but kept walking. A moment later, they heard what was now a distinguishable two-tone chirp, followed by Barley's voice.

"Apologies for the delay, we made contact with Raven-One. They were separated during an engagement with the enemy outside Creekmoor. No casualties to report, but their progress has been stunted."

She took a breath before proceeding. Popov and Russo accepted the time to have small swigs of water, while Vlada took a sip of her Apofuel. She figured now was better than later, not wanting to explain to the men what its ingredients were.

"Right now we have you on Sycamore. Maintain course, but be advised—the road ahead shows massive signs of wreckage, and a few Drones on patrol, but nothing more. Elgin is teeming with activity, including two Behemoths and four Warriors."

She let that sink in.

"Any idea what they're doing?" Vlada asked.

A few seconds passed. Likely Barley exchanging words with Aleem on how to structure a response.

"The Captain and I are wondering if you might have any input on the matter."

Vlada sighed. "Of course," she said, without radioing it. Then she pressed her transmitter. "Negative. Only a *hunch* that they're privy to my presence, and that I am both something familiar, and something very hostile."

"Right. Uh, copy. Just avoid Elgin, and attempt to rally with Raven-Two. Proceeding to make contact with them now. Over and out."

Faintly, Vlada could hear the RQ-8 Shadow fade as it flew north. At an altitude of three-hundred feet, it was silent to anyone below. Except Vlada, and she suspected, the Apophids. An eleven-foot unmanned drone with a fourteen-foot wingspan, the Shadow was likely piloted by a crew in the back of a specialized Humvee right outside the southeast Q-Wall, providing Aleem and Barley with a live aerial video feed of Keign.

With a stamina of six hours before refueling, the MSOT could expect consistent updates for the first leg of their stay in the city.

Had planning and resources been better, they could've had two Shadows on standby to provide aerial updates for both Raven squads upon deployment. A third emergency UAV would've been splendid, too, especially when Vlada and the others branched off. A decision she half-expected to see reprimand for once back on Base. Who would receive the brunt of said punishment was anyone's guess, but she feared likely not her; it would instead befall Gaspar first, then Popov and Russo.

She would, of course, dispute this if it came to it.

Avoiding any discussion regarding the possible status of Raven-One, per Barley's update, Vlada picked up the pace a little. This forced Popov and Russo to do the same, indirectly making them focus on their progression and nothing else.

The second they crested the hill midway through Sycamore, they were gifted the visual confirmation of Barley's caution. An almost gridlocked array of vehicles, some charred by flame, others mangled by collision, or Apophid contact.

A sporadic glimpse of Drones moving amongst the wreckage could be spotted from their position. The van-sized creatures were only so visible, and with Raven-Three's approach, they would probably use larger vehicles such as buses, trucks, and actual vans to obscure their movement.

"On me," Vlada said, advancing on quick feet and with her rifle raised.

Once the street flattened out, their view of the Drones became nullified. It was like navigating a maze of metallic obstacles, a vehicular necropolis. Glass occasionally crunched beneath their boots, be it from a window, headlamp, or taillight. Bodies were intermittent, often hanging out of cars half-eaten or caught under tires.

The putridity of the scene was jarring.

For Popov and Russo. Although both had seen their fair share of similar scenes overseas, Popov especially, civilian corpses were usually bullet-riddled or charred from explosions. They were never mangled beyond recognition, much less *eaten*.

This was a uniquely unnerving spectacle.

The occasional contact of an Apophid with the cars surrounding it made for a jittery stage. Vlada seemed immune to tics, never flinching or directing her aim based on the smallest sound. Although the two men followed her as close as they could, without stacking up, they maintained different routes through the gridlock so as to encourage multiple lanes of fire.

After a nerve-wracking fifteen seconds in the mess, Vlada raised a distinct violet fist and the two operators stopped in their tracks.

"I'm going to use the rooftops for a better view, and hopefully draw their attention," she radioed. "If this works, I'll direct them toward the far shoulder, against the soundwall. There, we can light 'em up."

"Solid copy," Popov said. He exchanged the G6 for the Rattler, as its compacter design made navigation easier, and more confident. "Proceed when ready."

Vlada nodded, slung the G6, and climbed onto the roof of a silver SUV. Its chassis rocked, the noise alone seeming to lure the attention of two Drones she could immediately see once up there. They shrieked and focused on her, one about thirty feet ahead of Popov, behind her left shoulder, and the other about sixty feet ahead of Russo, behind her right.

"Two inbound, twelve o'clock," Vlada radioed. "Moving

to lure them away from the cars, *do not* engage, unless necessary."

Russo felt that if an Apophid so much as looked in his
direction, it could be classified as 'necessary.' But he understood what she meant, and kept his forefinger extended past the
trigger guard.

The Drones ahead seemed to take the bait.

They fixated on Vlada as she jumped from one vehicle to
the next. As the nearest one did something similar, no longer
between vehicles but instead crawling on top of, and crushing
in their wake, smaller cars—she descended into the bed of a
pickup truck. She drew her Taurus, fired at the Drone's skull,
but with no intention of killing it outright. The heavy round took
out a chunk of bone and enraged the creature. She disembarked
the truck just as the Drone reached it, a scythe coming down to
impale the floor of the bed. A loud, metallic, jarring sound cut
through the air.

For a moment the truck was anchored to the asphalt, as
the tip of the Drone's scythe had stuck into the road.

Vlada fired in the general direction of the other Drone. It
cut across the gridlock, crushing vehicles as it advanced toward
her. She squeezed between the front bumper of an SUV and the
back hitch of another pickup. Vlada reached the oncoming lane,
and then put her back to the noise barrier.

She watched the one Drone finally dislodge itself from
the truck, just as the other crossed the oncoming lane. This time
she fired, deliberately at the Drone's eye, barely hitting it. The
eyeball was scored by the bullet, but didn't pulverize it. Nonetheless suffering a searing pain, crippled vision, and a burst of
ire, the Drone shrieked in its final charge.

Vlada side-stepped at the last moment, her torso leaning
back simultaneously. Evading a stab from the Drone's right
scythe. The creature slammed headlong into the barrier, fracturing it and making the single twenty-foot section wobble in its

concrete frame. The other Drone didn't just charge her, it pounced. The briefly airborne creature took two rapid rounds from her revolver into the underside before it landed in a tumble. She rolled free, and reached for her transmitter.

"Now, hit 'em with all you got," she radioed.

Clearing the gridlock but staying out of the oncoming lane, Popov and Russo let their weapons roar. A volley of well-placed 6.5mm Grendel and .300 Blackout rounds battered the creatures. They slumped at the end of a five-second barrage, while Vlada relocated to the top of a panel van four cars ahead of the others.

She thought she had...*felt* something.

Like a quiet whisper in her blood, one she 'heard' even over the operators' gunfire and the Drones' shrieks.

She could see the end of Sycamore Blvd, and not because of her telescopic vision. The intersection with Mayfield Drive was about half a mile away. Named after Curtis Mayfield, a legendary African-American musician native to Illinois. Considering the road was the second longest in Keign, favoring the art districts of the city, this made sense.

Vlada believed she saw movement at the intersection— but not of the Apophid kind. *Humans*. Whether they were Raven-Two, or civilian, she wasn't certain. A sudden thorn in her side made her flinch, taking her attention off the intersection.

Vlada's teeth grinded as she folded where she stood.

"Vlada, what's wrong?" Popov asked, noticing.

He and Russo moved up toward her, having slain the two Drones. But a mere few strides later and a startling sound snared their focus. They turned, facing the noise barrier. The twenty-foot section before the one where the Drones had been killed began to wobble. Their eyes lifted to the top. The sharp, minutely curved scythes of a Warrior appeared like grappling hooks. Dread filled the men as they watched the concrete begin to crack, and the panoply on a Warrior's skull summit the top of the barrier.

Behind it.

The Apophid was literally scaling the wall, from Elgin Park. The noise barrier was erected along an earth berm nearly ten feet up from the flat ground of Elgin, which meant the creature had to climb some degree before reaching the top of the barrier.

"V! We've got a Warrior, uh, on your seven—" Russo's voice ended in exchange of gunfire. G6 shouldered, he began firing at the Warrior's peering face. Popov returned the Rattler to its carabiner and unslung his G6.

The barrier suddenly split like glass, in so many areas that it crumbled beneath the Warrior's force. The Apophid fell out of view, but it had not failed. An immense gap in the noise barrier gave the operators view of a sycamore tree in Elgin Park. Seconds later, two Drones crawled through the hole, snarling and salivating.

"Vlada!" Popov shouted, not radioing.

He and Russo retreated back into the gridlock of wreckage. Firing in semiauto, training their shots. Behind the two Drones now crossing the oncoming lane emerged a Warrior, possibly the one that had brought the barrier down.

Vlada's right hand clutched her head. In hopes of making the pain stop, she began to squeeze. Her alien digits applied five points of pressure against her skull, threatening to crush it.

In an abyss within her mind, the darkness cleared away. She saw herself in a prison cell, and a Military Police officer sitting guard. Her chest suddenly hurt, as she watched this unfamiliar version of herself fashion a torn coil of cot spring into some kind of weapon. The vision, which she feared was an obscured memory now presenting itself for a reason she couldn't place, began to sink back into the abyss. A tar-like substance dripped over it, as if she was watching the memory through a periscope in a sea of oil.

Or black blood.

And then this military prisoner that was Vlada an indiscernible amount of time ago thrusted the metal spring into her own throat. Vlada, on top of the vehicle, screamed. The vision sank into the void again, and her eyes shot open. Her muscles froze up and she fell off the roof of the van.

Popov rushed to her aid, while Russo followed, firing in between vehicles at the nearing Drones. One of the Apophids walked over the tops of them, periodically impaling a roof or hood and having to wiggle its leg free. Windows shattered, windshields splintered, and tires popped.

Shaking her aggressively, Popov shouted as well.

He didn't know what to do. Vlada looked catatonic.

"Russo! Can you pick her up!?" Popov stood, once more swapping his G6 with the Rattler. A Drone stepped onto the panel van where Vlada had been impaling the body of the vehicle. Glass crumbs sprayed his face, cutting his brow and cheek. His thumb toggled full-auto and he fired the Rattler up at the snarling Drone. In addition to the spray of .300 rounds that battered the Drone's chest and skull, one caught its left eye just as its jaws came within arm's reach of Popov. The creature crumpled, and Popov dove out of its path.

Behind him, Russo dragged Vlada across the asphalt, before the Drone collapsed in a narrow space between vehicles, partially crushing a sedan that had been behind Popov.

Russo exerted as he slung Vlada over his shoulder.

She was maybe a buck forty, proving that her alien arms and cellular bonding had not affected her weight as much as it did her strength and resilience. It was not easy, but manageable. For how long, he didn't know—especially with Apophids hot on his trail.

Russo strode in the opposite direction at first, but the other Drone and approaching Warrior encouraged he cut across the lanes, toward the Optima luxury apartments.

"Optima!" Russo radioed, freeing a hand from holding Vlada. His other hand stayed on her, keeping her body slumped over his shoulder. "Fall back to Optima, Popov."

Of course. Where they'll have trouble falling.

Vlada had suggested this much when she decided to take Sycamore Blvd instead of Elgin.

Not that it seemed to matter much in the long run.

Whether the Apophids knew they were on the other side of the noise barrier because of their engagement with the Drones, or because of Vlada, was anyone's guess. This also likely didn't matter. The lingering threat would always be there, and it was their job to survive, to neutralize the enemy. At all costs.

Russo knew that by *carrying* Vlada away from the fight, his own confidence in survival had dropped into a bottomless pit. Seeing Vlada crumple was a major hit to his and Popov's faith. Not necessarily in her, but in their own chance of making it out alive.

Much less rallying with the others.

Just as they reached the nearest building, specifically an outdoor patio-like area for Optima residents, their earplugs chirped.

"Raven-Three, sitrep?" Barley sounded stressed. *"I've got a Little Bird en route to your pos for air support. Another assisting Raven-One. Raven-Two has eliminated hostiles just down Mayfield, not far from Sycamore. They're moving to assist you."*

"Negative," Popov said. "Direct them to Raven-One."

"This is not a negotiation, Sergeant."

"He's right, ma'am," Russo panted. He kicked a door shut in his wake, and nearly tripped over chairs as he carried Vlada toward a main entrance. "Vlada is decommissioned, but it's temporary. Once she's up, Raven-Two's help will be nullified."

"*That's...quite a statement, Corporal.*"

"He's not exaggerating, ma'am," Popov said, also panting. He had made it inside an Optima lobby, where a Drone followed him through a massive glass pane, shattering it in its wake. But no Warrior could follow them inside. Popov vaulted a counter, then used it as support as he fired his G6 in full-auto bursts, keeping the Drone at bay. He raised a hand to radio in the interim. "Vlada is a certifiable one-woman army. We just need to batten-down for a few minutes."

Barley took a moment to respond.

In this time, Popov killed the wounded Drone in the lobby, and then reloaded. Simultaneously, he radioed to receive an update of Russo's location.

"Heading to the laundry room," Russo replied. "I think we're in the same building."

"*If she's unconscious,*" Barley said. *There's no telling when, or if, she will resurface.*"

"We have faith," Popov said. "Just as we do in Raven-One and -Two, but once they rally, they'll be an unstoppable force. *That* is a priority. Ma'am."

Barley sighed over comms.

"*Copy. Just stay alive, Raven-Three. Air support is twenty seconds out.*"

The transmission ended.

And so did Vlada's unconsciousness.

6

Before being thrust back into the tormenting reality Vlada had come to know as this stage of her life, she had been incarcerated in a featureless void. It rivaled no nightmare she had ever experienced before; it was pure, haunting emptiness. Her awareness of the void was the single worst aspect of it. But toward its unexpected end, Vlada's mental image of herself in a military infirmary had presented itself. She was being treated for the jugular wound, which had resulted in one carotid puncture, but not enough to drain the artery, and she had never reached the other.

While people tended to her, a strange shadow stood in the corner of the infirmary. It appeared humanoid, at first. It was a deep, dark, near-black shade of violet. But when Vlada's body stiffened on the operating table, the shadow developed multiple appendages which descended from its 'head,' as if a skeletal umbrella. These limbs drooped, and then formed a claw that reached out for Vlada.

Her seizure persisted.

The men and women treating her stepped back. They stared at their feet and then each became a shadow in themselves. The stark white lighting of the infirmary flickered before cutting off, leaving only a single tube. It provided erratic lighting on Vlada's seized face.

The multi-limbed shadow in the corner—

Its outstretched hand had reached her. In the light, its

hand dispersed into a swarm of black spiders. They teemed over Vlada's face, which was no longer tensed in a seizure, but screaming wide-awake. In pain and fear. The tide of spiders coursed into her throat, and began to crawl out of her orifices, out from under her eyes.

Gasping, choking, Vlada came to. Instead of sitting up or bolting to her feet, she rolled off of Russo's right shoulder. Her sudden return to consciousness startled him, and she hit the floor—hard. Anyone else might have suffered a broken arm, shoulder, or rib.

Vlada was on her feet seconds later, violently gagging. She never retched, not even a single drop of fluid. When she finally stopped, Russo heard a strident crash of glass behind him. He had reached the back of an Optima lobby, unsure where to go next. He was outside a stairwell door, expecting to take it down to the laundry room.

The Drone that had pursued him from Sycamore Blvd was now inside the building. The creature doggedly advanced through the lobby, effortlessly crashing through signs and furniture. Two marble counters, a pair of steel turnstiles, and twin escalators were the other obstacles between Russo, Vlada, and the creature.

He raised his G6.

Outside, the chainsaw sound of a Little Bird helo's minigun firing in rapid bursts caught their attention. The charging Drone paused to half-turn toward the front of the building. Likely detecting, in some way or another, the death of its brethren. Russo hoped, that Warrior. More, ideally.

Every time the minigun paused, the clinking of spent casings on the tops of cars, or the asphalt, could be heard all the way inside the lobby.

Finally Russo began firing, grateful for his ear-pro, as the gunshots inside the lobby would have been especially deafening. Vlada suddenly screamed, startling him. Not in pain or fear, but anger. An unrivaled, unprecedented spite. She practically shoulder-checked Russo before charging the Drone forty feet away—leaving her G6 on the floor beside him. She leapt over a turnstile without a single misstep or hitch in her stride.

Dumbstruck, Russo watched Vlada clash with the Drone. She used its right scythe as a sort of gymnastic pole, swinging herself around until she stood on top of it. Her alien digits crept under the Drone's cranial panoply, ripping it off. She slung it behind her, and then began rabbit punching its exposed skull. The speed of her jabs was astounding, and the force immense. Within two whole seconds she had caved in its skull, but the Drone was still active.

Shrieking, its front legs tucked under, and it rolled forward, flinging her off. She rolled, too, but sprang up as if nothing had happened. Before the Drone could try anything, she had spun around and slid both hands into its jaws. With another scream, she ripped its mandible off, and then plunged one of the broken joints into its left eye. She shoved it farther, twisting simultaneously.

Reaching and penetrating the brain.

The Drone went limp.

She backpedaled away from the dead creature, until she bumped into the turnstile. She turned and vaulted it, then shook her hands until the mess had come away.

Sniffling, she walked back up to Russo, retrieved her G6, and nonchalantly asked where Popov was.

Russo radioed. "Vlada's conscious, Sarge. Location?"

"Took an elevator down. I think I'm in a different building, but I did just hear a ruckus up top."

"These buildings are bigger than they seem. That might've been us. Well, her." Russo turned around to face the stairwell door, and to the right of it, two elevators. He saw the circular lights above them illuminated. "Surprised the lifts still work."

"Yeah, the government didn't want to cut power to Keign, as it could help civvies escape or find better shelter."

"Smart. Well, I'm still taking the stairs."

"Suit yourself. I don't think a Drone can squeeze in there, either."

"That helo might've taken care of the enemies outside."

"No," Vlada said, radioing it. "There's more. I think all it did was attract more."

"Attract more just to be slaughtered?" Russo asked, brow furrowed. "That doesn't track."

"Stop trying to understand them," she said, bluntly. And then raised one of her arms. Looking at it, she added: "Nothing makes sense. Until it's too late, and they're chewing through your skull."

She lowered her arm.

"V, glad you're with us again," Popov said. *"Even if what you have to contribute is so fucking grim."*

Subconsciously, she didn't mind the casual abridgement of her name. If anything, she found it comforting that someone would want to; it certainly beat *21X*.

"Sergeant, request you come to us instead," she said, now looking toward the front of the building. "We need to advance, not hide."

"I don't know if that's wise right—"

"We got an update, Vlada," Russo interrupted him, looking at her. "Barley. She wanted to redirect Raven-Two from Mayfield to us. Raven-One is receiving air support, but is still split up. We insisted -Two rally with -One."

Vlada grunted. "Bold decision. Why?"

"You," Russo took a deep breath, and then his attention was drawn to the front of the building. Outside the lobby, the minigun from the Little Bird started burst-firing again, but grew more distant with every few seconds. It was likely running low on ammo, or perhaps trying to draw the Apophids away from Raven-Three's location. Russo shouldered his rifle and looked at her again. "We had faith in you. And deemed Raven-One in more need of the help. Besides, once *they* rally, that'll be a force no Apophid would want to fuck with, lest they regret it."

Vlada nodded.

She had never expected any of the MSOT to develop such a level of belief in her, much less after she lost consciousness out of the blue. It was borderline suicidal for them, but they chanced it and instead prioritized the greater good.

"I'd like to say you shouldn't have," Vlada said, "but it *was* the best decision, for the team as a whole."

"For Malathion."

She nodded at Russo, and then radioed Popov.

"Sergeant. Advise you rally with us. I have an idea."

"Am I going to like it?"

"Unlikely. But it may be our best shot of reaching the others before dark."

Popov sighed, over comms. *"Moving."*

Vlada dug her Apofuel out of a satchel on her waist, by the small of her back. It almost resembled a Capri-Sun pouch. She unplugged a small apparatus at one end and took a considerable gulp, still leaving seventy percent of its contents.

Russo watched, and didn't know how to feel.

She appeared genuinely refreshed. The color of the liquid, before she licked her lips, was a gray-white, like bad milk.

"The Doc make that for you?" Russo asked, brow furrowed.

She nodded, plugged it again, and returned it to her satchel.

"What's in it?" he reluctantly asked.

"You don't wanna know," she said, and there was barely any humor in it.

"That's fair," he said, his nose wrinkling. He looked away, squeezing the butt of his rifle into his shoulder.

"Still wanna kiss me?" Vlada asked.

He performed a double-take, and she smirked briefly. He opened his mouth to respond, but a sudden sound startled him. They turned, seeing Popov enter the lobby through the patio area adjacent it, the same one Russo had carried Vlada through. Popov's boots crunched on chunks of glass scattering the white and black tile floor, from when the Drone had breached the lobby. As it turned out, Popov *had* been in a different building, the neighboring one.

Vlada led Russo over the turnstiles, past the dead Drone, and they finally reunited with Popov.

"So, what's the deal?" he asked.

Vlada's stomach expanded with a deep breath, and then flattened again.

"We *cut across* Elgin Park, past the north end of the pond, coming out at the intersection of Mayfield and Grackle Ave."

"Grackle. Where's that?" Russo asked.

"The road parallel Sycamore, other side of Elgin."

Named after the common grackle, not native to Illinois but a frequent sighting. A blackbird with an iridescent, dark blue head and neck. The state bird of Illinois was the cardinal, which had taken the name of another road in Keign.

"That intersection, that'll put us…where?" Popov asked, thinking. "By the Sheriff's Office?"

"About," she said.

Popov nodded.

"Wait," Russo said, with a sarcastic chuckle. "Barley recommended we *avoid* Elgin. The high Apophid activity and all."

"If we keep taking Sycamore, and then use Mayfield, we'll probably be hit by Apophids every few hundred feet, and might not rally with the others 'til nightfall. You wanna be on the streets in Keign after dark?"

Russo sighed. He kneaded his brow.

Vlada didn't genuinely expect to still be separated from the others for the next several hours—dusk about four away—but even cutting it close was something she wanted to avoid. The sooner they assembled with Raven-One, and possibly -Two as well, the better.

"The second we're boots on grass," she said, "you two *run*. Reach that northwest corner, follow the signage. We won't be sticking to the Diamondback Trail, but it *does* cut across Elgin, past the pond, and have a route that goes up to that corner."

"Right," Popov said. "Barley mentioned that."

"And the Apophids that'll be on our ass?"

Vlada opened her arms. "What happened to all that good faith, Corporal?"

"Shit," Russo shook his head. Then he stared and pointed at Vlada. "As long as you don't go hara-kiri and 'take one for the team' just so we can make that intersection."

"Trust me, I'm not the suicide type," she said.

Popov and Russo stepped away to have a few words that might build their confidence on this crazy plan. As they did so, Vlada's last statement ran across the back of her mind, and a distorted flash of her memory in the military jail cell dizzied her. Jabbing the sharpened spring into her throat, puncturing a carotid artery and following the spray of blood down a dark path she didn't expect to wake from.

Only she had woken, seemingly claimed by the Apophid entity that…

Was it already on Earth at that time?

There was no telling when exactly that had been, supposing it was a real memory and not some fabrication by the Apophid hive to disarm her from within.

She didn't focus on it.

The sound of the Little Bird outside was now just as well a distant memory. Even she couldn't hear the thump of its rotors across the sky. Nor could she track nearby Apophids, suggesting that they had either been drawn away, killed off, or repelled. Temporarily.

"We should move," she said. "Now."

She led them toward the front of the lobby, across crunching glass. And then the sudden staccato rhythm of staggered gunfire caught her ear. Seconds before the other operators heard it. The din lured her out of the Optima apartment lobby quicker, and the men decided to abandon any irresolution to follow her.

If anything, they felt safer in her immediate company. Upon emerging onto Sycamore again, which was now littered with four Apophid corpses—three Drones and a Warrior—they were glad they had.

Two operators from Raven-Two had made their way up the road, on the Optima side of the gridlock. They took turns firing back at a pair of Drones that followed them up Sycamore. One of the two creatures took a wide berth, appearing to use the far lane of stalled traffic as cover.

"The literal fuck are you two doing here?" Russo asked.

Corporal Graves and Sergeant Arrington separated, the latter trying to keep an eye on the evasive Drone. The machine gun he toted helped suppress it even with rows of vehicles between them.

"Barley instructed Seb take us to rally with Raven-One, after an initial order to direct us toward you." Graves took a deep breath, shouldered his G6, and fired a few well-placed shots that briefly deterred the approaching Drone. Vlada stepped past him to keep drilling it with superior aim, knowing she could hear Graves better over the gunfire. Not complaining, Graves continued. "Marco's dumb ass insisted on finding Pops, so Seb let him go, as long as it wasn't alone. So here I am."

It wasn't common for the operators to regard each other by their first names, or monikers, during an op. But some men, like Graves, didn't care.

Vlada had inferred Seb as Sebastian Lebeau, and Marco as Arrington. Pops as Popov was one she had not been aware of, but might have to store.

Just as the latter two neutralized the Drone crawling over the tops of vehicles toward them, its alien body slumping down between cars, shoving a few aside, Vlada delivered the final eye-shot that put the other Drone out of commission. Fifteen feet away.

Arrington and Popov exchanged fist bumps, then rallied with the others. Vlada received a nod from Arrington, which was a hint more of respect than she expected. Although, he and Graves were, to her belief, relatively neutral toward her before the op had begun. Having heard what Graves had to share, it certainly made sense that Fuller wasn't going to be the one to volunteer to join Arrington.

"A shame," Vlada said, looking at Graves. "I was hoping to see Fuller again."

Graves smirked wryly. "I bet."

"Had to practically hold that asshole back from coming along," Arrington said, his voice devoid of humor but the sarcasm thick as tar.

Russo smirked and shook his head.

"How was MOCA?" Popov asked.

"A regular shit-show," Graves said. "Might've been a nice visit, once upon a time. I think that eight days ago, that all changed."

"Bodies, everywhere?" Russo asked, brow furrowed.

"You'd expect more," Arrington said.

"They're eating most of them," Vlada said, grimly. The look on her face expressed a sort of regret and sadness in making that statement. But that didn't keep her from continuing. "And taking others. Possibly for larviposition."

"For what-now?" Graves asked.

"Hatching their young in rotted flesh," she said. She

watched their expressions sour. She tilted her head. "Sorry, I just figure complete transparency is the best recourse right now."

"Can't say I appreciate it," Arrington said.

"But we do," Graves said, squinting. "Kind of."

"I understand. Listen. We were just about to move." Vlada nodded toward the demolished section of soundwall. But before she explained their plan, she asked Graves: "How's Mayfield look? Similar to this, or better?"

"Less gridlocked, but still bad. Our last word from Barley was that Grackle is virtually untouched. Not much has changed since Downpour's debriefings. Civvies still trapped, or hiding, in the office buildings. Raven-One found some survivors held up in Celestine, but virtually no enemy activity. Not 'til they moved outside."

Graves took a breath and checked the magazine of his G6. He proceeded to exchange it for a fuller mag.

"So, what's the plan?" Arrington asked. He and Popov were now the highest ranks among them. Yet he was asking Vlada, directly.

"We had about decided," she said, and gestured at the hole in the noise barrier, thirty feet away.

"Elgin?" Arrington scoffed. "What, leap-frog over to Grackle?"

"Beats taking Mayfield, much less finishing that stretch of Sycamore," Graves admitted. "Especially for us, Marco. What? Not hyped for a lil' change of scenery?"

Arrington shook his head.

"I assume this plan involves bolting across the Park, *movement is life* sort of deal."

"Faster the better," Popov said. "And that's coming from the least fit of us all."

"Look, I'm not blind to the benefits of taking the shortcut," Arrington said. He brandished the RM338, its belt of cartridges clinking softly, his exposed muscles wet with sweat, giving his dark skin a light sheen. "But this fucker slows me down a bit."

"Would you mind?" Vlada asked, slinging her G6 and extending her hands.

Arrington didn't look excited. He tilted his head and his eyes expressed uncertainty. He looked over at Popov, who nodded once.

"I guess if anyone is…" he finally said, and lifted the heavy-duty sling over his head. Then handed the 22-pound weapon to Vlada. She accepted it with such ease that immediately sparked an unexpected jealousy in Arrington. Despite this, he was just as quickly relieved of not having to carry the weight, especially with a run ahead of him.

When he began to reach for a .338 Norma Mag belt-pouch, Vlada shook her head.

"Hang onto those, you'll get this back as soon as we hit Grackle," she said, and secured the sling around her torso, adjacent the G6. Then she squeezed the LMG's buttstock under her left arm, and used her right to lift the feed cover, investigating the loaded belt. After securing the cover again, she unzipped the pouch for an instant; roughly thirty of the fifty-round belt remained. "Should be enough for this run."

"If you say so," Arrington said. "Just don't drop it."

"I won't," she said, revealing a tiny smile. "Point is, everyone focus on running. If you have a Rattler, carry it. Fire only if necessary. I'll handle most of that, keep them at bay."

Only Arrington and Popov had Rattlers. The others would just run with their G6, although Graves, not as tall as Russo and thus a shorter reach, considered slinging his rifle and just running with the Taurus.

"Everyone ready?" Vlada asked, proceeding across Sycamore.

"I suppose it doesn't matter if we are or not," Graves

113

mumbled.

As she neared the opening in the noise barrier, concrete chunks littering the narrow shoulder of the oncoming lane, Vlada heard some quiet chatter behind her. Arrington's whisper was inherently deeper and huskier than anyone's else, barely qualifying as one. Even if Vlada didn't have superior hearing, she believed she could have heard him. Graves's mumbles were far quieter, not meant for anyone except whoever he stood directly beside to hear.

"So what's the 411, she the real deal or what?" Graves asked Russo.

"This bitch crazy or what?" Arrington asked Popov.

"Nothing realer than wringing out a Warrior's brain through its eye socket," Vlada said, turning to face them, her eyes on Graves. She had raised one of her hands, wiggling her fingers before clenching a fist and letting her arm hang at her side. Then she stared at Arrington. "I don't know if that counts for 'crazy' or not, but I'm *present* if that's what you mean."

The men from Raven-Two nodded before exchanging glances and then shrugging.

"Stop bullshitting," Popov said to them, and then gestured at Vlada. "Lead the way."

"I won't be, though," she said. "Anyone here with a greater sense of direction than the others?"

"Marco's ex-DEVGRU," Graves said.

"Gray Squadron, no?" Vlada asked Arrington.

"How'd you know that?"

Vlada simply shrugged.

Arrington sighed. "Yeah. Mobility and QRF."

"Take point, guarantee the others reach Mayfield," Vlada said. Somewhere in Elgin Park, maybe a hundred yards away, a cluster of Apophid shrieks rose into the sky. Vlada put her boot on the jagged base of the broken barrier, and beckoned the others. "Follow the footpath if need be. I'll draw their attention, and repel them, before I follow."

"Copy," Arrington said, and advanced.

The drop on the other side was a grassy slope. The earth berm was lightly grassed, dense soil. Arrington landed without his legs buckling, and jogged down until he was on flat ground. A sycamore tree was fifteen feet away, its lush canopy providing green-tinted shade in a forty-foot radius. He unfolded the buttstock on his Rattler and aimed it southeast of their position, far left of where they touched down.

The mass of a Behemoth could be seen, eighty yards away. The other side of Opeka Pond, the nearest edge of which was about fifty feet from where Arrington stood. Around the huge Apophid teemed Drones and a couple of Warriors, the latter like lieutenants.

"Eighty yards and closing," Arrington announced. "Mostly Drones, but…"

Popov and Graves assembled behind him.

"Just go, run, make that intersection!" Vlada shouted.

"Moving!" Arrington barked, and led the others across the Park in a diagonal route.

"Right behind you," Vlada assured Russo, who nodded and followed the others. His legs tucked under him and he rolled down the berm, springing to his feet without issue. He trailed Popov by a few long strides. When he glanced behind him, just as he cleared the canopy of the sycamore, Russo saw Vlada descend from the Boulevard.

Wielding the RM338 with one hand, she fired it from the shoulder as she ran. Although the others couldn't tell, and were mostly focused on following Arrington to the far northwest corner of the Park, most of her shots were landing. The suppressed machine gun was still loud; their ear-pro mitigated this, but the reports certainly drew the Apophids' attention. There was far less muzzle flash from the weapon because of the suppressor, but the imposing rounds striking the creatures was indication enough.

She focused on the Drones, knowing the Behemoth would take much more and at a closer range. Meanwhile, the two Warriors fanned out—one focusing on the Sycamore Blvd side of the Park, the other on the Grackle Avenue side.

A large pavilion-sized gazebo on their right was a sight Russo and Graves wished they had not seen. Arrington and Popov had tunnel-vision toward their objective, not noticing the scattered civilian corpses, dismembered and eviscerated.

Vlada approached the nearest end of the pond, and set her feet shoulder-width apart. She put both hands on the RM338 and began firing at the Warrior along the Grackle berm. It wove around the occasional tree, but her aim was too precise and consistent to make its attempt to use cover effective. The .338 Norma Mag rounds devastated the Warrior's exoskeleton, especially where it was thinnest. She managed to blow off one of its scythes as it came within sixty feet of her.

Then she swung the machine gun around, firing at a pair of Drones bold enough to cut right across the pond. Although nearly the area of a small lake, Opeka was classified as a pond due to its shallow depth and rich aquatic life along the bottom. Water tumultuously splashed around the Drones' legs and bodies; Vlada's burst-firing occasionally cut divots through the pond's surface, but primarily hit their marks. One Drone dropped before reaching the end, in a spray of water and blood.

She began to backpedal, and glimpsed the belt of ammo fed from the pouch to the weapon grow thin. She had maybe eight rounds left.

She lowered the RM338 in her left hand, drawing the Taurus with her right. She fired two rounds at the Drone, nearly obliterating its skull in the process. Then she resumed her progress, as the Warrior along the Sycamore berm came in behind her, thirty feet away. The one along the Grackle berm ignored her, fixating on the operators heading up the footpath toward

Mayfield.

Russo had passed Popov, leaving him to trail.

He turned on his heel to fire at the encroaching Warrior. His Rattler hosed out rounds in full-auto, battering the Warrior's face with .300 Blackout rounds. It barely recoiled, its pace still advancing, despite the wounds it suffered, including a destroyed eyeball.

Vlada emptied her belt into the side of the Warrior's face, pummeling bone into brain. Its massive body slumped midstride. Leading the pack but stepping aside to assist, Arrington witnessed this. He made brief eye contact with Vlada before shouting at her. Vlada turned and raised her right hand, just in time to catch a Drone's downward scythe. She shoved it away, at an angle and force that fractured the limb close to its shoulder socket. The Drone shrieked and latched its jaws down at her face. Vlada let the machine gun sag in its sling, raising her left arm to guard her face.

The Drone's jaws clamped around her forearm.

She screamed through her teeth, drew the Taurus from its holster again, and thrusted the five-inch barrel into the Drone's left eye. She squeezed the trigger and the explosive, messy result left the Drone to collapse where it stood. Its slackened jaws released her arm. She watched inch-deep puncture holes in the purple flesh quickly return to form.

"On us, move your skinny ass," Russo said into her ear.

She looked back toward the footpath that led up to Mayfield. Around a sagging oak branch of leaves she could see Russo and Graves firing their rifles where they knelt. Behind them, up at street-level, Arrington and Popov seemed preoccupied with something else. Vlada could hear men's voices, even women's as well.

Civilians.

Vlada pulled away from the pond, putting her back to a Warrior that had gotten dangerously close to her, and more

Drones as they crossed the pond.

Graves stepped past Russo, clearing the paved footpath for a better shot. He began putting one round after the other into the Warrior as it pursued Vlada. She picked up the pace, going from a light jog to a bounding sprint. Witnessing this nearly startled Graves out of his marksmanship.

"Sergeant!" Vlada shouted.

Popov heard her, but was out of her line-of-sight. Arrington turned away from the street to look down at her, running up the footpath. She singlehandedly lifted the RM338, ducking out of its sling.

"Maybe you should keep it," he said.

"Don't be outrageous, just let me reload it," she said.

He dug a fresh belt-pouch out and tossed it to her. She knelt on the sidewalk and swiftly reloaded the machine gun at a speed and dexterity that embarrassed even Arrington. Once finished, she handed it back to him, and noticed Popov waving at a scattered group of civilians on the other side of Mayfield. Three men, including two in tattered sheriff's department uniforms, and a woman with a teenage boy.

Not a single speck of clean, unsullied skin among them. They were mostly tarnished by dirt or soot, likely gunpowder residue as well.

Between the deputies was a Winchester pump-action shotgun and a black six-inch Smith & Wesson revolver.

"Inside, anywhere, inside!" Popov shouted.

Directly across the street was the sixty-acre parking lot belonging to a stretch of locally owned businesses and corporations alike, called Cedar Plaza. The primary shopping mall in Keign, whose interconnected storefront stretched the length of four football fields. Even the lot was home to three 'islands'—a Shell gas station, Panera, and Burger King, each about 120 yards apart.

There was no way the civvies were going to cross the lot.

The nearest building next to it and flush with Mayfield was a Rite Aid. Between it and the Museum of Cultural Arts was a Wells Fargo, one of two banks in Keign. Lacewing Place intersected Mayfield and bordered Cedar Plaza, dividing it from the residential streets of Creekmoor. Opposite the Mayfield-Lacewing intersection was a PNC Bank, and the Sheriff's Office.

The Plaza, including its vast lot, was the only property this side of Keign that wasn't packed like sardines. It made sense if a lot of civilians had found some form of solace hiding inside buildings, where Drones would have to struggle to get into.

When Vlada asked where they were headed, Popov wasn't of much use.

"Hell if I know," he shouted back. "Seems they came from Iron Mill, down that way."

He pointed, but didn't need to.

Vlada remembered the map. Iron Mill Court was a road perpendicular Mayfield, between Cedar Plaza and the edge of North Village. They could have been shopping, or at a restaurant in Novi, when Keign was first hit, and had been hiding or trying to relocate since. With two of the men being from the sheriff's department, it was possible they were frequently on the move, trying to help others.

This gave Vlada hope—however thin and frail a hope as it was.

Gunfire behind her was incessant.

Until it wasn't.

She turned, noticing a Warrior that had gotten all too close, part of its skull sloughing off. A close-quarters barrage of .338 Norma Mag would do that. Arrington lowered the machine gun and led the others around the corner of the noise barrier, on the sidewalk, until they were officially alongside Grackle Drive.

Vlada's hearing narrowed.

She could hear gunfire and voices down Grackle, across the street somewhere.

"Raven-One, I can hear them!"

"Where?" Popov asked.

He had turned away from looking down Mayfield, or at the civvies. The latter had navigated into the Rite Aid, which unfortunately had a sizable double-door entrance that a Drone could likely 'squeeze' through.

"Down Grackle, probably still in the vicinity of the hospital, but closer to Creekmoor." She shook her head. "The Behemoth on the other side of the pond, it didn't follow. It could think of flanking the far side of Grackle."

Not great news, but that it was keeping its distance—for now—*did* provide a crumb of relief. Behemoths were simply too big to wander into the Labor District, anyway.

"We need to make Cedar Plaza and Novi our next AOs," Graves said.

"Once we link up with Raven-One," Russo said.

"Or -Two."

"Negative," Arrington said, firmly. "We prioritize -One, and *then*—"

Vlada's head whipped to the right. She nearly knocked over Popov as she marched down the sidewalk on the Park-side of Mayfield.

"The hell she doing?" Arrington asked.

Vlada watched one Drone in the middle of the road get peppered with gunfire from across the street, in the direction of MOCA. She couldn't pinpoint the shooters, or even the muzzle flashes, which meant they were well sheltered. The second Drone had deviated toward Rite Aid, but instead of fixating on the windows or entrance, it scaled the side of the brick building.

"Do *not* follow!" Vlada shouted, crossing Mayfield and bounding over cars as if they were mere stones. She waved her left arm away, as if telling a dog to scram. "Go! Find Raven-

One!"

"Like hell," Russo growled, frustrated. He began to follow her, but Arrington seized a fistful of his vest and kept him from advancing.

"We're *moving*, got it?" Sergeant Arrington demanded. "*Now*, Corporal."

Russo pulled himself free, but didn't follow Vlada. Popov slapped his back and followed Graves down Grackle.

"She can handle herself, and you know it," Popov insisted.

"Unless she collapses again," Russo snapped.

"Say what?" Arrington asked.

"Just move, goddammit," Popov pressed. He shoved Russo in the back.

Arrington cursed under his breath and led them down Grackle, quick to cross the mostly vacant road. It wasn't long before they, too, heard the echo of gunfire somewhere behind Celestine Hospital, between the partially demolished office complexes and the residential Creekmoor behind them.

Meanwhile, Vlada reached Rite Aid. She clambered up the side of the building, her booted feet bending to accompany the wall, but her digits acquiring purchase via shallow holes in the brick. Prior to this moment, she had not realized she could literally scale a building, although she suspected it would be different if it was a perfectly smooth surface like glass.

More than halfway up the structure, she glanced over her right shoulder. The Drone in the middle of Mayfield had been neutralized and the gunfire ceased. She could hear voices overlapping, somewhere out of sight. She began to fine-tune her hearing but then the huffing breaths of the Drone on the roof made her focus again. She scaled the wall the rest of the way, flinging herself onto the flat rooftop.

The Drone had just begun to burrow into the composite tile floor around an A/C unit when she rose to her feet. It lifted its ugly head and snarled at her.

Vlada just glared at it, arms at her sides, negating the weapons on her person.

After a brief staring contest, the Drone warbled and charged her. She side-stepped the beast at the last second, simultaneously delivering a quick jab at its face. Her fist pulverized its left eyeball, just before its limbs scurried helplessly at the edge of the roof. The parapet crumbled in its wake, and the creature fell twenty-four feet. It landed with a crunch, and rolled into Mayfield, knocking a car aside.

She peered down at it, and unslung her G6.

Two well-placed rounds penetrated its skull and made it go limp. She dismounted the roof with one hand dragging down the brick to slow her descent. She peered into the Rite Aid through one of the glass double-doors, not wanting to fully enter. The sight of her arms might terrify the woman and boy, or trigger a hostile reaction from the deputies.

Most of Keign was familiar with Project Outreach, but given the city's condition, a cameo from her might not be the wisest decision.

"Please, stay put!" she requested, her voice both authoritative and civil. "We will not rest until Keign is safe. Try to seek a small, secure room. Innsbrook is secure. Trinity is secure. Hide and stay quiet. Thank you."

The deputies began shouting something at her, not far from "who are you to tell us what to do," but Vlada didn't pause to hear them out, or provide a response. She retreated, circled the building, and navigated through alleys to home in on the others. She assumed it was Raven-Two, or what remained of them. How they had not gotten farther from MOCA she didn't understand, unless they were delayed by both enemy contact and helping civilians.

She hoped Russo and the others didn't perceive her sudden departure as *abandoning* them. She trusted they were close enough to Raven-One to assemble without her assistance. A mere duo of operators in Keign—even if one of them was Gunnery Sergeant Lebeau, whose familiarity with the city during Operation Downpour counted for a lot—didn't fill her with a lot of confidence. It said nothing about the soldiers themselves. But she refused to let them wander about when her group was so close to rallying with Raven-One.

The original plan was to have the MSOT split into two squads, so that they could "divide and conquer" the threats of Keign. But the situation had quickly presented itself as a problem best dealt with as a single force. The Apophids were simply too agile, smart, and resilient to be handled any other way. The sheer firepower and teamwork capable of an amassed MSOT would spell certain doom for the Apophids in Keign.

This was what Vlada, Popov, and Russo had tacitly established when they refused Barley's instruction to direct Raven-Two to their position. While this wasn't completely fulfilled, it was a start.

Had Vlada not been supplied with Arrington's RM338, it was quite possible she could've lost Popov or Russo during their daring shortcut.

Every little iota of help mattered.

Vlada held onto this smidgen of truth as she hunted down Lebeau and Fuller, in hopes of helping them reunite with the others.

"So we can all be one big, happy family again."

As if she had any right to deliver that cheesy line.

7

The Duckworth Center for Veterans was originally planned to have a plot in the North Village, but property space and the abundance of employment called for a larger building. Therefore it wound up in the Labor District, and was one of the more attractive structures amid a throng of near-identical glass and steel behemoths. The Duckworth Center was a two-story V-shaped concrete building with far less windows than most of the other architecture in the District, without being a prison. Staggered blue- and yellow-tinted vertical panes gave it some color, one more aspect that made it stand out from its neighbors.

Named after Ladda Tammy Duckworth, a U.S. senator and Army veteran from Illinois, the purpose of the Center extended beyond helping military veterans. It helped lower-income residents with banking, managing taxes, and other monetary issues, as well as resolving homeless concerns in neighboring cities.

It was here, in the second-story offices, that a fragment of Raven-One found themselves. Taking shelter, and a sliver of respite. Only made possible with the aid of a Little Bird that had swept in to provide aerial support when the operators were in a tough spot against the enemy.

The helo, a remote-piloted drone, had departed from the area to do another pass over Keign before RTB for refueling.

"We shouldn't be here, not when Roback is out there," Wilson said, pacing around. He kicked an already toppled chair in frustration.

"If anyone can handle themselves, for a moment, it's Roback and that three-three-eight," Gaspar said. He wiped sweat from his brow with the back of a partially gloved hand.

"Just give us a moment, yeah?" Lloyd asked, draining a quarter of his water supply. He gnawed off a corner of a protein bar, without fully swallowing his water, and then finished. All while Wilson glared at him.

They had just come up here not thirty seconds before Wilson started off.

"I'm going to the roof," Gaspar said. "Might be able to reach Roback on comms."

"The *roof*?" Wilson scoffed. "We're on the shortest building in the District, go figure. You'd be better off jumping up and down, on the ground, trying to raise him."

"Worth a fucking shot, Corporal," Gaspar snapped.

He left them in the office, emerging into the elevator lobby, and then kicking open the stairwell access door. Inside, three civilians in tattered suits flinched and whimpered.

"Shit." He peered out of the stairwell and shouted. "Civvies, on me!"

Wilson didn't hesitate. Lloyd packed his provisions and followed. They assembled on Gaspar, and looked in on the office workers. Two women and one man, all of who had seen better days. The man looked borderline malnourished.

"How long have you been in here?" Gaspar asked. "This stairwell, I mean."

The man wetted his lips before speaking, but barely a word came out.

"Three days," one of the women said.

"Christ. Anything to eat, drink?"

"Sam's gotten us stuff from the breakroom, before the collapse crushed it."

The woman had tugged on the man's partially torn, but

devoid of blood, blue button-down shirt sleeve, when she said his name.

Gaspar silently praised the man's selflessness.

He began unearthing his own provisions, and insisted Sam accept his water and a single MRE.

"It isn't delicious, but it's better than nought," Gaspar said.

Wilson had already begun to do the same for the women. He provided them with what he had to offer. Lloyd started to follow suit, but Gaspar interrupted him. Then he leaned in, whispering against his ear.

"Look for the breakroom, yeah? Hit me on comms second you find it."

Lloyd simply nodded once and retreated.

It didn't take the Gunnery Sergeant long to locate the office breakroom. It was on this floor, down a narrow hall on the opposite side of the elevator lobby. Employee restrooms were at the end of the tapered hall, but the breakroom itself was a different story altogether.

Lloyd pressed his transmitter.

"Found the breakroom, boss. She was right. Some kind of collapse has crushed most of it. I can see through, not all of it is demolished, but might not be safe to be inside the room."

Gaspar copied, and told Lloyd to regroup.

When he did, Gaspar was already halfway up the stairwell. Wilson was kneeling on the landing nearest the civvies, trying to console them and distributing his provisions. Gaspar whistled, quietly, snatching Lloyd's attention. He rushed up to follow Gaspar to the roof. Once they were outside, it was not so distant from Wilson's annoyed statement. They *were* in the squattest building of the Labor District, surrounded by structures no less than twice as tall in every direction. Through a narrow alley at one corner of the Duckworth Center's V-shaped rooftop, they could glimpse an opening and the façade of a three-story luxury home.

Creekmoor.

"Knowing Roback, he'd want to break out of this area," Gaspar said, "and hold up in a Creekmoor house."

"Not the wisest decision, seeing as how Drones could better scale a house than cram themselves into an office building's bathroom, but yeah, that's Roback to a T."

"Truth be told," Gaspar sighed, shaking his head. "This isn't about long-term survival, not for us. We're here to eliminate threats. And if that means showing our ass for a minute in the open, then finding a more actionable location, we'd sooner do that than hide for a minute."

"Fuckin' A, boss," Lloyd said. "But where's that leave us? We gonna goose-chase a *possibility* that Roback's in Creekmoor? Shit, you heard that gunfire. Raven-Two's gotta be in the area, maybe even -Three. Coming down Mayfield, at least."

Gaspar nodded a few times.

He looked around, and then jogged toward the widest end of the V-shaped rooftop. He stopped about thirty feet shy of the edge, because there was no choice to do otherwise. A section of the neighboring office complex had collapsed, likely after lingering in an unstable state from the day-one meteor shower. Then, three days ago, according to the civilian in the stairwell, it finally gave way. A three-story plank of cracked yet intact glass and twin beams supporting it had fallen. When it landed on that section of the Duckworth Center's roof, it had partially crushed the breakroom, barring easy entrance.

"I've got an idea, Lloyd," Gaspar said. He sucked his teeth and looked away from the sloped plank of glass, to see Lloyd's bewildered face. "And you ain't gonna like it."

"Nah, I don't just not like it, I *hate* it. Wilson, though. Roback's his brother-from-another-mother. I think he'd go for it. Question is, *why*?"

"Better comms, if we can get closer to Creekmoor without taking the alleys. I bet Drones are patrolling 'em, we just can't see right now. Vlada was right. Fuckers are smarter than we've noticed, smarter than me and the other boys realized during Downpour, even."

"Y'all come down this way during Downpour?"

"Passed by, not really through. That op was an absolute shitshow, brother. Hardly no organization or strategy. Made us Raiders and SEALs look like Coast Guard poofs."

"Hey, my second cousin's in the Coast Guard."

"Sorry, sorry," Gaspar raised a palm, smirked, and shook his head. "Fact is, that op was doomed from the start. If we can rally with Raven-Two, even Vlada and the others, supposing Barley's last contact holds up, we can give these alien freaks a run for the money."

"Fuckin' A."

They bumped fists, and then heard metal creak somewhere behind them. They turned, and relief eased their chests. Wilson was peering through the open stairwell door. Gaspar beckoned him, and Wilson jogged to meet up.

"What's up? Make contact yet?"

"Not quite," Gaspar said. "Got an idea, though. May not like it."

"This is Keign," Wilson said. "The fuck's to like?"

Gaspar smirked, wryly. He exchanged looks with Lloyd, whose eyebrows raised as if to say *told you so*.

What ensued was another story altogether. Much to Gaspar's relief, Wilson didn't adamantly reject the idea of crossing over to the neighboring office complex, despite its 'decapitation' as Lloyd put it, let alone via a creaking, warped plank of glass supported by two steel beams twenty feet apart. However, Wilson did oppose the necessity of it.

"If you can think of absolutely no better option," Wilson said, sounding significantly more composed than he had been ten minutes ago, "I'm all-in. A hundred fucking percent, sir. But frankly…I just feel like there's gotta be a sounder alternative."

Gaspar nodded, and gave Wilson's shoulder a firm slap. He looked around, unafraid of putting a foot on a knee-high parapet before looking down. The narrow spaces between buildings were enough for a Drone to navigate, but with little forgiveness. It made sense that Roback wouldn't want to stay here, but for him to go so far as Creekmoor worried Gaspar.

Lending one more scrupulous, unexcited gaze up the makeshift bridge of glass connecting the buildings helped Gaspar decide. The bowed section extended from the top of the two-story Duckworth Center to the fourth floor of the six-story office building. To make the trek, they would have to use one of the two intact steel beams as a massive handrail, since the glass itself, despite its many cracked grooves, wasn't sip-resistant.

"Maybe SAR will be crazy enough to make that trek," Gaspar ultimately said, withdrawing his boot from the edge of the glass. He signaled his comrades back toward the stairwell door on the other side of the roof. "Right now I say we keep our feet on the ground, hunt down Roback one block at a time, and if we get a Drone on our ass, pull into a building. Bottleneck it, kill it, and continue."

"No objections," Lloyd said.

Best-case scenario, especially at this point, after Operation Malathion has run its course, and the MSOT was taken back to Base, SAR teams would be dispatched. Mostly via helicopter, including rappelling crews to enter taller structures and extract civilians without ever having to put boots on the ground. Again, anyway.

Wilson and Lloyd were back in the stairwell, Gaspar within arm's reach of the door, when his comms crackled with life. A distinctly low, raspy voice he would recognize anywhere in the world entered his ear.

Marco Arrington.

"Crossing Grackle, westbound, anyone read? Raven-One, copy?"

Gaspar backpedaled, briskly. He raised a finger to his mouth, and whistled. Lloyd and Wilson regrouped, back on the roof. Gaspar pressed his transmitter.

"This is Raven-One, I hear you, Lima Charlie." A pause. "Arrington?"

"Master Sarge, that you? Goddamn."

"Come to the Duckworth Center, not on Grackle, but a road down, uh…Lloyd, what's the addy?"

Lloyd had already run to one end of the rooftop, and peered over the parapet. He radioed his response, instead of shouting at Gaspar from eighty feet away.

"204 Lincoln Street."

"204 Lincoln, it's the *fourth* building down *Lincoln* Street, how copy?"

"Lima Charlie, en route. I can…I can see Lincoln from here, sir."

"Fuckin' A. Keep an eye out for patrolling Drones. Who are you with?"

One by one, as if taking rollcall over the radio, Arrington's company responded on comms. Gaspar felt relief hearing their healthy voices in his ear.

Popov, Russo, and Graves.

No Vlada, though.

Or the rest of Raven-One.

"Where the hell's the rest?" Wilson asked, without radioing the impulsive question.

"Solid copy, come to us and we'll reboot." Gaspar rallied with Lloyd by the streetside edge of the roof. Wilson followed. "I've got Lloyd and Wilson with me, Sergeant. We're on the roof. Avoid the…"

Lloyd snapped his fingers and pointed.

Gaspar's finger released the transmitter.

"I see 'em. Excellent."

The three operators watched as their four comrades emerged into view, ninety feet from the Duckworth Center, at the intersection of Grackle and Lincoln. Arrington led the way with his RM338. Single-file, they advanced down the narrow road that was Lincoln, between office structures much bigger than Duckworth. Most vehicles occupying Lincoln were on the curb, parked or crushed.

"Thank God we don't have to worry about snipers," Graves radioed. "Or else y'all would stick out like sore thumbs."

"You, too, bud," Wilson replied.

"Lookin' clear, Raven," Gaspar said. "Go ahead and cross, you won't be entering through the front."

"Say again, sir," Arrington asked, before leading the other three across the street, two buildings down Lincoln.

"You are to avoid the main lobby," Gaspar replied. "Got a Drone corpse that might be taken at any minute, or could be watched by another. Cut around 203 and take the back door by a red dumpster. How copy?"

"Wilco," Arrington replied, and then put both hands on his machine gun before vanishing between buildings 202 and 203 on Lincoln. Popov, Graves, and Russo followed, respectively.

"Let's go," Gaspar said, redirecting his men toward the back of Duckworth. "Cover their entrance, on me, on me."

Twenty feet shy of the parapet, and the men heard a distinct sound. The stabbing 'feet' of a Drone scampering across pavement, paired with the occasional brush of its panoplied limbs against walls. Gunfire in the opposite direction of the approaching operators pulled Raven-One's attention far right. Gaspar only glanced, before looking straight down; he saw a Drone pause by the red dumpster, consequently blocking access to the back door of the building he occupied. The door led down into the maintenance level beneath the Duckworth Center's ground-floor offices.

Shouldering his G6, Gaspar began firing down at the Drone. Simultaneously bursts were coming behind it, through a narrow alley in the direction of the hospital.

"Holy shit, it's Roback!" Wilson exclaimed.

Leading a column of operators, Arrington maintained point and battered the front of the Drone with his own RM338. Clusters of rounds chewed away the Apophid's skull, and even when it lowered its cranial panoply like a shield, Arrington's rounds slowly punched through the violet carapace. All while Roback's LMG battered it from behind.

With Gaspar firing from above, the Drone was decommissioned for good in a matter of ten seconds. If that. Trouble was, it collapsed in the most inconvenient spot.

Arrington led the others closer to its corpse, that dark red dumpster a perfect waypoint. Once within arm's reach of the seemingly dead creature, he punched two rounds into the riddled skull, ensuring its demise. Then, in a feat of human strength and bravery, he put his own back to the creature's thorax, and shoved it away from the door. Popov followed, opening the door and holding it for the others.

"Where the literal fuck you been, man!?" Wilson shouted down at Jayson Roback as he hustled down the alley.

"Killing bugs, how 'bout you?" Roback responded.

He reached Arrington, who gave him a passing fist bump as if they had missed nothing at all. Roback entered the building and then Arrington followed. The dead Drone's body slackened, its limbs effectively barricading the door from the outside. The sound briefly startled Russo.

"Ease up, brother, we're safe," Roback said.

"How's that?"

"Our boys wouldn't be perched on the roof if this place wasn't secure," Roback said, wasting no time in finding a way topside. Upon finding an open stairwell, he looked back at the others and shrugged. "To some extent, anyway."

"En route to you," Arrington radioed.

"Copy," Gaspar responded. "Head's up, there's three civvies in the stairwell. They've been tended to."

"Good to know."

"Imagine we'd crossed that crazy shit," Lloyd said, pointing at the glass bridge-like debris, "just for Roback to come running down the back alley."

"Fuckin' hell," Gaspar shook his head. "Don't even bring that up."

The three men shared a fleeting laugh.

Then, emerging onto the rooftop, was the Sergeant himself. Roback, followed by Russo, Popov, and then Arrington. Roback was eager to let the RM338 sag in its sling, freeing his hands to greet the others.

"Raven-One, once again," he grinned.

"Shit, missed you, brother," Wilson said.

"Same," Lloyd said.

"Don't lie, Lloyd. You just missed the three-three-eight."

Lloyd shrugged. "You're not wrong."

"Glad you're in one piece," Gaspar said. "Fuck happened, though?"

"When we broke from the hospital," Roback explained, in between heavy breaths and sips of water, while the others assembled around them, "that Warrior along Grackle damn near made me piss myself, no joke. I put a burst into it, pulled back, lost sight of you, caught up, then a fuckin' Drone cut me off. Rest was history. Had to snake through alleys trying to make it fuck off or die, before I knew it I was circling back to Celestine, thinkin' maybe that's where y'all would go."

"Shittin' hell," Lloyd said, shaking his head.

"I hear that," Roback said.

"Why didn't you ping us?" Gaspar asked, tapping his

transmitter.

Roback turned his head, pointing at his empty ear.

"Lost my plugs when that Drone's scythe caught my vest. Knocked the wind right outta me, damn near broke my neck in the process."

It was only then that the operators noticed the distress to the center of his vest, above his ammo pouches. The fabric was torn around the impact spot, but his CyTech ballistic plate had absorbed the damage, and allayed the pressure.

"Gonna hurt like an absolute bitch tomorrow," Gaspar cautioned him, having endured the same during Downpour.

"I'll take it."

Gaspar nodded. Then he let his rifle sag on its sling and reached behind him. He dug something out of a small pouch. It was a round case, half the size of his fist. He handed it to Roback.

"No way. You just so happen to carry an extra?"

"Got one more," Gaspar said. "Lebeau has two additional pairs himself. What? You think we'd go into Keign, expecting a two-day excursion, and not have extra plugs?"

Roback shook his head before letting his sling take the weight of the RM338, freeing his hands. He then inserted the CyTech plugs, and synced them with his transmitter. He took a moment to test them; meanwhile, Popov and Russo had taken to the front edge of the building, facing Lincoln Street.

"You think she's linked up with the rest of Raven-One by now?" Russo asked.

"We'll know soon enough."

"How's that?"

"Far as I can figure, that woman isn't about waiting around. And she'll find a way, somehow or another."

"That *woman*, huh? Not…alien? Hybrid?"

"Semantics," Popov said. "She was, and far as I'm concerned, still a woman."

"I'd like to believe you're right."

"Then believe it," Popov said, adamantly, before turning away from the parapet. He regrouped with the others, meeting Arrington and Graves halfway.

"The prodigal return," Arrington said, smirking and exchanging hands with Popov.

"Raven-Two almost feels complete," Graves said, giving Popov a fist-bump. "You think Lebeau and Fuller are in one piece out there?"

"If Vlada has anything to say about it, I'd think so."

"Shit, let's hope she doesn't hold a grudge against Fuller for being such an asshole," Graves said. "I wasn't exactly a big fan of her from the get-go, but…seeing is believing."

"Then he'll just have to see for himself," Popov said.

Someone suddenly whistled. Shrill and curt.

The three operators turned to face the others. Gaspar was beckoning them. They rushed across the roof to rally with him and the rest of the group.

"Bad news, fellas, we gotta move," Gaspar said. He pointed, left of the Duckworth Center. In the direction of Grackle Ave. At the far end of the alley, a massive, violet shape was skittering to and fro. Probing the mouth of the alley, barely wide enough to fit a large vehicle down. Much less a—

"Behemoth," Roback said.

"No way that thing can come down here," Wilson said. He looked at everyone else. "Right?"

"It shouldn't…but it could," Lloyd said.

"Lloyd is right. If that Behemoth so much as tries to cram itself down here, it could severely damage, possibly even bring down some of these buildings."

"But the people hiding in them…" Graves said.

"Exactly. We can't risk that." Gaspar pulled away. He advanced to the far end of the rooftop—the upper limb of the V. It pointed toward Cedar Plaza. Was a bit of a trek, but it gave

Gaspar an idea. "I say we push for the Plaza, lure it into the open, we've got enough manpower to really make a difference without relying on cover."

"Bold, but I'm in," Roback said.

"Half the point, too. Show these fuckers we're more than just rats in a maze. Running and hiding. Besides..." Gaspar nodded at Roback, then Arrington. "We've got two heavies with us, now."

"Three, if we manage to regroup with Lebeau," Graves said. "Which I trust Vlada is making possible as we speak."

Roback scoffed. "I wouldn't trust that bitch far as I could throw her."

Gaspar shook his head and began to say something.

"You wouldn't be doing the throwing," Russo said.

"Fuck you just say?" Roback scoffed, stepping up to Russo. Arrington was quick to park them, and the only one that could physically push Roback away.

"Look, we've seen her in action," Arrington said. "Fact is, she can fire a three-three-eight with one hand, reloads it faster than you can take a belt out, and kill a Drone with her hands alone."

"A pair of Warriors, too, for that matter," Russo said.

"Bullshit," Wilson scoffed.

"We've seen it," Popov said.

"Listen, I don't care if you think 21X doesn't belong here, or any other train of thought regarding her for that matter," Gaspar spewed. "Fact is, we've still got *at least* two of our own people out there, and now we have a Behemoth on our asses."

A loud, grating sound lassoed their attention back toward Grackle. They turned and saw the Behemoth begin to shove itself down the alley. The jagged edges of its carapace, with no apparent difficulty, started ripping through the concrete wall of one building, while gouging the reinforced glass of another.

"First," Gaspar snapped, "we need to lure it back onto

Grackle, and take it down Lincoln. Then we hang a…"

He looked around, to confirm his sense of direction, and memory of the city's map.

"A left onto Lacewing Place, which takes us west of the Plaza. From there, we cross into the parking lot and handle that fat fucking pest."

The operators gathered. No more objections flew.

"Wilson, Russo, Lloyd—you're the fastest of us. Get down there, cut over to Lincoln, then Lacewing. Make sure the Behemoth follows, pepper it with rounds but conserve."

A brief pause.

"*Now*, gentlemen!" Gaspar snapped. Popov wished Russo luck, which he returned. Then he joined Wilson and Lloyd as they ran to the stairwell door. Gaspar called out: "We'll meet you at the Plaza!"

The operators emerged from the back door less than twenty seconds later, albeit with a minor struggle. The legs of the dead Drone outside made opening the door a tough task, one that two of the men turned into light work once they collaborated.

Peering over the parapet, so as to reduce their visibility, Gaspar and Arrington witnessed the Behemoth notice the three operators emerge from the building. They advanced toward it, firing at its putrid face, and then hanging a left between two buildings. Lincoln 201 and 202, tremendously close to the massive Apophid's scythe-reach.

They hung a right onto Grackle, in the opposite direction of Lacewing, briefly confusing Gaspar. And then they started putting rounds into the Behemoth's ass, slowly luring it into a backpedal. The creature returned to Grackle, the horn jutting from its skull briefly goring the corner of a building. It turned away from the alley it had started to violate with its massive presence, and belligerently snarled at the operators. Then it pursued them, and from the front of the Duckworth building, the others watched Wilson lead the way, across the mouth of Lincoln Street. Behind him, Russo and Lloyd took staggered turns firing back at the Behemoth. Its speed in a wide enough space was unnerving, so they watching their footing to avoid tripping, and didn't shoot back at it when the creature seemed certain enough of its speed.

It followed them right down Lacewing Place.

"Let's shine, boys," Gaspar said, leading the others down the stairwell, giving the civilians there a comforting word in passing, and then taking the lobby entrance instead of the back door. The dead Drone Gaspar had warned Arrington of earlier reeked to high heaven but was no longer a point of concern. They navigated around it, but instead of taking Lincoln to Grackle or Lacewing, Gaspar led his men in the opposite direction. He hung a right onto a backroad whose left would have taken them toward Creekmoor.

The street sign at the intersection of Lincoln indicated it was Braun Drive, named after Carol Moseley Braun, the first woman elected to the U.S. Senate from Illinois.

"Braun takes us to Lacewing, but too soon," Gaspar said. "We're gonna cut left onto Brooklet Road, via the last alley, and then should wind up behind the Behemoth, on Lacewing."

Braun Drive bisected more office complexes. Small restaurants, bakeries, and coffee shops occupied the bottom floors of many. The occasional alley between buildings offered a glimpse onto Lincoln to their right, or Brooklet to their left. Gaspar neared the last alley about forty feet from the end of Braun. He slowed, approaching the corner of a Starbucks at the base of an office tower, and his nose wrinkled.

The front glass window had been shattered, and mangled bodies of civilians were strewn about. Some hung on the edge of the broken window, their grisly wounds seemingly caused by the glass, but more than likely an Apophid.

Arrington cut across the open space, ignoring the aftermath of carnage to instead focus on the alley. Aiming his RM338 with purpose.

"Clear," he announced.

Gaspar advanced down the alley, eager to leave that bloodbath behind him. It was just as well motivating, though. And to his displeasure, the alley wasn't as spotless as the one behind Duckworth. It was congested with a small car that had tried to escape down it, only to be attacked by an Apophid, by the looks of it. A jagged hole in the windshield left behind a bloody mess inside, and most of the windows were shattered. Only one body occupied the passenger seat. It had not been eaten, so most of the woman's body was intact, save a gruesome hole in the left side of her chest.

"Focus, focus," Gaspar reminded his men as they passed the vehicle.

An alcove twenty feet ahead of the vehicle and to their right featured a dumpster, a UPS truck, and two lurking Apophids. *Waiting* for them. The second Gaspar noticed the loitering Apophid, impossible to hide behind the UPS truck like its accompanying Drone, he announced it.

"Warrior!"

Gaspar didn't radio it. He shouted, and turned to face the creature, rifle shouldered. The G6 spat rounds out toward its face. But the creature shrieked and flung the dumpster toward him. It screeched across the pavement, one corner colliding with Gaspar's right elbow. His radius shattered and his ulna fractured. He exclaimed in pain, and his arm went limp. Still wielding the G6 in his left hand, he kept firing at the Warrior while side-stepping down the alley.

The other operators surged forward to volley the Warrior with gunfire. The Apophid took two swings with its serrated limbs, one stab with a scythe, all out of reach, before the barrage of high-caliber rounds brought it down.

In this time, the Drone had circumvented the UPS truck to attack Gaspar, who was some thirty feet away from the nearest other operator. Arrington swung his RM338 left, battering the Drone's left thorax and skull with armor-piercing rounds. The Drone might have reached and impaled Gaspar had it not been for Arrington.

Gaspar found himself backing into a concrete wall, draining his G6's magazine into the Drone's face before it reached him. A scythe came down, stabbing concrete eight inches to the right of Gaspar's face.

Arrington was joined by Roback, and together they neutralized the obstinate Drone. It collapsed in a bleeding, rancid heap.

Popov and Graves went to Gaspar's aid.

They administered a makeshift sling, but had nothing to compose a splint. Gaspar insisted it was fine, albeit through painful groans.

"They were *waiting for us*?" Roback asked, in disbelief.

"Smarter than we've given 'em credit for," Popov said, reiterating Vlada.

Roback appeared angry. Gaspar realized he was on the verge of saying something negative about Vlada again, or possibly along the lines of "don't tell me you admire these things," which would be even worse and poorly founded.

"We still have a chance," Gaspar growled, "to prove we're smarter."

Roback nodded firmly.

Popov, too.

"Graves, take point. Arrington, on his ass. Roback, our six. Help me keep pace."

"You got it," Roback said.

They moved, Popov in between Arrington and Gaspar. The latter was wounded, but just his right arm. Like most MARSOC Raiders, Gaspar was ambidextrous. He had slung his

G6, though, in exchange for the lighter Rattler. His legs and the rest of his body unaffected, he moved just fine. But the pain in his arm wasn't an idle thing, and he appreciated Roback following the order. Keeping pace. Ironic, considering Gaspar was three ranks higher than Roback.

Graves, now the fastest among them despite his shorter stature, maintained point. They emerged onto Brooklet Road, hung a right, and then a left onto Lacewing.

"It's taken the bait, I see 'em," Graves radioed.

"Advance," Gaspar replied. "Let's kill this fucker."

Riding the coattails of Gaspar's voice was the familiar thump of a helicopter's rotors.

8

Corporal Dylan Fuller was reloading his Rattler when a different indication of movement stole his attention. Behind him. At the mouth of Graffiti Ave, the scenic road he and Lebeau occupied. They had come about sixty feet down it, pursued by two Warriors and a whopping seven Drones. The latter disseminated moments earlier when the operators were nearly run over by a pair of civilian vehicles on Mayfield. The pickup truck and hatchback were carrying as many as ten people, some of who carried firearms. They seemed to be on some sort of vigilante course, but how effectively, Fuller couldn't determine.

Much like the civvies in Innsbrook during their initial flyover, probably not very.

Even now, over the staccato beat of Lebeau's RM338, Fuller could hear the vehicles' engines and occasional screech of tires as they tried to evade the Drones. Perhaps the civvies were the ones pursuing the Drones, but Fuller deemed this unlikely.

As with the bulk of Keign's population, they should have followed the announcement preceding the MSOT's deployment. To stay indoors, maintaining shelter and quiet.

The movement back toward Mayfield suddenly worsened Fuller's expectation of his and Lebeau's survivability. They were estranged from the others, out of comms range, and the last update they received from Barley was forty minutes ago. Every ten minutes, for about ninety seconds, a Little Bird would cross their airspace and deliver support. The helo's minigun was a blessing, but Fuller didn't like that it was a drone. The remote pilots were good at their job, but something about having a real man or woman in the cockpit was of greater comfort. Since the Apophids had no air force, he didn't understand the prioritization of using unmanned craft.

At any rate, if the movement he saw was another Warrior, he might have to play bait. Lure the creature into an open enough space down Graffiti Ave for Lebeau to pick it apart with his LMG.

Named after the rows of art and music studios, clubs, and warehouses whose outer facades had been surrendered for graffiti artists, the road was nearly as wide as Mayfield and easily the most vibrant place in all of Keign. More colorful than Elgin Park, albeit artificially, Graffiti Ave was the most frequented street in the North Village, but primarily for pedestrians.

Much to Fuller and Lebeau's relief, once they found themselves down the Avenue, it was far less blemished by carnage than they expected. This led them to believe—hope—that the bulk of its attendees had found substantial shelter inside the buildings.

Unfortunately, the sheer lack of vehicles, given an abundance of no-parking signage, provided significantly less cover for them than any other road in the city.

After managing to kill one of the two Warriors, Lebeau and Fuller witnessed the other scamper off and periodically emerge from an alley to take a swing at them, before retreating again. Paired with the occasional wave of Drones, it was becoming an extremely daunting experience.

He was regretting not bringing a G6.

Fuller didn't have the body mass or brute strength to carry as much as an RM338, G6, *and* Rattler on his person, like Lebeau. Who had offered Fuller his own G6 moments ago, only for them to be interrupted by two different Drones in either direction, dividing their attention.

"I've got movement down Mayfield way," Fuller radioed. He looked in that direction, but saw nothing. A glance over his shoulder showed him Lebeau on a knee, reloading the RM338.

"Busy," Lebeau radioed.

Fuller noticed a Drone accompanying a Warrior into the open, thirty feet from Lebeau.

"I'll say," Fuller said, and then radioed: "Moving to you."

He literally *heard* the air woosh above him, and flinched, half-expecting a Drone to have leapt from the roof of a building. Or to witness the first-ever winged Apophids. Instead, when his eyes scanned the sky, he saw a human figure leaping from one rooftop to the other, crossing the forty-foot gap with virtually no effort.

21X.

The alien-woman hybrid landed a few feet behind Lebeau's right shoulder. Fuller felt a surge of hatred, distrust, and anger. He raised his weapon, but spared a hand to radio Lebeau.

"On your six!"

Lebeau impulsively rolled left, popping up on his robust legs, wielding the machine gun. But in this time, 21X had sprung into the air again. She landed in a forward somersault, and the second she was upright, ten feet in front of the Drone leading the Warrior, she drew her Taurus. The revolver barked twice and the Drone collapsed in a tumble that she side-stepped to effortlessly avoid. Then, scrambling right, she took to a sidewalk, catching the Warrior's attention. It snarled at her and swung a bladed arm, but she shrunk to her knees, sliding across the pavement and evading the Apophid limb by maybe ten inches. When she was on her feet again—

"Close," Vlada said to herself, out of the others' earshot.

144

She spun to face the Warrior but before it could even rotate away from Lebeau to face her, she had shouldered her G6. Rounds barraged its exposed petiole, the lead mushrooming inside the muscled mass, steel cores providing deep wound channels.

The Warrior uttered something that Lebeau could only describe as a vocalization of pain, as its footing weakened.

Vlada surrendered the G6 to her sling, ran a circle around the wounded Warrior, then used its limbs as stepping stones, its appendages as ladder rungs. She vaulted herself onto the back of its elongated cranial panoply, and reached for its left eyeball. Instead of plunging her fist into the socket, her alien digits clawed for the sensory organ, sinking in for grip, and then yanking it out. Optic nerves severed and bloody pus poured from the socket. She flung it onto the asphalt, dismounted, and backpedaled—making eye contact with Lebeau.

"Now," Vlada radioed.

He nodded and sidestepped for a better angle, before firing up at the Warrior's injured face. With Lebeau's superior aim and the Apophid's wounded composure, he was able to deliver a fatal shot to the eye socket in as few as three trigger squeezes. The towering Warrior slumped, with not so much as a twitch afterward.

Vlada lifted her G6, eyeing the magazine window. Eighteen of the original thirty rounds left.

"Nice of you to…drop in." Lebeau approached her.

"Hey, lovebirds, got a sitch unfolding," Fuller in their ears. Down the opposite direction of Graffiti Ave.

Lebeau rolled his eyes and began to jog toward his comrade. Vlada reached Fuller in a third of the time, and began to raise her weapon. But paused.

"Civvies," she said, watching the hatchback approach.

"At least we know you aren't blind," Fuller said.

"You have no idea," she said, the nonchalance and ambiguity of her statement appearing to trouble Fuller.

She walked past him, and the hatchback swerved to a stop. It mounted the curb about fifteen feet away, went into reverse, and began to make a U-turn.

Vlada raised a hand. "Wait! Come to us."

Fuller stood from when he had been kneeling, and cupped his mouth.

"Don't go!" he shouted, and then beckoned them.

Through the passenger window, a man in plainclothes wielded a Glock and began firing at Vlada. She cursed under her breath and angled her robust forearm. Bullets plinked the alien flesh, dropping without penetration. Fuller flinched from how close he was to the impacts, shockingly looking up at her, noticing the fallen rounds, and then navigating to the nearest sidewalk.

"Cease fire, cease fire!" Lebeau roared, firing into the air, to Vlada's right.

The hatchback turned around to head back toward Mayfield. Just then the other civilian vehicle, a pickup, fishtailed past the end of Graffiti Ave. A pursuing Warrior swung its bladed arm, catching the back right fender. The truck barrel-rolled across Mayfield, colliding with the corner of an ornate stone sign that read 'Optima Suites.'

From the cab leapt two men. Stuck in the cab was a woman who screamed in pain. From the bed had spilled three other men, two of who were fatally crushed in the process.

Up across Mayfield, crawling across the tops of gridlocked vehicles on Sycamore Blvd, were two Drones. They reached the pickup wreckage. The men now on their feet looked back in horror, two of the three managing to run in the process. The third still held onto a pump-action shotgun, and fired it up into the face of a nearing Drone.

Vlada had long since departed the spot beside Fuller.

She rebounded off the wall of a nearby building down Graffiti Ave, landing in front of the hatchback. It screeched to a stop. She shouldered her G6 and began firing at the Drone that had reached the man with the shotgun. Ignoring the bullets peppering its skull, the Drone's jaws came down, vanishing the man's upper body inside them. The creature whipped its head back, leaving a grisly V-shaped gap in the man's torso.

Vlada screamed and leapt across the hood of the idling hatchback, firing her G6 at the other Drones. But the Warrior that had derailed the truck intervened, swinging its arms at her, and threatening to impale her with its scythes.

In exchange for her bare hands, Vlada released the G6, evaded the Warrior's melee attempts, and then used the stalk of its torso to swing herself around the creature. Behind her, Lebeau and Fuller targeted the Warrior for nearly a hundred feet away with their weapons, focusing on the head and petiole.

The driver of the hatchback attempted to drive away, seeking to hang a right onto Mayfield. But there was discordance inside the car, and eventually three of the passengers disembarked. They took equal care in defending those that had been flung from the pickup, while the hatchback veered off down Mayfield.

A Drone pursued it, nearly trampling one of the former passengers in the process.

Meanwhile, Vlada reached a Drone about to impale one of the other truck passengers. She caught its left scythe, and was about to rip the limb away when its other stabbed down, and her left shoulder was grazed in the process. The tip of the exoskeletal limb punched into the civilian's sternum, shattering it before jutting out his back, between his shoulder blades. He had been struggling to stand, one leg broken from the truck wreck. Now blood shot out of his mouth, misting Vlada's waist.

She pulled at the Drone's other scythe, breaking it off at the joint. Screaming at the same time, she turned the scythe around and impaled the Drone through the throat with the limb. As the creature sagged to the pavement, the two operators far behind her had advanced, and slowly killed the Warrior trying to flank her.

Two of the three passengers from the hatchback had reached the survivors of the truck wreck. Helping them away. But one didn't. He crawled into the overturned pickup, trying to help the woman caught inside. Her legs were crushed, and a piece of shrapnel was lodged in her spleen.

Vlada heard the woman's sobs of pain and fear.

The blood from another man painting her stomach.

Stench of failure suddenly reeked far worse than a dead Apophid.

Another Drone was in the process of snapping its jaws at those who hobbled across Mayfield. Around abandoned vehicles and mangled bodies of civilians long dead. She drew her Taurus and fired at it, trying to distract the creature from its prey. The thing tried to ignore her, until its wounds amassed. Forced to reload, Vlada instead holstered the revolver and lifted her G6.

At that same moment, Lebeau incapacitated the Drone with his machine gun, before lowering it. Fuller raised his G6, but Lebeau put a heavy hand on the barrel.

"Conserve ammo," he said. "Allow her."

Vlada had already leapt onto the Drone's back. She scooted forward, her heels digging into wounds around the base of its stubby neck. Her alien hands reached toward the inner corners of its mouth, fingers navigating its terrible teeth. With a scream of exertion and rage, Vlada ripped the Drone's upper jaw off. Blood and saliva gushed from the joints of its mouth, sundered brain slop spilling from the open cavity in its skull.

The body went limp on the pavement.

"Jesus," Fuller mumbled, before rushing across Mayfield. He helped the man in the overturned truck, but the woman was difficult to move. He radioed to Lebeau. "This woman's stuck, sir. Her legs are crushed and she's got shrapnel in the abdomen. Please advise."

"Moving to you," Lebeau responded.

As he crossed Mayfield, the man helping his friend, possibly relative, away from the scene turned to look Vlada in the eye. He appeared afraid, but nonetheless thanked her.

"I, I don't know who or what you are, but, but thank you."

"Just…find shelter, a small space," Vlada requested, panting. She wasn't tired, not physically. "Hide. Please."

The man nodded and helped the other one hobble across the street.

"What do we do?" Fuller asked Lebeau, who was now looking inside the truck.

"Move," Vlada said, firmly.

She stood by the hood of the flipped truck.

Fuller appeared confused. But Lebeau looked at Vlada, nodded, and then helped the other civilian back. Then he looked at Fuller, who still seemed puzzled. Or against this idea. So Lebeau grabbed his vest and physically pulled him back, before ducking into the truck to speak with the wounded woman.

"This is going to hurt, a lot, but it's all we can do to get you out," Lebeau said. He gently squeezed the woman's outstretched hand, and then let go. She nodded, crying. After emerging and standing, Lebeau gestured that the other two men step back. Then he nodded at Vlada.

Gripping the front axle of the of the truck, with some semblance of strain, Vlada rotated the vehicle. Left hand staying there, her right relocated to the front left fender for stability, and finished. The truck sagged on its blown tires. Inside the cab, the woman was now on the partially crushed dashboard, no longer stuck.

Lebeau and the civilian man helped gently pull her out. Her legs were not in as terrible shape as they had feared. Only one was broken, and it hadn't compounded. Vlada circled the truck, drawing Lebeau's attention. Her head suddenly jerked to the side, and she seemed to stare into the sky above Mayfield.

"What is it?" Lebeau asked her.

"Helo. But not a Little Bird."

Lebeau's brow furrowed.

"Merlin?" Fuller asked.

"I think," she said.

"We've gotta move," Fuller said, looking at Lebeau.

"Optima," Vlada said, and then turned to face the woman and who she suspected, believed, was her husband. "Go to them."

"B-But we live in Creekmoor," the man said.

"It's too far, too dangerous," Vlada insisted. "Go to Optima, as soon as you clear the lobby you'll be safe. Try to find a room, someone will let you in."

The man sniffled and nodded. But in trying to move her, he struggled. She could limp, but even her working leg was in pain. And neither were in any state for him to carry her.

Suddenly Vlada looked up again.

It was such a brisk, abrupt motion that it made the man and Fuller both flinch. Fuller immediately shook his head, mortified and ashamed.

"Barley," Vlada said. "The drone, it's—"

"Raven-Two, how copy?" Barley's voice in their ears. Fuller and Lebeau were staring at the sky, which had begun to grow dimmer with cloud cover and the approach of dusk. Albeit still two hours out.

"Lima Charlie," Vlada responded. "Update on Raven-One?"

"The others are on the move, handling a Behemoth threat in Cedar Plaza. More Apophids are en route there as we speak. Merlin-Three should be making contact with them at any moment. Sitrep?"

"Complicated," Lebeau said. "But alive. Civilian casualties, unfortunately."

"Copy. A refueled Little Bird is en route to help escort you to the Plaza. Rally with the rest of the MSOT there, eliminate threats, and then seek shelter. Await further update."

"Wilco, out." Lebeau released his transmitter and looked at Fuller. He gestured down Graffiti Ave. "We take that down to the end, Cardinal Boulevard cuts across the north side of Novi, and circles the Plaza."

Fuller nodded. He gulped. "What about—"

He was in the process of indicating the civilians. But Vlada stepped forward.

"Sir, can you walk?" she asked him.

His brow furrowed as he looked at the others, but then shrugged.

"Yeah, I'm...I'm not hurt."

"Ma'am?" Vlada asked.

Apophid shrieks could be heard down Sycamore.

"I won't hurt you," she said, her expression relaying compassion and concern, even a sort of empathy, considering her outstretched alien arms.

The woman nodded, and reluctantly surrendered herself to Vlada. She hoisted her, carrying the woman with ease; her nape in the nook of Vlada's left elbow, and her bent knees across her right forearm.

"To Optima," Vlada told the man. "Follow. Try to keep up, but I won't leave you behind."

Gulping, the man nodded. "Thank you. I, f-for the record, I don't know why Frank shot at you. S-Scared, I guess."

"It's fine," she said, and then looked back at Fuller, her voice, eyes, and face devoid of hate. Only empathy. "I understand."

Fuller felt a pang of guilt in his chest.

"I'll meet you at the Plaza," she told Lebeau.

151

He nodded once and they watched Vlada effortlessly carry the wounded woman toward the nearest Optima building. She periodically glanced behind her to confirm that the husband was following fine.

Lebeau grabbed Fuller's shoulder and his eyes alone indicated urgency. Fuller swallowed and followed his CO back across Mayfield. They advanced down Graffiti Ave, subconsciously reflecting on how great of a town Keign was, especially for artists. A reputation that they didn't expect to survive this ordeal.

A shame.

Something well out of their control.

As they reached the end of Graffiti Ave, hanging a cautious left onto Cardinal Blvd, the unmistakable chop of helicopter rotors drew their gaze skyward. The space above Keign was growing dimmer by the minute. It was mind-numbing, and a touch terrifying, to acknowledge that nightfall would be upon the city in just over an hour.

The human-piloted Little Bird that Barley had mentioned came into view.

"This is Scout-Two, your friendly escort to the Plaza," the pilot radioed Lebeau and Fuller.

"Copy, lead the way," Lebeau replied.

The Little Bird took point, its shadow staggered across the buildings of North Village below it. Within three minutes they had reached Iron Mill Court, an uneventful journey they immediately regretted taking for granted. Gunfire echoing across the sixty-acre parking lot of Cedar Plaza was faint, but discernible where they were. Scout-Two banked right, its dual wing-mounted miniguns spraying lead down at multiple targets. A small, for lack of a better word, swarm of Drones and Warriors had come up Iron Mill and begun to cut across the parking lot. Four-hundred yards away, the rest of the MSOT had circled a Behemoth and were in the process of repeatedly volleying it with meticulous gunfire. These were details neither Lebeau nor Fuller could make out from their range, only deduce, with Barley's intel filling in the gaps.

Farther west, the distinguished MV-75 was performing a flyover of the Creekmoor exurbs and Labor District. De Horta periodically fired bursts at targets below, whenever an opening appeared.

Lebeau and Fuller inferred this much, from sound and the occasional glimpse of the tiltrotor craft in the distance.

To their left, part of the Apophid horde branched off from the rest, flooding the parking lot, to instead fixate on the two operators. Drones scampered down the asphalt, around empty vehicles and across sidewalks, with unnerving agility. Lebeau and Fuller targeted them with accurate bursts, from their RM338 and Rattler, respectively. The Little Bird, mobile above them, focused its miniguns on three Warriors. Their multi-legged footing made them more difficult targets than their size and lack of projectile weapons should be.

The buzzsaw-like sound from the miniguns would be almost overwhelming to untrained ears, but in a beautiful kind of way. The operators' earplugs handled the frequency without muting it. Occasionally a stream of armor-piercing 7.62mm rounds caught a Warrior and chewed into its exoskeleton. After the first half-dozen bursts, one severed two of its shoulder limbs, and made the creature topple into another.

If only the domino effect had been more fruitful.

The creatures' agility proved more difficult since the helo pilot couldn't freely fire from every angle. Surrounding buildings could very well be harboring hiding civilians. Frequent misses, and bullets that cut right through an Apophid, spit up divots of asphalt or concrete in the process.

After collaborating on two Drone kills, Lebeau and Fuller navigated onto the grassy median between Iron Mill and the Plaza parking lot. Using the lean trunk of a ten-foot hackberry tree, Lebeau stabilized his RM338 and let out six-round bursts. A Drone was sundered down the middle, at least from skull to thorax, before he redirected his aim. Another had leapt from one roof of a truck to the overturned side of a panel van, and then landed on the parking lot pavement ten feet from Fuller.

A spell of panic made him drop the magazine he was in the middle of reloading. It clattered onto the pavement and he dropped to a knee to retrieve it. Lebeau shouted his name, pivoted his aim, and put a meaty burst into the right side of the Drone. It let out a blood-curling shriek, turning to face him.

A Warrior that had slipped past Scout-Two's minigun strafes had reached Lebeau. A scythe came down, damn near cutting the ten-foot hackberry in two. A pair of broken branches fell onto him. He tried to somersault free, but one pinned his left leg to the ground. It wasn't tremendously heavy, just enough to momentarily immobilize him.

Fuller secured his new mag, put the Rattler's name to practice, and in full-auto slayed the wounded Drone staring him in the face. Dollops of vile alien blood landed on his chest and neck. He ran toward Lebeau, firing the Rattler with its protracted buttstock anchored against his right ribcage. Bullets hosed at the creature's chest, some penetrating its exposed muscle and stalling it.

Above, the Little Bird swung around to target the Apophids streaming across the parking lot toward the MSOT's location. A baker's dozen of Drones and five or six Warriors. Despite not having the clearance to deploy explosives, the pilot determined it was a wide enough expanse devoid of civilians or friendly fire—only scattered vehicles, which he had inferred to be empty.

Lebeau had drawn his Taurus and fired it up at the looming Warrior, which, with Fuller's assistance, began to backpedal. Fuller himself was too short, despite his own strengths, to truly help hoist Lebeau to his feet—but some aid went a lot way. He was barely upright when they heard the distinct hissing sound of a Hydra 70 rocket being loosed from its wing mount. The trail of fumes followed the twenty-pound forty-inch-long blue rocket to its target.

An explosion the size of a convenience store blossomed amid the moving throng of Apophids. Chunks of charred Drones and Warrior limbs scattered about, but the blast was bigger than expected due to igniting surrounding vehicles.

The result was nonetheless effective.

Unfortunately, the other half of the enemy's force continued on as if unfazed by their losses.

Contrary to previous observations on Apophid reactions to casualties and aerial assaults. Perhaps it was different because of the Behemoth's presence. Although at this rate, the Apophids would be arriving to a corpse.

"Good splash, Scout-Two," Lebeau radioed.

He grimaced as he stood up straight. A light limp would be worked out in the next few strides. He gave Fuller a firm slap on the back, in gratitude.

"Copy, permission to follow targets before—"

The pilot didn't need Lebeau's go-ahead, only Base's. Barley's or Aleem's. But the Gunnery Sergeant respected his adamancy. Unfortunately, it was short-lived. The pilot stopped talking midsentence when the Little Bird suddenly faltered in the air, a good sixty feet above the asphalt. It had just passed over one of three small buildings strewn across the lot, a Burger King. The fast-food joint was about a hundred yards from where Fuller and Lebeau were, who had just begun to cross the lot.

They paused to cautiously watch the Little Bird wobble in the air, as if hit by gunfire. But both roof and tail rotors appeared healthy; not a single puff of smoke spilled from anywhere on the helo.

"How copy, Scout-Two?" Lebeau radioed. "You're all over the place."

"Uh, I…I don't know, I just…d-dizzy all of a sudden."

Hearing a pilot sound that uneven and fazed wasn't a good sign, much less what he had to say.

"Feeling better, Scout-Two?" Lebeau asked, after a three-second pause. The helo appeared to have leveled out, but was still a sight from perfect flight.

"Uh, that's a, that's a negative, Raven-Two. Engaging autopilot, clearing the area, I, I think I might p-pass out."

Lebeau and Fuller exchanged bewildered looks.

"Advise you RTB, Scout-Two," Lebeau said regrettably. "Appreciate the help, no fucking joke."

"Copy, I'll…I'll…" The Little Bird banked east and cleared the Q-Wall behind Cedar Plaza six seconds later. The operators were befuddled, but didn't get lost in the moment. Fact was, the pilot *had* helped them a shit-ton, and the bulk of the Apophids no longer seemed interested in the operators trailing them by sixty yards.

As they passed the Panera, the creatures fanned out and drew the attention of the operators behind the Behemoth. Lebeau and Fuller watched its bloodied legs give out, and its bullet-riddled mass sag to the asphalt. Had it not been for Arrington and Roback's RM338s, they wouldn't have been able to penetrate the Behemoth's resilient carapace. The most superior panoply of any Apophid.

Something that Dr. Ginley had theorized was the "hardened, shell-like version of Vlada's sarcous arms."

Lebeau and Fuller navigated to the right side of the Panera, around parked vehicles, for a better angle on their targets. They were now a mere 120 yards from the nearest operators, who surrounded the dying Behemoth in a vast space between the Shell gas station and the storefront. In passing the entrance of the bakery, which was entirely glass, Fuller noticed he could only see himself in its reflection. The lights were off inside, not so much as a spark illuminating the interior. Contrarily, the greater Cedar Plaza storefront appeared lit to some degree. Fuller briefly wondered if maybe the owner had individually cut the power to enhance the quality of his hiding. Fuller hoped that, if this was the case, other civilians were in there as well, taking advantage of the quiet and, thus far, effective shelter.

After all, none of the glass was shattered.

No Drone could've entered any other way.

"On me," Lebeau whispered, vigorously.

Fuller advanced. Lebeau pivoted, unslinging his G6 and handing the rifle to Fuller, who gratefully replaced his Rattler with it.

"Raven-One, at your six," Lebeau radioed.

This side of the dying Behemoth stood Wilson, Russo, and Lloyd. They glanced back to see one-half of Raven-Two by the front corner of the Panera.

There was no time to rejoice, though.

Apophids were attempting to flank the MSOT at their seven o'clock, circumventing the gas station and using it as cover. On the other side of the Behemoth were the rest of the operators, Graves and Arrington nearest the station. They turned to engage the elusive Apophids, Arrington careful to avoid the pumps.

In case civvies were hiding inside the convenience store part of the Shell.

Meanwhile, the storefront windows along the other side of the lot crowded with faces of people that had been hiding there for days on end. And not a single one of them could have predicted the events that were about to unfold in Cedar Plaza.

9

All feelings that she had done something good during her time in Keign, something genuinely selfless and directly helpful, crumbled away on Vlada's approach of Cedar Plaza. She had effectively relocated and saved two civilians, only to be plagued with the fear that in turn she wasn't there for her teammates. Naturally, Vlada could not be everywhere at once, not even two places. For a fleeting moment of dry humor, she had mused to herself—would such a capability be possible had she literally sold her soul to the Apophids?

Then again, these last few weeks, she had begun to dread that this exchange had already happened. Unbeknownst to her, and in ways without her permission.

Vlada's voluntary involvement with Project Outreach didn't count as giving her explicit consent to the forfeiture of her *soul*…did it? Whether the soul was synonymous with heart, or a core of one's mind, or even something far less corporeal, she couldn't think of a price worth surrendering it.

Serving her nation and the betterment of humanity was at the top of the list, though. Reasons for making such a sacrifice.

Regrets were easy to come by, as a human.

For someone in Vlada's circumstances, they were a miring abundance.

Her galloping trek from the northwest corner of Trinity Housing to the southeast end of Cedar Plaza could have been taken across rooftops, but she found it faster on the ground. Instead of taking Iron Mill Court, she cut down Mayfield and then hooked a right onto Yerkes Street, a road named after Illinois' own Mary Agnes Yerkes, a notable impressionist painter. An apt choice for the street that traveled down the west end of Keign's Museum of Cultural Arts.

The MOCA property had seen a great number of civilian casualties and even structural damage, possibly from residual debris when the meteor shower hit the Labor District two blocks over.

Much to her surprise, and initial relief, Apophids were nowhere to be seen. She suspected they were all swarming toward the rest of the MSOT, likely in response to a Behemoth in trouble. Had Keign felt like a ghost town earlier, now it was a necropolis waiting to be buried by time or some immeasurable bulldozer.

It made Vlada's heart hurt, the grave losses the city had suffered in the span of eight days.

What pained her more was an unseen attacker.

Her sojourn to Cedar Plaza could have been made in less than two minutes—had she been unobstructed. She was less than halfway down Yerkes when a searing pain in her chest staggered her. She might have tumbled headlong into the pavement had she not instead run into the fender of a stalled vehicle. She bounced off it as if any other object, her insane momentum debilitating as she collided with an overturned SUV.

Finding herself on hands and knees, Vlada's eyes clamped shut as a paralyzing jolt surged down her spine. Her teeth ground, and around them spilled a wordless utterance of anguish. Her digits curled inward, an act which would have been devastating to any human, but for her just dug troughs in the asphalt.

In the darkness behind her closed eyes, she could see Dr. Ginley and his team of CyTech bio-geneticists surrounding her on a medical slab. Except the slab was composed of rugged stone, and instead of the floor it was the sweeping, gaseous void of scintillating space. More disconcerting, Ginley and his team were not their human selves; they had humanoid outlines, but were each a smaller version of an Apophid Behemoth. The sight made zero sense, but her mind had managed to illustrate it as such, without error. Every detail fit together, disturbingly so.

Their vague faces articulated intelligence and intent, but were vacant of emotion.

They were instruments of a coming genocide.

Tools of an extraterrestrial scourge.

As if apostles of the Apophid horde, themselves.

Of course, even in her paralytic state, Vlada knew better. Their intentions were never anything beyond the pursuit of scientific breakthrough. Blinded by the timeless adage of *could versus should*, Ginley and his team were inherent faults of humanity. Vlada could not blame them any more than she could herself, for winding up in a U.S. Army jail.

There it was again.

The bars, her uniformed self, with a scar on the side of her throat, her whole neck gauzed, and a sullen look of futility in her eyes. Any shade of brilliant green that previously inhabited them was now a deep, dark, featureless black. It was only when Vlada looked outside the bars, at herself, spectating, that her mind witnessed a horrible transmogrification.

Her face began to expand between the bars that she clutched, with very human hands. Then her eyes filled with a tar-like black liquid, the corneas themselves inundating with the lightless filth. She screamed in pain, while her cheekbones reached away from her skull, stretching the skin and creating caverns beneath her sunken eyes. Through these gaping wounds, and around her clenching teeth, swarmed hordes of tiny Apophids. Drones, specifically, but each no bigger than half an inch.

These tiny, wretched abominations marched in droves out of her crumbling face, until her screaming grimace became a silent expression, one that very slowly inverted. Now grinning deviously, her face a festering microcosm of Apophids, she *spoke*.

The words were as crisp and intelligible as they could be, as if she was whispering them directly into her own ear.

"He deserved it," she said.

And Vlada screamed herself into an upright position in the middle of Yerkes Street. Her eyes came open, tears pouring down her cheeks, jaw slack but torturously sore. Her ears popped, and in the distance she could hear a clamor of gunfire, shrieking Apophids, and helicopter rotors. When she tried to run, she could only lumber forward, each step half her normal stride, and an agony to do so.

Until it wasn't.

Vlada willed herself out of the crippling siege of her body. One that, perhaps, the Apophid hivemind was manipulating. A surgically psychological tactic to impair her. If even for a few minutes.

Accepting this as the case, and loathing the Apophids tenfold more for it, she galloped ahead with increased brio. As she neared the end of Yerkes Street, all the sounds she heard before became more precise, and she could even *smell* each of them. The acridity of gun smoke was familiar, but the Apophid stenches she had not yet grown accustomed to. From their hormonal adrenaline to their spilt blood, it was all so dizzying.

Vlada leapt onto a covered ladder on the back wall of a cinema theater. She climbed the steel cage, whose lock broke away in her wake, before vaulting onto the flat rooftop, and moved to the nearest parapet. She had a grand view of Cedar Plaza's parking lot from here, but her location was closer to the west end of it, where the bulk of the action was unfolding. A dead Behemoth occupied the center of the scattered MSOT, who were engaging an arc of flanking Apophids around a Shell gas station; she was maybe sixty yards from it. She noted two operators on this side of a Panera toward the center of the parking lot, before dismounting the roof. She landed mid-stride, sprinting toward the Apophids using the gas station as cover.

The Drones remained too distracted by their human enemies to notice her, half of them suffering the effects of being bullet fodder. But the Warriors spun to address her sudden cameo, and the rage casting from every movement made Vlada a plight for the Apophids.

Most of the MSOT could not see her fight from their side of the parking lot. Only Lebeau and Fuller witnessed glimpses of her manually dismembering Warriors, impaling them with their own scythes, literally punching their eyeballs out, and in one instance digging a clawed hand between a Warrior's ribs before pulling out what could be an Apophid organ.

The sight, even from eighty yards away, was nothing shy of a spectacle. Fuller's regret for misjudging Vlada was humbling, to say the least. But scarring their visibility of her efforts were scattered vehicles in the lot and the other Apophids stretched thin between the MSOT and themselves. They engaged the creatures, whose numbers began to dwindle thanks to overlapping gunfire from Russo and Lloyd.

To everybody's terror, another Behemoth appeared the last place they expected. It must have crept around the northeast side of the city, adhering to the narrow greenbelt just inside the Q-Wall. Had there been less enemy activity in the parking lot these last two minutes, one of the operators surely would have noticed the swaying tree canopies along the Q-Wall at the end of Lacewing Place.

On approach of Cedar Plaza, Merlin-Three's pilot apologized for the delay in regards to scattered clusters of Apophids over Creekmoor and the Labor District.

Hearing his voice in her ear as well, Vlada decided to free

a hand during a brief respite to radio in.

"Likely decoys to keep you busy," she said. "But if they're dead, now, then I'm not fuckin' complaining."

The ire in her voice was not directed at the pilot, and there was no uncertainty about this to everyone listening. Vlada's hatred of the Apophids had never been clearer than it was now.

She had reduced the three Warriors and eight Drones behind the gas station down to only four of the latter. She then leapt onto the canopy over the pumps, and from there jumped onto the lower rooftop of the attached convenience store.

The MSOT was torn between waving at her and engaging the Behemoth. Vlada was not even aware of it until now. She immediately shouldered her G6 for the first time since assisting Lebeau and Fuller. Without hesitation she began plinking rounds at the creature's ghastly face, and the small pockets of exposed muscle around its forelimbs.

Two Drones worked on scaling the sides of the building she was on top, to flank her during this period. Lebeau advanced, joining Lloyd in firing at them; one fell off, tumbling over. The other took its wounds midstride, reaching the rooftop twelve feet to Vlada's right. She let the sling carry her G6 in exchange for her Taurus. Although she drew it in time, the Drone was upon her before she could fire it. A nimble sidestep left its right scythe to anchor in the rooftop, briefly immobilizing it. She fired at the sinewy socket where the scythe-limb was anchored, and with an acrobatic roundhouse kick severed bone from meat. The Drone shrieked in pain, and a steady burst from Lebeau near the base of the building, behind a parked vehicle, annihilated the creature's skull.

Vlada shook herself of its gore.

"Appreciate it," she shouted down at him.

"Anytime," he responded, in his exceptionally deep, husky voice.

The previously wounded Drone rose up to attack him in

his moment of lowered guard, but with Fuller and Lloyd's help, the creature stood no chance.

The arrival of the MV-75 eighty feet above Cedar Plaza welcomed a sweeping avian shadow across the parking lot in its passes. Dusk was nearly upon them, making the aircraft's shadow disproportionate and seemingly darker. Lampposts at scattered intervals across the lot turned on per a schedule. The casting nimbuses of light helped the operators keep their wits, and awareness, sharp.

With the helo's assistance, more specifically De Horta's, the Behemoth below would be dealt with in seconds. Vlada had just dismounted the gas station to rally with Lebeau and Lloyd when they witnessed several things happen at once.

Wilson had retreated from the Behemoth, toward Fuller, who stayed close to the Panera. Mid-reload, Wilson looked up to see the Behemoth charge him, despite gunfire assailing its carapace from above, and more directly into its rear. Suddenly Wilson and Fuller both dropped to a knee, screaming and clutching their heads.

Vlada's brow furrowed. Her heart pinched from within her chest, as if an unseen force had squeezed it into a vice grip.

"No," she growled through her teeth.

Lloyd and Lebeau shouted at their comrades, firing into the right side of the Behemoth, fifty yards away.

The aptly named Apophid reached Wilson and Fuller, its left scythe catching Wilson's skull and obliterating it in a split-second; the exoskeletal scythe continued downward, impaling Wilson's body from neck to groin. His limbs went limp. Fuller, horrified, tried to dive out of the way. The Behemoth's other scythe cut across his back, catching the base of his nap and leaving a grisly trench all the way down to his coccyx, simultaneously shearing his plate carrier away.

Merlin-Three spun around above the Panera, without the

need to bank wide, as any other helo would. Its tiltrotors allowed it this maneuverability. The pilot gave De Horta a clear angle down at the Behemoth's stubby head, but a horrible debacle altered this plan in a split-second.

For a reason unknown to those below, the helo suddenly faltered in the air. De Horta's aim went askew, and the minigun burst too late to correct cut across the parking lot. Popov thought he saw the divots in the pavement come toward him, but then he was thrown down, and in his place Gaspar crumbled. Armor-piercing rounds had gouged his torso, devastating his organs and producing irreparable blood loss.

Vlada had witnessed this at a slower speed than anyone else, and it enraged her to no end.

The paralysis in her body persisted, but she managed to scream. Without radioing it, while the MV-75 pitched down in her direction, she shouted two words.

"Get inside!"

The sound of the massive aircraft plummeting, despite no sign of engine failure or damage, was itself an explosive sound. Realizing she was paralyzed, Lebeau and Lloyd hauled Vlada away from the gas station, back toward Yerkes Street. Meanwhile, behind them, the Behemoth had turned away from a severely wounded Fuller to charge Graves and Arrington. Russo and Roback had gathered Popov en route to their nearest form of shelter, the Plaza storefront.

Amidst the chaos, two Drones that had broken away from the gas station earlier had successfully flanked Arrington and Graves. A scythe came within ten inches of impaling Arrington, but instead caught his RM338, destroying it and taking his right hand with it. Graves was assisting him while hip-firing the Rattler in full-auto to repel the other Drone—but its persistence was uncanny, and savage. As if some unseen force was propelling it forward despite the wounds battering its face.

Jaws still functioning the creature locked them onto

Graves's head, the tips of its teeth scoring his shoulders before the pressure pancaked his skull inside its mouth.

Arrington had watched this unfold, and felt the vile, warm splash of his friend's brain matter on his own face.

The MV-75's nose dipped toward the spacious parking lot behind the Rite Aid. De Horta managed to leap out of the aircraft, after unharnessing himself from the gunner's seat, landing in a painful tumble on top of the gas station canopy. At a reduced speed and altitude, the helo did not explode on impact, and since its tiltrotors were vertical at the time, they remained intact. But its momentum didn't let it rest until after it demolished more than half of the Rite Aid, whose building was only slightly bigger than the helo itself.

Vlada witnessed this as Lloyd and Lebeau flinched, now redirecting them back toward the gas station—per her instruction to seek shelter. Vlada could only pray that the four civilians she had insisted stay there, earlier inside the Rite Aid, had since relocated.

An improbable optimism.

Feeling returned to her legs just as the two operators pushed into the convenience store. Glass doors clanged shut behind them, and scattered merchandise crunched beneath their feet. The partially illuminated interior was an absolute mess. The store had been thoroughly ransacked by survivors, likely days ago. They could hear the faint murmur of civilians hiding behind the front counter, and noticed a few cowering faces at the back of the first two aisles.

The second Lloyd and Lebeau eased Vlada into a corner by the refrigeration units, a middle-aged civilian man fifteen feet away hissed at them. Shouting, in whispers.

"Get that freak the hell out of here! Gonna bring those fucking *things* right to our door!"

Lebeau stood, vehemently, and marched over to the man.

He didn't point the RM338 at him, where he cowered in a corner with, presumably, his wife; but Lebeau did let the weapon sag heftily in its sling, barrel pointed at the floor by the man's feet. Scowling down at him, Lebeau spoke in a voice that, despite its hushed nature, would not be dissuaded.

"That *freak* has saved more lives than you could dare dream of, and those *things* are already here, so I don't *fucking* want to hear it."

Lebeau then turned away, back toward Lloyd and Vlada.

"You're…such a gentleman…" Vlada groaned in pain, wincing around her sarcastic words.

"What's wrong?" Lebeau asked, kneeling. He let the buttstock of his machine gun rest on the floor, and hung onto it like a prop.

"I…I don't know, there's…something else at play here." She shook her head. "Fucking body seizes up, did it earlier when I was with Russo and Popov. Russo saved my worthless ass. Did it again, on my way here, but worse than before. So much…worse."

Lebeau didn't know what to say.

It hurt them all, in more ways than one.

Not only the losses they had suffered, some of which these two operators were unaware of, but now that their greatest asset was inexplicably incapacitated. Her legs were working and she sat up on her own volition, but pain still arrested her features.

Pain.

Vlada was supposed to be virtually immune to pain.

"Well, if nothing else, you aren't *worthless*," Lloyd said. "So I'll have none of that shit in my ear."

Vlada nodded, respectfully.

"But the helo?" Lloyd said, after a moment of reflection. "The fuck happened to Merlin?"

"I don't know, but…same thing happened to our air support, when me and…and Fuller were coming to Cedar. Scout-Two. Pilot was great, saved our asses, but then he suddenly just…lost control for a sec, said he felt sick and might pass out. I ordered him to RTB. He made it out, but…"

Lebeau was shaking his head.

A hand raised to push through his shallow hair. His woeful eyes were clearly recalling the sight of Anthony Wilson's gruesome death and Fuller's terrible injury.

"Maybe some kind of, like…jamming technique," Lloyd said, scowling as if offended by the mere notion of it. He was essentially betraying logic by suggesting it, but it wasn't like the existence of the Apophids followed the rules of their reality.

"Whatever it is, I, I can't be here," Lebeau said, now heartily shaking his head. He got to his feet and returned the machine gun to his hands. He commenced a tedious reload. "Fuller's down, and he can't tend that wound himself. If that Behemoth is still out there…"

Lloyd stood, trying to convince him not to go until they had all their eggs in one basket.

"It is," Vlada finally said, looking up at them. "It *is* still out there. Prowling. I can't *see* it, but I can…I can *feel* it. Almost like a second-sight."

She shook her head, and felt the scrupulous eyes of that man and his wife on her, twenty feet away. But Vlada didn't look their way. She kept her eyes on the operators.

"The others made it to shelter, I…I think. But the Behemoth and a few Drones are still out there. Warriors may be on their way, too."

"Drones could get in here," Lloyd said, suddenly uneasily. But then his brow furrowed with confusion. "Or the storefront. I…I don't know why they haven't tried yet."

"Something about this area, it's…it's *wrong*," she said. "Off. Like they're doing something we don't know about. I…I

168

fear the Apophids have a special plan for the people hiding here."

The operators looked at her for a few long seconds, and then at each other. Their features grew increasingly worried.

"Gaspar, he's…" Vlada croaked, staring straight ahead. Tears cut down her pale, high cheeks. Both men appeared confused. Her jaw moved a few more times before finally eliciting words. "He saved Popov, but…the minigun, he…he's dead."

In the span of a long breath, Lebeau went from grief to anger. He practically shoved Lloyd aside, marching away from them both. Lloyd cursed under his breath and followed Lebeau down a dark aisle, whose ceiling fixtures were out. Those still intact and functioning wafted a dim white glow onto their broad shoulders.

Lloyd reached out, grabbing Lebeau's right vest strap. He gave it a firm tug and Lebeau paused midstride, turning to face Lloyd. To glare down at him; Lloyd was 6'1" but Lebeau still had three inches over him.

"You know what this means, Seb. You and I are the highest ranks in the city. You wanna go out there, try to save Fuller, or anyone else, *right now*, you're gonna make *me* the highest rank. And I gotta tell ya, boss. I ain't up to it. Not alone."

Lebeau shook his head. He seemed like he was genuinely considering Lloyd's suggestion, something that Lloyd himself couldn't have expected. It would be a major win, one they desperately needed right now. But when Lebeau's mouth opened to respond, their comms came to life. It was almost startling.

"This is Barley. The Captain is here, too. Who all can hear me right now? I believe you're out of range from one another."

Lloyd took the initiative to respond.

"This is Lloyd, ma'am. I am with Lebeau, and…Vlada." He paused. "We believe that Gaspar is KIA and may have other casualties."

A few seconds passed.

"Copy, Gunny. You three are to stay put. The RQ-8 Shadow is maintaining a higher altitude than usual, so as to not alert the Apophids that we have eyes-on, or ears for that matter. Do not *engage them, unless absolutely necessary, and only if clear of civilian presence. For now, just stay put, replenish, and rest. Understood?"*

They did, although nobody acknowledged it right away. Being contacted by Barley initially was the closest thing to a shot of adrenaline, as it meant they had eyes in the sky and might be able to arrange a safe exfil. Not by helo, but on ground. Anywhere but here. Now, though—Barley's words had the opposite effect.

Lloyd was right back to where he had been, trying to convince an obstinate Lebeau from leaving. Even as a Gunnery Sergeant, Lloyd knew that Lebeau was notorious for getting on his own CO's nerves. He wasn't *exactly* insubordinate, but he had the propensity to lean toward that nature. Especially if it meant doing something for the proverbial greater good.

"How copy?" Barley asked.

"Lima Charlie," Vlada said, just before Lloyd began to say something comparable. *Loud and clear*. Except that Vlada had an addendum. "Would advise keeping air support on standby, ma'am. As much as I hate to say it. Fact is, we've had two birds experience troubles above the Plaza."

Vlada let off her transmitter just so she could piece together her next words better, but in that narrow time, Barley responded. Her awareness of the situation was…mildly comforting.

"Can confirm. Scout-Two made it back alright, pilot is in the infirmary, but scans are crystal. He said he felt dizzy and feared blacking out. Our last contact with Merlin-Three was from the copilot. She said the pilot was having a seizure, *and according to our records he is, obviously, not epileptic or prone*

to them in any way."

Barley relented for a few seconds.

This didn't sit pleasantly with the operators.

"Until we figure it out, follow the Captain's orders as I've given them, and we'll make contact again at first light. I will proceed to have the remote pilots circle the Plaza, raise the others, and inform them of the same. Then, they will conduct citywide reconnaissance before RTB for refueling. Understood?"

"Yes, ma'am. Over and out." Lloyd's hand fell from the transmitter at his chest. He stared back at Lebeau, whose reaction was an all-too-lackadaisical shrug.

"Makes no difference," Lebeau said. He poorly suppressed a chuckle of desperation. "Not you, not her, not even the Captain—you just can't. So stop trying to."

Lloyd knew that there was no deterring Lebeau. If anyone was going to do something they had set their stubborn heart on, it was Sebastian Lebeau. Regardless of his rank. With their very own Master Sergeant Cris Gaspar reportedly KIA, it was all the more incentive for Lebeau to *try*. If it wasn't for Vlada's condition, Lloyd suspected both of them would be joining Lebeau. She wasn't one to wait anything out, much less hide.

"You better goddamn stay safe," Lloyd said, firmly.

"I will," Lebeau said, and walked away. Pausing at the glass entrance, he looked back at Lloyd. "Once the others are."

10

Keign after dark was a place no human wanted to be. Even after spending consecutive days in the city with far less qualified weapons and teammates, Seb Lebeau dreaded this moment more. Slinking around closely neighbored buildings at least provided cover and shelter from the bigger Apophids, and a more manageable combat space with Drones. But the openness of the Cedar Plaza parking lot, while effective in circling and eventually killing a Behemoth, was a death trap at night, much less alone. The scattered lampposts helped his outward visibility; the decision to not bring night-optic devices for Operation Malathion was one both he and Gaspar had actually voted on.

The way they saw it, carrying NODs was just one more item of equipment they could've done without, because nobody wandered anywhere after dark. During Downpour, nightfall was spent either inside the safe confines of a building tending to wounds, hydrating, consuming provisions, and resting—or on rooftops. Providing lookout in addition to firing on exposed Drones, when the shooter felt confident enough for a kill.

Which was, with their weapons and ammo at the time, far too infrequent.

Lebeau now dreaded the absence of NODs.

After leaving the gas station, Lebeau slinked around one corner of it and kept low, as if avoiding enemy fire. It was all too strange to be in an urban combat zone where the enemy didn't have projectile weapons; it was in ways a benefit, and in others an outright nightmare. Lebeau did notice a lack of Apophid corpses scattering the pavement, despite how many Vlada had left in her wake earlier. Some Drones remained, but all three Warrior bodies had been dragged away, pulpy blood trails left behind.

From the corner of the gas station, Lebeau could see a couple of Drones patrolling the dark parking lot. Their pale exoskeletons were visible even at night, more so whenever they neared a lamppost—even when they avoided direct exposure.

Utilizing vehicles as cover, Lebeau eventually made it as far as the general radius of the Panera building. Eighty yards had never felt so far. He had found a hint of solace on the driver's side of a black Ford Super Duty. The pickup truck, despite its mass and power, had seen much better days. Two inhabitants had been slaughtered through a gored windshield, the male passenger reduced to only his waist and legs; the top half had likely been devoured through the window before the rest slumped back inside. The driver seat was empty, of a body anyway; coagulated blood slathered it from headrest to pedals.

Even outside the truck, Lebeau could smell the vile punch of days-old bloodshed.

Inching toward the tailgate, peering around it, Lebeau thought he heard the muffled groans of an injured man. Fuller, possibly. In a strange way, *hopefully*. Out this far from the storefront, nobody else should be in the open, except Fuller—unless Lebeau wasn't the only one going to his aid.

Part of him hoped this was true.

Another part, the leader in him, prioritized everyone else's safety. Thus praying they remained wherever they had found shelter.

To his suspicious surprise, Lebeau spotted Dylan Fuller about forty yards away. Behind the Panera, just out of the nearest lamppost's reach. He was crawling toward the front of a parked sedan—beneath it. Unlike trucks, cars had lower ground clearance; Fuller really had to squeeze himself under there, and with his severe back wound that must have been torture. He also likely had shed most of his kit to do so, supposing the bulk of his vest had not come off when the Behemoth's scythe cut away his rear plate carrier.

Lebeau pressed his transmitter but kept his gravelly voice to a whisper.

"Fuller, I see you. It's Lebeau. Stay put. I'm coming to you."

Slowly, just before Lebeau prepared to emerge from cover, Fuller responded. Weakly; the pain in his voice was straining to cut loose.

"Don't you goddamn dare, Seb. I'm done."

"Fuck off," Lebeau scoffed. "If that was the case, you wouldn't be crawling under cars like a psycho."

"I...I know what I'm doing."

"How's that, fuck-face?"

Thirty feet away, slowly meandering around vehicles, a Drone chittered. Lebeau felt his blood quicken, but he stayed calm.

"Everyone else made it to the storefront. Except you, Lloyd, and Superwoman."

"She's paralyzed, sick or something. Apophids getting to her head, I think. But what's your point? Lloyd didn't want me to come. Here I am. I ain't gonna leave you."

"You won't have a choice. Listen." Fuller paused, groaning in pain over comms, but biting his tongue to keep it down. "The team will survive as one. But not the way it is right now. Let Lloyd stay with the Alien Goddess. Beauty and the Beast will figure it out."

Lebeau smirked and shook his head. *This fuckin' guy,* he mouthed, knowing that Fuller meant 'Beauty' was Lloyd and the 'Beast' was Vlada.

"But *you*…you need to rally with the others. A…A distraction is your only chance. That fuckin' Behemoth is down by the BK. It'll head back any minute."

Realizing that, if Fuller was correct, the Behemoth was way down by the Burger King—nearly three-hundred yards away—all this time, he could have made it to Fuller and possibly taken him to shelter. Be it back to the Shell, to the storefront, or even inside the Panera.

This made him move, almost immediately.

No more bullshitting.

"Coming to you," Lebeau radioed, before tucking the RM338 into his chest and booking it toward Fuller's location.

"Goddammit, Seb, *stop*!" Fuller snapped, at regular volume. A pair of Drones forty yards to his far right—Lebeau's left—immediately shrieked, and fixated on the sound. Then, Lebeau's movement. Fuller had started to haul himself out from under the car; Lebeau reached him, hoisted the wounded man to his feet, and only then realized just how bad Fuller's injury was. He ought to be dead, but the Behemoth's scythe had missed his spine by inches. Still, from blood loss alone, Fuller would be dead in minutes.

It was nothing shy of a horrid miracle he was still alive, much less speaking.

Lebeau helping him stand was another nail in his coffin. Fuller unavoidably screamed in pain. Regrets began to fill Lebeau, despite his good intentions. Selfless heroics were suddenly realized as a fatal mistake.

Nonetheless, Lebeau forced Fuller to limp along, away from the car. They were halfway to the large pickup when Lebeau swung his weapon right and hip-fired the machine gun. High-caliber steel-core rounds battered the charging Drones, slowing them.

Fuller craned his head left, as he hopelessly held himself onto Lebeau and limped alone. Fuller witnessed the terrifying

Behemoth rush toward them from the Burger King. Unlike the Drones, it didn't have to meander around vehicles, only trample or push them aside. Its speed was hampered by the amount of damage it had taken earlier, but it was still disturbingly fast for its mass.

"I hate it when you're right, Fuller," Lebeau groaned, reaching the pickup.

"Think she'll forgive me?" Fuller asked, through a painful groan, as Lebeau leaned him against the rear left fender.

"She already has, trust me," Lebeau said. He popped the fuel cap off the truck with two strikes of his weapon's buttstock. Then he backpedaled, swung left, and fired at a nearing Drone. The creature began to crawl over the truck's hood, a limb driving the engine block through the compartment and into the pavement. The pickup's whole bed bounced on its rear tires, and Fuller fell away, hands keeping himself from landing on his face. The Drone hissed, salivating onto the asphalt within arm's reach of Lebeau's feet. His machine gun kept firing up at it, bullets shearing away its mandible and then parts of its skull.

The Behemoth to his far right was suddenly much closer. Fifty yards would become zero in seconds.

"Now, Seb!" Fuller shouted. Another Drone began to crawl over the truck, impaling the cab with a forelimb. Fuller looked left, and saw the Behemoth's ghastly face nearly twenty feet away. "Fucking do it! Do it right—"

Sebastia Lebeau directed his weapon at the fuel spout of the pickup. He fired the machine gun on full-auto. Every five rounds on the belt was a tracer. The tiny pyrotechnic flare sufficed to ignite the fuel inside the truck. An explosion consumed Fuller, killing him instantly; paired with a fatal shard of shrapnel from the vehicle's body, the blast killed Lebeau half a second later. The fireball devoured the other Drone that had just reached the truck, and swathed the front half of the Behemoth in flame. Shrapnel embedded the giant Apophid's exposed leg muscles, but the rest was deflected by its panoplies.

From a storefront window, the rest of the MSOT witnessed the explosion, and had heard fragments of the operators'
dialogue leading up to it. But the blast was nearly a hundred
yards away, and they had to believe both men were dead.

"Fuck was that?" Arrington asked, the only one not by
the window. He had refused help in bandaging his injury, a kind
that only a man of his experience and conviction could handle
himself. That Apophid had taken his whole left hand off, and
not 'cleanly' at the wrist, either. His thumb remained, and by
some miracle the radial artery between it and his wrist had not
been damaged. The pain was paramount, though, and had warranted a single cap of morphine.

"Vehicle," Popov said, turning away from the window.
His voice and face remained glum with grief, which had not
dissipated since Gaspar's sacrifice.

"Them or us?" Arrington asked, between winces.

"Both," Russo said. His brow furrowed. "I think."

The other civilians that had taken shelter inside the clothing store stayed toward the back. They didn't try to
communicate with the operators, but were likely confused by
those last few words.

Russo knew what Arrington was asking.

Whether or not the vehicular explosion was *caused* by the
enemy, or their own. And, who suffered from it.

The ensuing radio silence proved that both Fuller and
Lebeau were more than likely KIA from the blast. That the Behemoth was still moving about wasn't comforting, but its
distance from the storefront was a tiny shred of relief.

"Why's it keep wandering toward BK?" Russo asked to
nobody in particular. His hands were cupped around his eyes
against the glass. The store was dark, apart from a few ceiling
fixtures in the far back.

"Patrolling that end of the lot, probably," Roback said,

tiredly. He withdrew from the window to sit back down on an upended crate of shoes. "Especially after Lebeau and Fuller came from that way. Doesn't wanna be flanked again."

"Why aren't any of the Drones seeking us out?" Russo asked. He stepped back and gestured at the floor-to-ceiling storefront window. "It'd be a tight fit, but doable."

Popov, behind him, scoffed.

"Keep that shit to yourself," he said.

The civvies at the back of the store were within earshot, regardless of them staying quiet.

Russo nodded, apologizing mutely.

The operators were nearly decommissioned from woe alone, when suddenly their comms buzzed with life. Everyone but Arrington stood rigid, hands cupping their ears. Hoping it was Lebeau or Fuller. When Corporal Oscar De Horta announced himself, they were disappointed, but not in a cruel way. Having already been demoralized by Barley's last transmission, knowing that *someone* had survived from Merlin-Three's crash was good news.

It was still possible either of the helo's pilots had made it, but for now this was all they knew.

"I'm on top of the gas station, the canopy. Bailed when the 75 went down. Bruised up but unbroken. Must've blacked out, though; head hurts like a bitch. Some blood. Otherwise fine. Who can hear me?"

"You might have a concussion, Corporal," Popov said. "It's Sergeant Popov, by the way. I'm with…most of the others. Those that made it. You have eyes on anyone else?"

"Uh, negative. That explosion rocked me awake. It's hard to tell, but I…I think two of yours were taken out by it."

What the operators inside the store proceeded to hear were fractals of a transmission somewhere else. Possibly inside the gas station itself, others communicating with De Horta but unable to secure an unbroken link with the rest of the team.

It was too fragmented for them to discern whole sentences, but after a moment Roback declared some good news.

"Lloyd, it's Gunny Lloyd and…and Vlada."

He didn't say it with the same contempt he would have before the events of Cedar Plaza. His reconsideration of Vlada's merit had only started to fluctuate back when he regrouped with the others on the roof of the Duckworth Center. Gaspar's praise of her always felt unsubstantiated; training, Roback would say, was incomparable to live combat. But then Popov and Russo adamantly defending her after spending operational hours in her presence had stricken a chord in him. Then, hearing Arrington's dogged reinforcement of their words was another. Roback was a stubborn asshole to the core, but he *was* self-aware. And given the circumstances, he had been willing to sway his opinion of her if given proper proof.

When that evidence presented itself in the Plaza earlier, Vlada mounting the roof of the gas station and without any hesitation engaging the Behemoth despite immediate threats to her own safety—Roback had accepted fault.

He now dreaded Fuller's death, and Lebeau's, the most moral part of him hoping that the woman, supposing she was more human than alien, could forgive them moving forward. Should the rest of them make it out of Keign alive, Roback was prepared to humble himself.

The ordeal in Keign had proven too dire a place for ego to get in the way of others' safety. Civilians and operators alike.

Vlada included.

"I think they're in the gas station," Roback said.

"Read me? Sergeant Popov?" De Horta asked.

"You're a go, Corporal," Popov said, with a lick of renewed morale. "Fill us in."

De Horta took an audible deep breath over comms, before continuing. Inside the gas station convenience store, Vlada and Lloyd hydrated, ate, and rested their bodies as they listened to

De Horta tell the others, who they couldn't hear, their own situation. Including the recent departure of Lebeau from their ranks, and Vlada's belief that the Apophids were "up to something fishy"—his words, not hers—in the area.

Lloyd took the opportunity to quietly hunt down proper, quality protein bars while they were inside the store. And a Gatorade to boot. Meanwhile, Vlada all but finished her Apofuel, wishing it, and Dr. Ginley's specialized provisions, would combat these spells of paralysis and intense visions. The latter of which she had not shared with anyone else, as they were too muddying and concerning by her lonesome.

If she even suggested that she wasn't of sound mind, she feared the others might not trust her. Or, trust her *less*. She felt as though some great degree of breakthrough had occurred among their ranks, in her favor, but couldn't be certain of Roback's progress in that field. Or Fuller's, whose fate she feared had met its end.

He and Lebeau…and Gaspar, among the others…had all fought so brazenly, so devotedly.

Part of Vlada felt unqualified to share this fight with them. But this had grown beyond proving herself to anyone else. If any of that battle remained within her, it was a private war. Proving herself *to* herself, and no one else. Not for the selfish betterment of her mind, but to provide others with the most superior version of herself available.

The unparalleled warrior that Dr. Ginley saw her as.

The fruits of so many men and women's labor.

As the night progressed, it became clear that their first business would be to help De Horta down from the canopy. He was safe for now, especially since it wasn't attached to the main building, and was higher as well. The only way an Apophid could get to him would be a Warrior's scythes or a Behemoth demolishing the support beams.

At this rate, it didn't seem like the Apophids had any intention of hunting the operators down. At all. At least not for now. What awaited their near future was a troubling uncertainty for everyone involved.

With this in mind, Vlada and Lloyd convinced De Horta to stay where he was, maintain low visibility, and be patient. They were doing the same, sitting with their backs to the glass-doored refrigeration units.

"Apo-fuel," Lloyd said, slowly, his head tilted as he read the generic label on the liquid pouch's side.

Vlada plugged it, licked her lips, and her brow furrowed. She brandished the pouch as an offering.

Lloyd' head recoiled. "What's in it?"

"You don't want to know," Vlada said. A speck of déjà vu with Russo earlier this afternoon.

"Yeah?" Lloyd said, offering a tiny smirk. "Try me."

"Electrolytes, synthesized genetic crystals from Apophid DNA, and... cockroach milk."

Any humor was sapped from Lloyd's handsome face. He scowled.

"No shit?"

"Zero shit. Seventy-percent cockroach milk." Vlada said this with an unwaveringly stern expression. It broke Lloyd. He laughed under his breath, shaking his head. Vlada shrugged and returned the pouch to its satchel. "Dr. Ginley can be quite convincing."

"Hell, I'd have to be hypnotized for that."

"Who says I'm not?" Vlada said, without processing the impulsive thought before speaking it. The voice that carried the words had the debris of lingering humor in it, but was largely solemn.

Seriousness returned to Lloyd's face. That and genuine concern. He sat forward, turned his head, and looked at her. *Really* looked at her. Not judging, but trying to understand, and in some odd way, relating to her anxiety. Or some of it. She could feel the selfless civility of his sympathy. It pained her, in a strange way. One that reminded her of her own humanity.

Even if she was becoming less and less human with each hour spent in this seemingly forsaken city.

Vlada faced forward.

Then her eyes befell her own hands. But were they? Her own. They had been refashioned in the image of Apophid flesh. Yet she found herself fidgeting in only a way that a human would, as she spoke.

"I just…I know I volunteered for Outreach, but this…this is something else. I expected pain, expected *torture* even. Death! I had accepted it as the more likely result than actually enduring. Was *told* it had superior odds. But this, I…"

Vlada turned her head to look at Lloyd again.

He was on the floor. Supine. His arms straight at his sides. His hands had formed semi-fists, fingers clawing inward, and frozen apart. His expression was almost blank, apart from an unnerving fear inhabiting his chiseled features. His eyes were locked open but unmoving, and if it wasn't for the slow heave of his chest, Vlada would have believed him dead.

She immediately tried to wake him, to rouse Lloyd from this disconcerting paralysis. But he was unbudging.

When she sprang to her feet, an impulsive glance around the mostly dark convenience store revealed that the other civilians were asleep. Possibly dead asleep. She began to dread that some sort of toxin had been released into the air, by the Apophids. It could account for Lloyd's state, and her immunity. If this was the case, she feared De Horta's condition on top of the canopy. Urgently, despite Barley's orders, Vlada emerged from the gas station. She hung a left and then scaled the side of the squat structure, leaping onto the roof once more.

Facing the canopy, she jumped onto it.

De Horta, who had been so civil with her when she was

aboard the MV-75 at the beginning of the op, now looked the same as Lloyd. Catatonic, features stained by horror. It made her chest tighten with grief and anger. She obeyed the latter emotion, which led her to the asphalt of the parking lot, sprinting across it as if she knew exactly where to go. In her mind's eye, she was seeking out that wretched Behemoth, hoping to rip the innards of its throat out through its mouth, and then delight in its slow, painful death.

Instead, she wound up outside the Panera. Before approaching it, an unusual detail occurred to her. The sky's darkness was scarred by a purple glow, with very little white to it. Some shining through that dark violet haze.

The moon. Its fullness was overwhelming, tantamount the sun. But it was not itself. It seemed to drip rotted purple flesh, akin to an Apophid's panoply. Or Vlada's arms.

Although the sight would have normally been a spectacle no human could turn away from, Vlada found herself walking toward the Panera. Its glass entrance intact like most of the other storefronts, including the gas station. Her brow furrowed and she entered, noticing how much smaller the interior was compared to the others in the Plaza. But what made it especially smaller was the sole inhabitant.

Despite the darkness inside the business, her eyes gleamed over and she could see as if it was illuminated by direct, unobstructed sunlight. Or isolated moonbeams—filtering down through a pinhole in the roof of the structure.

There was no detail lost on her.

A Behemoth's horn jutted up through the floor. Tile was warped around its rigid base, the distinct panoply of an Apophid having pushed them apart. The horn itself, which Vlada's mind assigned the word *spire*, was atypically long. Behemoths' horns rose three to four feet above their skulls, no more. This one stood nine feet, and nearly perfectly vertical. It also tapered to a finer point than any scythe, horn, or spine in known Apophid anatomy.

The way moonlight gathered at the tip was almost mes-merizing. Hypnotizing, even.

Vlada felt her skin sweat, which she had not been capable of since the procedure sixteen months ago. Despite this, her bones and gums grew alarmingly cold. Against all signs that should have directed her out of the building, Vlada strode to-ward the spire. As she neared it, voices overlapped inside her skull. Not just her mind, but it seemed as though the voices were literally slithering around the microscopic confines of her cra-nium, snaking inside her auditory canals and probing her cochleae.

"You...volunteer. He deserved...didn't volunteer. You had accepted...isn't death...worse."

Vlada's face twitched. She reached out, both hands.

The voices melted together into a single source. The in-flections changed, slightly, but the speaker was one person. As her fingertips grazed the spire, the inner curvature of her digits falling into place around its foot-wide circumference, the voice growled clarity inside her skull.

"You didn't volunteer. He deserved it, but you didn't vol-unteer. You had accepted death. This isn't death. This is worse."

The speaker was Vlada.

Her hands locked around the spire, as if magnetically. Pain shot through every nerve in her body, and had it not been for the resilience of Apophid DNA in her, her teeth would have shattered. Blood leaked from a flaring nostril and her eyes went bloodshot as they shot wide.

However, sight abandoned her.

Externally.

It shifted, and she could only see into the mutating cav-erns of her own mind.

As she watched, small details not perceptible by sight or

sound came to her like flashes behind her eyes.

Vlada was wearing the OCP camo pants of her U.S. Army regulation uniform, but a black tank top above it. She was completely human, shoulders and arms included. Her long black hair was fastened into a snug ponytail, and kept back with a dark green headband. She circled the brick foundation of a large, lovely chalet. Reaching the back veranda, Vlada fixated on a window with a gap between it and the sill; on the other side, gauzy curtains billowed softly in the spring breeze. She slid her hands through and pulled it open before slipping inside the house.

Slinking through the sunroom, she honed in on a man's voice upstairs. She crept up the stairs like a predator stalking its prey on the savannah. One of four doors down the main hall hung open, shower water running and steam already curling out of the bathroom.

A man whistled Taps in an opposite room. His voice wasn't on-key to a bugle, but rivaled it.

Vlada gently pushed the door open.

The man was disrobing his full dress uniform. The dark blue jacket was on his bed, light from the overhead fan catching the single gold bar affixed to the shoulder loops. The anodized glint reflected in Vlada's green eyes but an ember of pure wrath burned brighter.

The U.S. Army Second Lieutenant still wore a white tank and his dress blue pants, when her knife plunged into the back of his right rib cage. She had surgically angled the carbon steel blade beneath the latissimus muscle, likely from weeks of meticulous training. The rigorous exercise she had been performing aided her strength as well. Vlada's sleek biceps flexed and veins embossed the backs of her hands as she strained. The inner serrations of the clip-point Ontario ASEK blade assisted its violent passage. She buried it to the hilt, nearly all five inches violating the gap between the man's ninth and tenth rib bones.

Vlada's superior officer buckled toward the foot of the bed, clutching at the right side of his back. The pain was unbridled, as he suffered a pneumothorax, blood filling the punctured lung. Despite the pain and ragged breathing, the Second Lieutenant mustered the strength to turn and face his attacker. It was a sudden burst of will that took Vlada off guard.

His hand latched around her throat.

"Was the funeral...not enough?" he growled, agony on his face, but also hatred.

"Maybe yours will be," she responded, and spit in his eye before driving her forehead into his brow. There was a sickening *thwack* and they both staggered. Her hand slid off the grip of the knife but when he fell back onto the bed, it angled toward his spine.

He released a cry of worse pain than before.

Dizzied, a single stream of blood trickling down her forehead, but not blind, Vlada lunged at him. She grabbed his pants by the belt, and pulled him off the bed. She slid forward, until the knife twisted a certain way and locked between his ribs. The man screamed out, a sound only escapable through the window Vlada had left open. But the beautiful trill of windchimes his wife had planted in the backyard last summer drowned it out.

Furiously working the dress pants off the man, Vlada began to pant and audibly seethe. Almost like a rabid animal. This terrified the man tenfold the stabbing wound, or the look in her eyes when she last spoke to him.

He lashed out at her, and even though the taller man had a greater reach, he was at a severe disadvantage. His partially collapsed lung was worsening with every painfully long second. Worse when Vlada stopped pulling his pants down to stand, and then drive the heel of her boot into the front of his right ribcage. Twice. There was a discernible *crack* and blood splashed past the man's lips.

186

"Atta boy," Vlada growled, frothing. She reached back, drew the four-inch boot knife properly sheathed above her heel, and, rotating the grip in her hand, swung it up between his legs. The double-edged Smith & Wesson dagger sank into his clothed scrotum. The man howled a sound previously unheard in his lifetime, except when hunting deer. A wounded, vocal, dying doe was vaguely comparable.

Vlada angled her fist as the man weakly slapped at her face in any attempt to strike her, to repel her.

She buried the dagger farther inward, pinning his deflated testicles into his perineum. Then she twisted it and watched with a wretched caliber of delight as an indescribable agony plagued his features.

"Atta boy," she repeated, her lip twitching, tears pouring down her cheeks. "Bleed for me."

Outside the house, his wife of nine years nonchalantly fumbled with her keys. Oblivious to the brutal murder of her husband, upstairs in their bedroom. But already down the street, sirens were echoing into the beautiful Sunday sky.

Vlada's forced voyeuristic observation retracted from the house, and swung around. Her view spun and spun, until the surrounding oak canopies blurred into bands of dark green. And, eventually, black. While her heart wept in the silence, light returned to her mind's eye. She found herself staring at a shelf of boxed, dated, and poorly labeled rations and perishables. From junk food to non-refrigerated contents that would inhabit a vending machine.

Her view pulled back farther.

A woman in a military uniform stood with her back turned to an open door. It was a storage room down the hall from the main cafeteria on base. Each of her sleeves wore a Sergeant First Class patch, composed of three chevrons over two arcs.

A black boot nudged the hard plastic wedge out from under the door. It swung shut behind the man that entered. The woman turned her head and reached for the boxcutter resting on top of a recently opened cardboard carton. But the man behind her was there quicker. He was five inches taller, and his large right hand had clutched her throat with an unrelenting presence. But the man, whose sleeves wore the gold bar patch of a Second Lieutenant, was left-handed. He used it to force the woman's pants down to her thighs, despite the fight she exerted in her arms.

A firm squeeze of her throat, one thumb digging into her right carotid, made her tense.

His mouth by her left ear, reminding her.

"The footage, it's something special," he whispered, uncouth pleasure already tinging his voice. "Amazing, how far technology has come. Got you *begging* for it."

His left hand dug his genitals out. He spit once, missing the target. Voices outside the door, passing down the hall, made his heart skip a beat. He shrugged and then buried himself inside her.

She began to make a noise, and the man tore off a flap of cardboard, balling it up and cramming it into her mouth. He swore as he thrusted, madly. Seconds passed. He reached down, ensuring he was still where he wanted to be. It was warmer, moister, than before.

His hand came away red.

The man's grin violated the side of her face.

"Atta girl," he snickered. "Bleed for me."

Two more thrusts and the man finished inside of her. She wept and groaned around the cardboard. It had cut her lips and the roof of her mouth. Bloodied saliva dripped off her chin, as she gripped the shelving in front of her.

The man rolled a tall cart of boxes across the storage room, behind her. A temporary concealment, while he clothed himself and then vigilantly slipped through the door. He unearthed a keyring, from which dangled three keys. He locked the storage closet, making it accessible only from the inside, or by certain ranked personnel with a key.

Vlada watched the woman crumple to the floor, sobbing. She ached to help her, to unshackle these invisible restraints keeping her immobile and powerless. Her own eyes stung with tears that coursed down her nonexistent face, in the darkness enrobing the storage room.

She had not seen the woman's face, until she struggled to stand again, slowly clothing herself. The grimaces warping her features made Vlada feel nauseous. Bile rose in the back of her throat but it was too tight to retch. There was a hand on her jugular, keeping her vomit down and her voice silent.

The woman's face upturned as pain and hatred painted it. The shame itself was a stifling mire that clogged her throat.

Vlada watched herself sob silently in the storage room, bleeding and devoid of strength. This version of her existence was a detached memory, shorn away by a culprit not alien, nor herself. Shown this for what reason except to further torment her mind, the feeling returned to Vlada's hands as she squeezed the Apophid spire. Wrenching it, until the exoskeleton began to fracture beneath her alien hands.

She screamed a sound she had suppressed that day in the storage room—suddenly realizing, in a blinding flash of violet-tinted memories, that it was not the only event. But the second. Nor the last time she would be betrayed by her fellow humans.

If they could be called that.

This version of reality bled away, until Vlada was back in the gas station, supine on the floor, stiff and catatonic. Her eyes frozen open, face awash in horror. Her hands had literally clawed troughs into the tile floor by her sides. Despite this, Evan Lloyd steadfastly tried to wake her, albeit futilely.

Until she finally did sit up.

With a jolt, Vlada was sitting upright, her hands lax on the floor beside her. Her eyes were no longer wide open, lids instead heavy and almost lethargic. Tears had welled beneath her eyes, giving her green irises a morose sheen. More to Lloyd's concern, her mouth was stuck agape. As if she was mid-scream, or anticipating one that could shatter glass.

No form of sound followed.

Lloyd's apprehensive hands on her inhuman shoulders, brow furrowed, he stared at her face from beside her.

"Okay…you're scaring me, V," he confessed.

"I," she finally said, a croak of parched voice at first. One of her eyes twitched. "I…I remember."

Solemnly, Lloyd nodded.

"What do you remember?"

She almost chuckled, in disbelief. The tears were flowing as if a faucet now.

"Everything."

11

Unstoppable. There were certain forces of nature that this could be applied to. Presently, a subsidiary of any number of them included Vlada Stoia. But a time for violence and aggression in its most absolute, unrivaled form was just on the horizon. A near-future she looked forward to as a necessary evil, but did not pine for. At the moment she had managed to convince Lloyd to stay put; it wasn't like he had any right, or way, to stop her, though. Nor could he follow. He did, just to the door, until he realized the truth in her words. Where she was going. And what she had to do, for a reason she couldn't profess.

"Stay inside. Give me your ears and heart on comms. I can only hope the others will as well. I'm going up to De Horta."

The last thing she told him, rapid-fire like a suppressed machine gun, on her way to the front of the convenience store. And then she emerged, slinking up the side of the short building with the kind of grace and ease only an insect ought to have. She leapt onto the canopy, startling a rested De Horta.

"You know you're not supposed to go to sleep with a potential concussion," she said quietly, crouching before him.

"I, uh…I'm not sleeping."

"Okay, Oscar," she said, extending her hand.

Brow furrowed, he stared it for a few seconds, and then at her. There was a civility, a sort of humanity, to her face that he wasn't certain existed before. He had never had a problem with her, not like the special forces guys, but this look was different. It was almost reformed, almost…placid. But there was also a pain in her eyes, a sadness he couldn't connect to.

And that terrified him.

Just not in the way an enemy would.

He slowly gripped her alien hand, and she shook it with the firmness of a girlfriend trying to impress her partner's father—without hurting him. The hypothetical father, or De Horta.

"Will you stay low," she then said, withdrawing her hand, "and listen?"

"For what?"

"Just…stay low. And quiet." Still crouching, she slinked toward the edge of the canopy, nearest the building. And thus the parking lot, a space between her and the storefront—the rest of the MSOT—populated by scattered vehicles, the occasional dead Apophid, and a few patrolling Drones.

She raised both of her index fingers to gently ensure her earplugs were in place. Then she lowered her right hand to the transmitter affixed to the left strap of her black sports bra.

"Raven," she said, letting a deep breath travel over the frequency before continuing. "This is Vlada Stoia. Subject 21X of Project Outreach. How copy?"

Two seconds passed.

"We read you, V," Popov said, his accent even more distinct than hers. *"What's up? We've got…maybe three hours 'til dawn."*

This had not even occurred to her.

It meant she had, in fact, been out of it—possibly genuinely asleep, even—for some time, before the whole spire thing. Further suggesting that it was, in fact, purely mental. A bridge built by the Apophids, one that she had to voluntarily, even if only subconsciously, walk herself.

"I need everyone's ears. I need to say something."

"Uh, yeah." Popov cleared his throat. *"We're all here, V. Except for, I mean…Gaspar and Graves. Wilson…Fuller, and Lebeau."*

"Right. I…I wish I could be speaking to them now, too. To thank them for what they gave this op; this city, and its people. Their sacrifice, be it deliberate or bad fortune, hasn't gone unnoticed. I know…some of you may not believe I deserve to be here, or that…I'm not *human* enough to fight this cause. But…and I say this not for pity's sake, not for sympathies. It's just…it needs to breathe."

Her vagueness to the operators weighed heavy on them, especially Popov and Russo, with whom she had built a greater rapport with than anyone else.

"You have the floor, Vlada," Popov said.

She smirked briefly. A nanosecond's worth. Although her chest tensed as she spoke, the pressure very, very slowly mitigated.

"From 2026 to 2031 I served with Lima Company, 3rd Battalion, of the U.S. Army. Our base was in Columbia, South Carolina. At the end of June, 2030, I was promoted to Sergeant First Class. In November that year, while overseeing perishables in a mess hall storage room, I was confronted by a CO, Second Lieutenant Thomas Axelsen."

Simply speaking his name pained her. Angered her. But she stowed it, only to the point that it made her voice shake a little.

"The grisly details are neither here nor there. He assaulted me, physically and…sexually. After he was…finished…he threatened me with a dishonorable discharge if I told anyone. How? I was lucky enough to get SFC, and he was eleven ranks above me. I didn't overthink it. I was stupid. Broken. I stayed silent."

She cleared her throat.

Found herself staring at the late-night sky.

There *was* lunar visibility. But it was not full, not quite. A waxing gibbous. Passing clouds of a normal dark shade left only filaments of argent light to pass through. She liked to believe she could feel them beneath her skin. The skin that was still human; if any of it was, anymore.

"A few weeks later, he blackmailed me with allegedly doctored footage of the event. There *was* a camera in that room, not even I had realized it. It wasn't like the cameras in the armory or entrances, it was…a joke, essentially. So his confiscation of the tape that day, didn't shock me. I…I believed him." Vlada coughed. "Early the next year, 2031, he followed me to that same *godforsaken* storage room. Shut the door and assaulted me from behind. Choked me. Reminded me of the tape. And then…raped me again. That time…anally. He made me bleed, and taunted me for it. After he finished and…left…it was without a word. Inferring my continued silence. And I was. Silent."

This time, when she cleared her throat, it was almost a growl. Something between that and a violent cough.

"I spent the next three weeks training. Arduously. Building my upper body strength, in tandem with improving my capabilities with a fixed blade, and learning how to induce a pneumothorax with a knife from behind."

She breathed through funneled lips.

"Nearly four weeks after our last encounter, Lima Company's own Major Casey Hebert died of natural causes. He was a good man, and had shown civil support for my small achievements over the years with 3rd Battalion. So, there was a funeral in Sumter, where the Major was born. We attended in our dress blues. It was…nice. But…after we left, I followed Axelsen to his home in Oak Grove, eight miles from Base. I parked a block away, shed my dress uniform, in exchange for my OCP pants. The same ones I'd wear on Base. In that room. I snuck into his house, knowing his wife could be home at any minute."

Despite never feeling so 'easily' parched since her procedure, Vlada suddenly had the urge to reach for a water bottle and gulp it down. Or Apofuel for that matter. But she didn't.

"I suspect some of you may be filling in the blanks by now. Fact is, the Army *did* do a good job at sweeping much of it under the rug. More so my name than his, surprisingly. But I imagine some of you might recall hearing about that officer in South Carolina three years ago, that was brutally stabbed to death, once in the right lung from behind, and again in the scrotum, into the perineum, from which he bled out while asphyxiating on his own blood. That sort of story sticks with most people, for some time anyway, even if you're so far removed from the goings-on of a lil' Army base in SC."

Vlada shrugged, as if they could see her.

Only De Horta, who didn't know where to look, but his eyes were wide with a certain kind of grief-stricken horror.

"At any rate, that wasn't the end of my hell. Apparently, a neighbor had seen someone suspicious—Yours Truly—approaching the Axelsen residence. Cops arrived on scene just as his wife had come home from the store. Their daughter, four, was at daycare. I was arrested, and a very short investigation followed. It was just my word against his sparkling reputation. A week later, awaiting trial, I attempted suicide with a cot spring in my cell. Only got one carotid, didn't die. A goddamn shame. Only to learn, shortly after my release from the infirmary, that MPs *had* uncovered recordings of Axelsen's assaults, in his personal office. Video *and* audio, separately. Sick fuck."

She spit over the canopy's parapet before continuing.

"Whether kept as a potential means to blackmail me, or for his own…amusement…neither the video-only tapes nor the audio files were doctored or edited in any way. He was bluffing the whole time. Against my fears, the Army *didn't* bury the incident, and his reputation was ruined. His wife was elucidated about her late husband's true self, and I trust, in the long run, especially for the sake of their daughter, for the better. Nonetheless, my crime was heinous and premeditated, so I was convicted and imprisoned for first-degree murder. Given the circumstances and my services, my lack of a record prior, I was sentenced to thirty years to life without parole."

Vlada's hand relinquished the transmitter.

Several seconds passed.

She continued her transmission. Her voice still burdened, but...slightly lighter.

"Thirteen months later, during Project Outreach's troubles, I was *selected* by CyTech investors as a new attempt to 'save good American lives' after twenty volunteers died on the table. Prior to the procedure itself, far from Pegasus, I was forced to endure chemically-induced amnesia. Dr. Ginley and his team were falsely informed that I had volunteered, given no other information about my "former life." It was a fabricated version of the lie that I had inherently accepted and been told my obscured memories were a result of the Apophid bonding."

Vlada took a deep breath over the frequency before releasing her hand. She didn't wait long to continue, but when she did, there was a renewed determination in her voice. It wasn't ablaze with spite or grief, though. It was pure resolve, unwavering fortitude.

"Point is, I didn't know *any* of this until half an hour ago. Before then, it was all a cesspool of repressed memories, most of which I had not even the faintest clue about. And *how* was I shown?"

She proceeded to inform the MSOT about her encounter with the spire in the Panera. She professed how ludicrous it sounded, and admitted to being unsure whether she physically walked there or it was just a convoluted mental process. And to what effect? Was it to redirect Vlada's hatred toward her fellow humans rather than the Apophids? Was it a cathartic, therapeutic attempt for the alien hive-mind to bond with Vlada on an emotionally psychological level—a feign of goodwill?

She acknowledged the possibility of both, but could not deny that what she was shown was the truth. She had only *seen* key events; the other details came to her like a computer processor ingesting waves of data. It was a tormenting yet unburdening experience she could not attempt to explain apart from divulging the facts as she just had.

To a sweeping opus of relief, none of the operators objected to her statements. Nor did they slather her with apologies or sympathetic sentiments. She wouldn't be upset if they did, but it was oddly comforting that nobody attempted to take that route.

However, she was surprised that the first to speak up was Roback. He didn't announce that it was him, but Vlada's fine ear identified his voice, even over comms.

"Do you think, then, that this spire *was what affected the pilots? If it does have any kind of telepathic power, it's possible that it…"*

She could picture him shrug, likely self-aware of how insane the theory sounded.

Given everything else that had happened today, and been discussed, it was actually the soundest postulation.

"Exactly my thought, Sergeant Roback," she said, hoping it was a surprise that she knew it was him speaking. "Which leads me to further believe, and I know this will be troubling to hear—that the Apophids are planning some form of…violating mental experiment…on the civilians hiding here. It would account for their abstinence from seeking us out, or breaching every storefront."

A theory that resonated with everyone listening, no matter how much they hated to admit it.

There was nothing less troubling than Vlada humanizing

herself in a long and thoroughly disturbing disclosure, only to perform a nonchalant heel-turn and refocus her devotion to the op. Nobody could begin to grasp the inner demons she was battling, not just the Apophids and their haunting telepathic link, but her past as well—that nauseating abrupt clarity. Any other human would dig themselves into a hole and avoid the jarring reality of their existence until all conflicts had been resolved.

If that.

Vlada was different, though.

Of all the second or third chances to be given, this topped them. Her abilities were inarguable. What she could do with them, the lives she could save, and the nightmares she could end, conquered all the hurt she was feeling.

"You mentioned that the spire, you think it's a Behemoth's horn," Russo said. Especially with the operators that remained, unfortunately how few, there wasn't one among them that Vlada didn't think she could recognize by their voice. Inflection, tone, even the faintest aspect of a regional accent. Russo proceeded: *"Does that mean there's just one massive Apophid buried under the parking lot?* Waiting...*to surface."*

"I do fear that, yes," Vlada said.

"How is that even possible?" Lloyd asked. *"The only place one could've burrowed under Keign is Elgin, but not without us noticing."*

"Unless it dug into the pond, and covered its tracks," Russo said, pausing. The outlandish theory was rattling. *"More or less."*

"We should consider," Vlada said, "that whatever is down there may surpass our understanding of Apophid nature. A nest, maybe. Insight into their reproduction. It could be the turning point *we* need—the pivotal reclamation of Keign."

"Which is probably what they're thinking, too, for themselves," Roback said.

"All the more reason we act as soon as we're able."

198

"You have something in mind?" Popov asked. *"Something...specific?"*

"I do. But it begins with some more rest. Get our heads on straight, mine especially. In this time, though, I'll need one of you...ideally Lloyd, as he is the highest surviving rank...to attempt contact with Barley. We'll need an Apache run, on our mark, to strafe the Behemoth with Hydras, *after* luring it with its thirty-mil, away from the cavity it leaves behind when it surfaces. If the size of that spire is any indication of this Behemoth's true mass, it's likely twice as big as the others."

Whether stunned speechless or struggling to process her plan, the team's silence was short-lived because she decided to take the initiative again.

"I also advise we give this particular Behemoth a call-sign, considering its unusual feature, size, location, and threat. Lloyd, you can relay this information to Barley so that the Apache pilot is better informed."

"You...really think she'll bite, and dispatch an attack helo against her previous orders? Much less, before daybreak?"

"I do, Russo. Those Hydra 70s have an effective range of *eight-thousand* yards. That pilot won't have to come close to the Plaza, and thanks to the location, plus Keign's low skyline, it should be an easy target."

The latter was especially true, if the Apache fixated on the Behemoth from above Elgin Park. Engaging the creature from the south of Cedar Plaza provided a clear lane of fire, with room to breathe.

"And the call-sign?" Roback asked.

"'Ultra,' after the CIA program MKUltra. In regards to the Behemoth's spire, and potential emanation of altering brainwaves."

There was an absolute absence of humor to Vlada's voice. This seriousness was hard for some of the operators to absorb, but possibly served as a reminder of her humanity. As if they needed any more, after the last baring of her heart.

"I can get behind that," Lloyd said. *"Sarges?"*

Someone sighed over comms. Maybe a few of the men, before anyone responded.

"Good as any, far as I'm concerned," Popov said.

"Sure, why the hell not?" Roback said, probably shrugging at the same time.

"Okay, good. Sound plan so far, V." Lloyd, with what seemed like a lick of light sarcasm. *"But* how*? How the hell do you plan on rousing that thing out of its comfy subterranean home? Much less without risking yourself again—it could incapacitate you at will. Could, I'm saying. It's possible you're less susceptible now."*

This was a great point, one that had occurred to Vlada earlier but had not stayed with her when it did.

"I appreciate the vote of confidence, Lloyd, I do. Because if ever I had a clear faculty, it's now. That said, I still don't want to take my chances with such a pivotal and necessary checkmate. An explosion will be needed, though."

"Splendid. And how? We're not carrying any grenades or Claymores."

"By taking a page out of Lebeau's book. I'll need a long article of clothing, ideally linen or cotton, something easily flammable. Stuff it in the gas port of a functioning vehicle, preferably an SUV, van, or truck—and drive it directly into the Panera building. I'll emerge, light it with a Zippo taken from the gas station counter, and get away in time. Oughtta do it."

A stunned silence ensued.

"I'm game," Roback said.

"Wish I could say that with a more gung-ho attitude," Arrington finally contributed. He sounded a touch defeated, to Vlada's surprise. She quickly learned why. *"But, more than half of my dominant hand is* gone*, thanks to a Drone. The same*

200

one that killed *Graves, bereaved me of my Rattler, and* destroyed *my three-three-eight. I've a Taurus, and I'm afraid I can't manage anything else with one hand, apart from a Rattler if someone wants to forfeit theirs."*

"You can have mine, brother," Roback said, over comms for Vlada and Lloyd's sake of clarity, despite being in the same room as Arrington. *"Rest assured, knowing it's in your possession is not forfeiture."*

They didn't hear Arrington's gratitude, but it was a given. Knowing the man wasn't out of the fight—she wouldn't have expected him to do, no matter how wounded, just as Fuller had been, but worse—refueled Vlada.

"Anyone object to this plan?" she asked. "I'm willing to brainstorm an alternative."

Several seconds passed.

Somewhere down in the parking lot spread out before her, past the convenience store and more extensively to her far right, muffled Apophid chatter could be heard. Grunts and chittering. A language not even she had cracked, but at this point she would rather not.

"Good," she finally said. "Lloyd, you need to raise Barley ASAP. If we're to do this before first light—have Ultra surface no later than immediate daybreak—we can't wait for that UAV's next flyby. She's supposedly having it run recon elsewhere in the city, but that Shadow has a wide infrared lens. You follow?"

"I'm tracking, yeah," Lloyd said. She could practically see him nodding with a kind of enthusiasm. *"Get on a roof, wave an IR laser. Get the UAV's attention."*

"Precisely. You're carrying, right?"

"Copy. CyTech IRL4."

Rescue lasers were nothing new, but CyTech's four-volt handheld device provided a 2° to 40° adjustable infrared beam, with a visibility range up to 1300 yards. Safe for the naked human eye, ideal for use with NODs and aircraft that had infrared targeting systems or cameras.

"Remember where I was when I first arrived? That rooftop? There's a ladder, facing the road. Yerkes Street. Take it."

"Copy. How soon should I move?"

"Trouble is, soon as you do, some Drones might home in on your pos. I'll cover you, but avoid gunfire. These things might be smart, but they still have eyes; don't want them to pinpoint us so soon.

"So, let's say, twenty minutes from now. In that time, gentlemen, we rest some more and gear up. The rest of Raven, only engage once you're clear of the storefront. Barley hit that nail on the head. Don't want to endanger any civvies."

"Confirmed," Popov said.

"Will await your mark," Lloyd said. *"How's De Horta fit into this?"*

She looked over at him and nodded.

De Horta touched his transmitter.

"How ever you need me, sir," he said. "But I'm a bit low on gear. All I've got is a sidearm, couple of mags."

"Which?" Lloyd asked.

"Glock 40, ten-mil. Fifteen-round mags."

"Not bad, really," Roback said. *"Could annoy a Drone, not much else. Unless you get lucky with an eye-shot."*

"I've a Rattler he can have," Lloyd said. *"De Horta, when Vlada comes down, you will, too. I'm in the store below."*

"Appreciate it, sir."

"Cut the sir shit. You got it."

De Horta smirked briefly at Vlada, awkwardly, and then nodded. She radioed the team again.

"The second half of this plan involves an incursion of the cavity that Ultra should leave behind. But I imagine that whatever Drones are in the area, possibly Apophids as well, will not be happy about that. Or us hurting Ultra. Since we won't know what's down there 'til we are, we can't afford to be followed by a horde of them."

She let off for a second.

Vlada knew she didn't need to spell out every single beat of the plan to soldiers significantly more experienced in stratagem than herself.

"Two to three go down," Arrington suggested, "while the rest hang topside, keeping the Apophids occupied."

"Ideally, Roback and Lloyd need to be among those that stay topside. Firepower wise. And, apologies for putting this so bluntly, but I am to believe that Lloyd and Russo are the best marksman here."

No audible objections, although she wouldn't doubt that some were passed between the men in the store.

"For that reason, I'd like to request Russo and De Horta come with me. The rest stay topside."

"Wait, wait, wait," De Horta immediately objected, not radioing it. "I, uh, I'm not, I'm not qualified to be—"

"Not qualified?" Vlada said, holding her transmitter. "Others would have sold their soul to insist I wasn't, either." For a blinking moment, she wondered what Roback's expression looked like when she said that. However, her reason for putting their dialogue on comms was more important. "But here I am. And here you are."

"That's not..." De Horta scoffed. He shook his head and then radioed his response. "That's not fair. W-We're hardly comparable. Tell her I'm wrong, guys."

"They don't need to, because I know you're right. And be that as it may, you're with us now. Besides, I know you're a little more than meets the eye, no?" She nodded at his 29th Infantry Division patch. "You can think of it as representing Fort Belvoir, all of Virginia, or Keign for that matter."

She had a point. Or ten.

"Rest assured, before I go find a working vehicle, I'm going to investigate the 75 to determine the fate of your crew," she added. "If they're alive, I'll move them here. No issue. But right now, I need your head in this. Once you have Lloyd's Rattler, I'm convinced you'll serve a better purpose in the confines of whatever's down there than you would up here."

De Horta sighed. He nodded, but stayed quiet.

"Okay, Raven," Vlada radioed, standing up. Her vision narrowed on the storefront windows over a hundred yards across the parking lot. She could see silhouettes of heavily geared operators through the floor-to-ceiling window of a clothing store at her eleven o'clock. But no clear faces. "I want to…wholeheartedly thank everyone for granting me a space, and the time, to speak."

She ended her transmission and looked down at De Horta. She extended her right hand. He tentatively accepted it and she helped him pop to his feet.

"There's one of two ways we can do this, you're not gonna like either."

He sighed and shook his head.

"Whatever you think is fastest. Not least belittling. Just get it over with."

Part of Vlada's face illuminated with a passing smirk. Then she guided him to the edge of the canopy, put a foot up on the parapet, and looked over at him.

"The speed of this will depend on your willingness. Don't doubt me. Just jump."

Before he could process or respond to her last two words, she dismounted the canopy. Landing on the forecourt pavement below without a hint of effort. She turned, looked up, and beckoned him with outstretched arms. The expression on De Horta's face was not excitement or confidence, but then he sighed and just leapt clear.

Vlada caught him at the waist without causing any damage, or slippage. She set him down with ease. All of this transpired behind a pump station.

"Don't worry," she said, as he looked around and straightened his uniform. "They didn't see."

The glass door into the convenience store pushed open. Lloyd stood, eyebrows hiking.

"But I did."

"Fuck's sake," De Horta shook his head, and rushed toward the building. Vlada looked around and followed, but paused at the entrance once De Horta was inside.

"Make sure he gets some food, water. Then grab a Zippo for me, collect someone's shirt—bigger the better—and radio me once you're done, if I'm not back before then."

"Copy. Where you headed?" Lloyd asked.

"Merlin," she said, thumbing over her shoulder. "No explosion, quite possible the pilots are alive."

"Let's hope. Be careful."

She nodded and turned away. But Lloyd reached out, to grab the kit belt secured to her lower waist. Except he missed; as his hand withdrew, he found himself grabbing her wrist. The skin was leathery, almost, but fleshy and quite alive. He felt awkward, especially when she paused to look down at his hand, then up at his face.

"I, uh…sorry. I was just going to say…" Lloyd pulled away his hand. "You're not armed. Uh, no G6, I mean. Or Rattler. Maybe—"

He gestured back into the store.

Vlada shook her head. She indicated her holstered Taurus, strapped to a thigh.

"This is enough, worst-case. But remember, I don't want to draw any more attention to myself than I might just by moving. I'll manage."

"Right. 'Course you will." Lloyd nodded, and then withdrew into the store.

After a breath that she didn't physically need, but felt psychologically deprived of, Vlada faced the south side of Cedar Plaza. The longest straight edge of the parking lot and where the MV-75 had gone down. Then she sprinted toward it, not glancing over her shoulder or ever looking back to see if any Apophids pursued her through the late night.

She bounded across the parking lot behind the Rite Aid, which had been scored as if by gargantuan claws. From one edge of a ditch to the other she sprang, along these gouges in pavement, until she leapt onto the V-shaped tail. The back end of the helo responded to her additional weight with a light creak, but no shift in movement. She crawled down the top of the fuselage, minding the warped steel rotors bent back toward the craft's body. The entire right tiltrotor was demolished, and although smoke poured from it, as well as the turboshaft engines, there were no fires.

Vlada counted every tiny blessing.

"Coming in from your six," she radioed, hopeful their headsets were still on, or they had plugs like De Horta. She also spoke just loud enough that anyone in the immediate vicinity should be able to hear. "I'm with Raven-One. We need to get you…"

She slid down the tapered cockpit, peering through the canopy. More than half of the reinforced glass had suffered major damage. Part of the cockpit's nose had wrenched backward and with it chunks of brick concrete had crushed the co-pilot. Vlada had never even learned her name, nor her wingman's; only knowing them as Merlin-Three.

Although his body was intact, the pilot's eyes were unquestionably lifeless. His seizure had been severe, and fatal.

Why or how he was affected worse than the pilot of Scout-Three could be debated for days on end…or proven, with enough testing and analyses, supposing Pegasus had something to go on.

Like the spire itself, from Ultra.

She wondered if it was directly connected to the creature's colossal brain, but the notion of incapacitating the huge Apophid without killing it was laughable at best. She didn't even consider it, and knew full-well that the operators wouldn't, either.

Vlada began to leave the scene, but paused.

She looked back at the partially demolished Rite Aid. Had those civilians from earlier remained, they were either dead from the crash or buried in the rubble. Vlada had known of miraculous events where even children survived plane crashes and building collapses, while others perished from less.

In the face of an urgency with her team's new plan, Vlada found herself investigating the partial ruins of the mostly brick structure. What glass had composed the outer façades and occasional skylight were now in small shards. Some ceiling support had fallen and impaled other clumps of debris. She began calling for survivors, hoping to hear a voice or two. Muffled, but with enough air to get their plea out.

Nearly a minute passed.

Vlada came around to the undamaged corner of the Rite Aid, far left of the MV-75's cockpit. She still had not heard any voices, so she performed a double-take when she saw them. Their faces. Terror stuck to them like glue. She stepped through a shattered window, ducked under a fallen girder, and approached the three civilians at the end of a narrow hall. Where the public restrooms were. The one deputy, a civilian woman, and her teenage son.

The latter two were most shaken.

The man in uniform was as well, but had a better grip on the matter than the others. At least ostensibly. Despite this, he *had* reached for his holstered pistol on her approach. Just not drawn it.

"I know, I know how this looks, but I'm not—" Vlada began, raising her strange arms.

"Outreach, right?" the deputy asked. His hand lowered. "I know what you are."

That hurt her a little, but that he didn't draw his gun to shoot her *was* progress.

"Are you a superhero?" the boy, maybe fourteen, asked.

Vlada's nose tingled. "No, but the soldiers I'm with are. We are about to perform a very big task, over in Cedar Plaza, so...we need you all to stay here."

The mother's brow furrowed. Her cheeks were caked with dust and tears.

"Y-You...You're the w-woman from earlier."

Vlada nodded. "Yes, ma'am. I'm...so happy that you're still safe." She looked over at the deputy. "Where's the other of you? There were two, earlier."

"Joey had to go. His wife was working at the hospital."

Vlada's brow furrowed. "The day of?"

The man shook his head. "Four days ago. She and many others that normally worked there flocked to Celestine to help people stuck there. Patients and staff. I...I haven't heard back from him, but these radios are shit and I left my phone in the squad car."

Vlada's chest hurt and tears welled into her eyes.

The strength and courage of normal people were super-human feats she could only aspire to.

"One of my teams secured Celestine earlier today, before you even came here," she said, looking around before her eyes returned to the deputy. It was a partial truth; she didn't know the full extent of carnage, nor survivors, at the hospital. "If nothing else, they're safely hiding just like you are now. Please...go into one of the bathrooms. Stay. You have my word...not another night will pass before SAR teams work their magic on

Keign."

"Mom, what's SAR?" the boy asked his mother, looking back at her.

"Search and rescue," the deputy said, assuredly.

When he looked back at Vlada, she was already retreating. She would have left without looking back had the boy not called after her, however quietly.

"Where are you going?" he asked, his face marred by worry.

Vlada tried to smile.

"To get rid of the bad things."

12

Against her insistence, but technically not orders, Evan Lloyd had not stayed inside the convenience store during her absence. He had swiftly retrieved a Zippo lighter from behind the counter, accepted a 'donation' from one of the heftier civilians hiding inside the building—specifically, a 3XL polo—and then left the items with De Horta, including his Rattler, before exiting. He maneuvered toward the end of Yerkes Street, taking notice of two dead Drones from earlier, at the base of the brick movie theater he would later be scaling. While there, he looked up and saw, in the sluggishly softening darkness, the mounted ladder Vlada had mentioned. Previously caged, it had since come open, violently by the looks of it.

Vlada.

Temporarily jealous of her abilities, Lloyd only let it amuse him, no more. Distractions of any kind couldn't be afforded right now. And when it came down to it, Vlada's revelation had left a sort of secondhand scar on his soul.

Regardless of her enhanced capabilities, it might be impossible moving forward to perceive her as anything but human.

It was, in his heart, her greatest strength.

"Now where are you?" Lloyd asked himself, in a whisper, looking around. Yerkes Street wasn't littered with empty vehicles, but it wasn't vacant of them, either. After checking two, whose batteries were dead, the third was missing a key, and the fourth had a thin film of smoke rising from the hood. When he touched it, detecting warmth, he felt a kind of relief. In knowing that people were still going about; it went against common sense, and the military's request, but he took it as meaning that people were intent on reuniting with loved ones.

While Lloyd didn't wholeheartedly condone vigilantes, primarily in this case as they were undeniably ill-equipped against Apophids, he respected the intention.

"Fifth time's a charm," he mumbled, checking the next vehicle. He skipped coupes, sedans, and hatchbacks. Only pickups, vans, and SUVs.

A burgundy Dodge panel van that would likely be reported if seen around Optima or Creekmoor, was his salvation. The '27 ProMaster was in decent enough shape and, to his immense surprise, had the key-fob in a cupholder. There were signs of blood on the dash and passenger seat, but not enough to indicate a devoured body. Praying the owners had made it to safety and abandoned any intention of being on the road again, Lloyd climbed in. He began to slowly pull the driver's side door shut. His right thumb was two inches from the push-ignition when the door became immovable.

He looked and flinched, visibly, clutching his chest.

"Fuck's sake, V," he said.

Vlada smirked, wryly and briefly. She let go of the door but still glared at him.

"The hell are you doing?"

"It's called *initiative*. Something a Gunny knows all too well."

"Right. You and Lebeau both, huh? The pigheadedness of Gunnery Sergeants."

Lloyd shrugged. His hands gripped the steering wheel in quiet anger and grief.

"That stubborn fuckin'…" He shook his head, staring at the dash.

"A page from his book, remember?" she said, touching his left shoulder. Just then, the scarcely lit lampposts down Yerkes turned off. Dawn was closer than they realized. Lloyd looked over at Vlada, who nodded before he did, too. "More than one, anyway. Just give me your IRL, I can make that roof quicker than you. The second you see me dismount, bring this around and direct it at the back of the Panera. I'll clear any cars that are in the way, and weaken the wall."

"What happened to you risking getting that close?"

"What happened to the vote of confidence, that I'm less susceptible now? C'mon, Gunny. I believe in myself, now."

Lloyd shook his head, trying not to smile.

"Once it's clear, I'll run to you and we'll swap."

"And what? You think the Apophids will stand by while we do this?" Lloyd scoffed. "We're lucky enough to have *all of this right now*. Nah. I got it. I'll wear my seatbelt, Mom. Promise."

Vlada shook her head, despite the small curve to one corner of her mouth.

"Just remember to scram as soon as you're through that wall."

"I'll do my best. Oh, yeah. I left the lighter and shirt, a triple-X-L, on the counter."

"'Course you did. Guess *I'll* light it, then. You just focus on driving, crashing, and getting the fuck out of there."

"Wilco, ma'am."

"No bullshit. Just wait for my dismount, then get in position. De Horta and I will keep 'em off you."

Lloyd nodded. He tilted his head, then, in thought.

"You really think he'll be better down there?"

"I do. A Rattler in close-quarters? That, and Russo, are all I need."

"If you say so." He dug out his IRL4, a two-by-four-inch remote-like device. The bulbous clear end was the obvious laser housing. She accepted it, and then backed away. She looked up, noticing a gentle dimness manifest in the far reaches of cloud-strewn sky.

"I do," she said, and then turned. Vlada *moved*. She scaled the theater building in less than half the time it would have taken Lloyd to, if not quicker. The instant she was flat on her feet, she armed the laser and waved the green beam through the air above her. Invisible to the naked eye, even hers, Vlada knew it would be impossible to ignore for the Shadow's infrared camera, even over a mile away.

To her relief, Barley raised her on comms twelve seconds

after she deployed the laser. Meanwhile, she noticed a slight increase of Drone activity in the Plaza parking lot. They weren't swarming or attacking, but chittering and moving more. She also spotted two Warriors in their ranks, albeit farther east of the Panera, where the wounded Behemoth was still loitering.

"Responding to the IRL. Shadow is en route, due southwest."

"Copy, ma'am. We're moving a little sooner than expected. Have critical news. A different kind of Behemoth has *burrowed* into the parking lot. It has a neural horn capable of disrupting brain waves. We have a plan to get it to the surface, and then investigate what might be a nest. How copy?"

A normal person would have to take a really big, deep, haggard breath after that one. Vlada didn't. She just waited; impatiently.

"Uh, I read you, 21X. Can this not wait until first light? Twenty, thirty minutes."

"Negative. Apophid activity is too wary of us. Besides, we fear that they are planning something awful and irreparable for the civilians present. Also…I have confirmation of Merlin-Three's fate. Both pilots are dead. One from his seizure; the other was crushed."

She knew that although the rest of the MSOT likely couldn't hear her, De Horta was listening.

"This is awful news, 21X. However…what is it you need?"

This sounded to Vlada like Barley was either reconsidering her initial incredulity in real-time, or was being given an order by Captain Aleem that contradicted her own. Possibly even his. Regardless…

"Hydra 70s, ma'am. An Apache could target Ultra from as far as Elgin Park, without risking the pilot."

"Ultra?"

"Confirmed. Raven's call-sign for the Behemoth. It may be as big as twice the size of any other Behemoth."

Some time passed. Vlada wasn't happy about it. She began tapped her booted foot against the flat rooftop. Then she glanced back, spotting the dark red commercial van in which Lloyd still sat. Her eyes lifted, noticing a Drone creeping past Yerkes, down Mayfield. Thirty yards behind the van. She hoped it would keep going.

Then—a new voice in her ear. New, but familiar.

"Vlada, this is Captain Aleem. How certain are you of this…Ultra…and its dimensions?"

"Eighty percent certain of its intentions, sir," she responded, sharply. Now staring out, down at the parking lot. Specifically, the Panera. "One-hundred percent certain of its size. The horn alone is more than twice as tall as any other Behemoth's."

Without a lick of hesitation, he responded.

"It will take the Apache nine minutes to reach Keign."

Vlada almost smiled. She began to thank him, but then realized the transmission was still open, still his.

"If possible," Aleem added, *"mark Ultra with your IRL as soon as it is clear to engage. Danger close is* prohibited, *understood? That includes you, Vlada."*

"Affirmative, sir. Thank you, sir."

Barley's voice returned. *"The Shadow will remain in the area to provide visual support for Raven, and comms from me. Once the Apache has entered Keign airspace, I will relay his readiness to you. The pilot's call-sign is Condor-One."*

A pause.

"How copy…Vlada?"

"Lima Charlie, ma'am. Thank you. Over and out."

Vlada disarmed the IRL, stuffed it into an empty magazine pouch on her belt, and then dismounted from the theater. Knowing that was Lloyd's sign to move, however, she suddenly hoped he didn't. Just yet. Because she realized that the curious Drone from Mayfield had in fact ventured down Yerkes. At the sight of her, it immediately charged down the street. The van's taillights illuminated, but not its headlamps, when Lloyd started the engine. The Drone did not notice, its gaze fixated on her at the end of Yerkes. She watched it approach, a red glow from the taillights passing over its pale body.

As soon as it reached her, she side-stepped, left hand reaching out. She grabbed its left scythe, below the knuckle joint, and thanks to the creature's momentum, was able to easily twist the limb off its body. The compound fracture agonized the Drone and it briefly rolled across the street, in a fury of discombobulated limbs.

"Don't have time for you," she snarled, and bounded toward it. She landed, but radioed Lloyd. "Get going, Gunny."

"Uh, copy." Lloyd drove the van with a new brand of resolve. He sped down the road, toward Vlada and the Drone. Just before he reached them, he added: "On your left."

Vlada swung her left leg in a roundhouse kick, effectively striking the Drone's mandible off its face. The creature staggered out of the van's path. She gripped its skull, punched its right eyeball, and clawed a fistful of its brains out when she withdrew her hand.

Then, she *ran*. Reaching the gas station in the time that it took Lloyd to take the van ten parking spaces east.

She burst into the store, without breaking anything in her wake. Waiting by the front counter, De Horta flinched at her brisk entrance.

"On me," she said, firmly, and snatched from the counter the two items Lloyd had left.

De Horta pulled his game face on. As if the 29th Infantry insignia was tattooed to his forehead. Lloyd's MCX Rattler slung and in his hands, four spare mags stuffed into separate pockets, De Horta followed Vlada outside.

She radioed the MSOT as she ran toward the Panera, weaving between vehicles in the softening darkness. An intermittent glance over her shoulder ensured De Horta was following.

"We're moving, Raven, Apache's ETA is eight minutes. Slight change of plans, Lloyd is driving and I'm clearing his path, weakening the wall, then lighting the torch. De Horta is with me, so I need everyone outside, find a target and make it regret ever entering our atmosphere."

She spoke like an automatic rifle, but with flawless coherency. No panting or grunting as she ran, augmenting her speed only so that she didn't vanish on De Horta.

"Copy," came Popov's voice. *"Moving."*

The second she reached the lot space behind the bakery, she could feel a wave of pressure lock onto her skull. Sauntering between the two cars parked there, Vlada uttered a frustrated shout and lashed out with both arms.

De Horta watched the two vehicles skid laterally, tires briefly shrieking against the asphalt.

Behind him, he heard the faint hum of an engine. When De Horta looked, he saw what he assumed was the van that Lloyd was driving. No headlights. They didn't need more attention brought their way.

This was plenty.

De Horta looked around, sorely missing the minigun platform on the MV-75. And the lives of its crew. He would have time to mourn them, once he made it out of Keign. An inevitability, he reassured himself.

Shouldering the protracted buttstock of the Rattler, he began plinking rounds at Drones as they crawled over vehicles toward him and Vlada.

The emergence of Raven squad from the storefront was the additional boost of confidence he needed. They fanned out from the sidewalk in front of the plaza shops, to avoid endangering any civilians.

Although De Horta could not see all of them himself, only glimpses of dark silhouettes between cars scattering the parking lot, their muzzle flashes and sporadic, trained gunfire were indication enough.

Just the same, none of the MSOT operators could clearly make out De Horta, or Vlada. The latter, they assumed, was behind the Panera.

"Barley here." Her voice in their ears. *"UAV is at two-hundred feet, Raven. Will call out threats in your blind spots."*

"Appreciate it," Arrington said.

Vlada struck the nine-foot brick wall in front of her as if

a martial artist training on a punching bag. She hit it with her palms, then her right elbow, and lastly a jab with her left fist. The pressure on her skull squeezed; part of her effort was giving her stress and pain a direct, albeit inanimate, target.

And then Lloyd hit the horn.

She snapped out of her stupor, just in time to notice cracks in the mortar and dust sprinkling off the bricks. The wall even moved, slightly, from her impacts. She scrambled away from it, peripherally noticing that Lloyd was already accelerating; she was proud he didn't wait.

Just as she slid over the hood of a car she had pushed aside earlier, Vlada saw a Warrior flanked by two Drones approach from across the lot. The latter had to navigate over or around vehicles that were discarded by the Warrior, not unlike she had.

And then, behind her, the van reached its destination with a loud crash. The sloped, stubby front end of the van had collided with the weakened brick wall going maybe twenty or thirty miles-per-hour. It would have been significantly more devastating to the van, and Lloyd, had the wall not crumbled upon impact. Bricks crumbled onto the roof and high, now severely cracked windshield of the Dodge ProMaster. The front bumper and grille, though warped from the collision, had even gone so far as wrapping around a commercial oven.

Vlada drew her Taurus, and waited until the Warrior was nearly within reach of its own limbs before she side-stepped and fired—arm at a seventy-degree angle, elbow locked. The Taurus roared and her shot decimated its left eyeball. The Warrior swung, madly, at her. A serrated appendage cut the air above her head, and she fired again, but not at the Warrior. A Drone nearly upon her took the heavy round to the skull, but it would suffer one more before it slumped to the asphalt.

A consistent stream of .300 Blackout rounds jackhammered the Warrior behind her. She spun to face it, firing into a space between its ribs, briefly faltering it. De Horta, marching toward it from the opposite corner of the demolished Panera wall, kept firing his Rattler in semi-auto.

Inside the bakery, Lloyd caught his breath and disengaged his seatbelt. He pushed the silicone-coated woven nylon airbag away from his face and chest, but not ungratefully. As he emerged from the van, having to force the door open and only succeeding on his third try, his comms came to life—but unevenly.

One of his plugs had fallen out.

It was too dark to find it. And when he looked up, past the van, he saw through the kitchen and over the front counter. In the center of the bakery, the enormous Behemoth horn Vlada had spoken of stood true. Immediately spurred into action, Lloyd ignored his comms, subconsciously acknowledging they were just Barley providing tactical call-outs for Raven, anyway.

He moved toward the gaping hole in the wall he had caused, momentarily tripping over chunks of mortar-bound bricks.

"Vlada!" he shouted, shaking a brief spell of tinnitus from the crash. Clear of the wall, he saw Vlada remove a Warrior's scythe from its own gut, between two exoskeletal ribs, slinging Apophid gore across the asphalt. De Horta was reloading his Rattler, and Vlada *threw* the scythe like a javelin, impaling a Drone that was nearly upon him.

Another Drone, apparently wounded, actually turned and scampered away. A sight Lloyd didn't think he would ever see.

"V," he radioed.

She turned, saw Lloyd, and immediately ran toward him. Then, past him. She brandished the Zippo lighter, flipping the steel lid open with surprising ease despite the size of her hands and digits. She looked over at Lloyd, her eyes wide.

"Go!" she snapped.

"Right," he nodded, and scrambled back toward Yerkes. Knowing it would be temporary.

"De Horta, follow!" Vlada shouted, as she stuffed the wrung T-shirt into the van's open fuel port. She stooped, putting her nose to it, and inhaled. Strong aroma. A full, or near-full tank. She nodded and flicked the steel wheel of the Zippo. The cotton wick ignited and a tall flame sprouted out. She had pre-ferred the Zippo over a Bic just in case she had to throw the lighter from a distance, which fortunately wasn't the case.

The shirt caught fire immediately and she capped the Zippo, pocketing it 'just in case,' as she ran from the Panera building. What was left of it, and soon, hopefully, only detritus.

Three bounding strides later, the van exploded. A blast that caved the roof of the structure, and weakened the lateral walls. When the coursing flames made contact with a tub of grease and bottles of cooking oil, the conflagration evolved in the blink of an eye.

Clear of the explosion, Vlada had rallied with De Horta and Lloyd to witness the fruits of their labor.

Before the blast had even begun to subside, several things occurred at once, all in the wake of a creeping lay of subtle sun-light. Of instant notice to Vlada and company were the other Apophids coming in front the direction of the Burger King. Even the Behemoth halted its hurried advance, among two War-riors and a small throng of Drones. The Apophids on the east side of the lot scattered as well. These were only Drones, and appeared more skittish in their retreat.

On the storefront side of the parking lot, Raven noticed jagged cracks in the asphalt begin to network along the center of the lot. When these widened and the ground itself shifted apart like tectonic plates, the operators could tell because rows of vehicles would move aside as if on sliding tiles. Of asphalt and earth.

These fissures all stemmed from one hub.

The Panera building.

As its walls crumbled and the interior of the bakery dis-assembled, the colossal Behemoth beneath it rose with a turbulent sound. It was almost similar to a jet engine stirring to life. Aptly named for more than one reason, Ultra was *more than* twice the size of a regular Behemoth.

It also had not four but six limbs, an additional pair pro-truding from the center of each side, to help support its bulk. The jointed legs carried it nearly thirty feet off the ground, the dimensions of its vaguely octagonal body equivalent to a four-bedroom ranch house. As it hoisted itself clear of the parking lot, leaving behind a craterous opening fifty by thirty yards across, the operators became aware of the damage it had endured. Not nearly enough to satisfy them, but the explosion had produced smoldering wounds around its skull, and crumbs of debris lodged in its exposed forelimb muscles.

"Hydras might not be enough," Lloyd hated to admit out loud, but did. He looked over at Vlada.

"We'll see about that," she said, seething. She raised the IRL4 in her right hand, engaging the invisible beam and directing the device at the left side of Ultra's skull. The bulk of its body extended between the remains of Panera and the Burger King, which further explained why most of the Apophids were amassing at that end of the lot.

"Jesus fucking hell, Vlada," Barley exclaimed, under her breath. *"You weren't lying."*

"I never do, ma'am," she responded, firmly. "Now where is our Apache?"

Three seconds passed.

Three seconds too long. Ultra plodded toward Raven, its crablike legs leaving sinkholes in the asphalt wherever it walked, each the size and depth of a Mini Cooper. If it wandered fifty feet to the right, it would effortlessly trample half the Plaza's storefront.

"This fucker's bigger than we expected," Vlada said, radioing Raven. "We need to keep it where it is, so that when it falls, it doesn't crush any of these businesses."

Before Raven could respond, Barley's voice returned. Incapable of contacting them until the frequency was open.

"Condor-One is twenty seconds out. Keep the target painted."

"Wilco," she responded, and then addressed the operators, some of who she could now see across the way. "May not seem like much, Raven, but open fire. Target the muscle hubs around its neck and forelimbs."

Immediately, while slowly retreating toward the east end

of the lot, the operators began firing bursts at these areas. Roback's RM338 had the greatest effect, but all together Ultra seemed genuinely…annoyed. Not hurt enough to show any signs of actual pain or damage, but…it was a start.

"What about that crater?" Russo asked, panic evident in his voice. Reasonably. Ultra's horrid gaze was fixated on his squad. "We not going down there anymore?"

Vlada began to respond but felt a sudden searing ache in her temples. Her reply got caught in her mouth, and warped into a groan of pain. She faltered where she knelt between Lloyd and De Horta. Their attempt to console her, that unexpected physical contact, despite their goodwill, triggered a physiological response. Fortunately, the sudden outward flare of her arms didn't hurt them.

"*With* or without you, *I* fuckin' am," she exclaimed. Shaking her head, teeth gritted, she mentally repelled the spire's assault on her brain. She looked over at De Horta, and as she spoke to him, she forced the IRL4 into Lloyd's hand. "Ignore my previous request. Stay with Lloyd. I need to move at my own speed on this one."

Both men felt the urge to shout "be careful" but didn't get that far before she was galloping away. Her movements were slightly delayed by the spire's incorporeal shockwaves, but she maintained her bearing. Behind her, Lloyd focused on keeping Ultra's head the destination of the laser. This was difficult to discern given its invisibility, but not impossible. For this reason, users without NODs or infrared gear could use the device's built-in sights to ensure alignment. This would have been easier if he didn't have to periodically fire his G6 at Drones trying to flank them.

De Horta did his best to help deter them from Lloyd as he controlled the IRL4.

Hardly four seconds after Vlada left them, everyone with an earplug heard Barley's words. They came through with a shot of adrenaline.

"Condor, fox-one, away!"

If there was any benefit to Ultra's size, it was its speed.

Or lack thereof. Immensely slow and ungainly. Finally, Vlada thought to herself, something that obeyed this planet's physics. To boot, its apparent awareness of Vlada's presence made it stop advancing toward Raven.

En route to the cragged, gaping crater in the parking lot below the enormous canopy of its underside, Vlada retrieved two things. The scythe and serrated arm from a single dead Warrior. She wielded the latter in her right hand, with which she would have to perfect swinging techniques. Her left had the versatility of thrusting *and* stabbing.

Less than twenty feet from the edge, and about that distance from one of Ultra's towering legs, the Hydra rocket hissed through the air above Cedar Plaza. The 70mm warhead detonated on impact, a shockingly direct hit. Nine pounds of Comp B-4 swathed Ultra's skull in a fireball. Vlada had paused to look up, in awe of the sight. But, to her disappointment, the flames and black smoke dissipated—to seemingly no effect.

Vlada radioed, vehemently.

"Fire again! Lloyd, keep that laser on its skull."

Barley's hesitation was null and void. Simply seeing that the target remained, and the infrared laser stayed on the huge Apophid, Condor-One probably didn't need an order to loose another rocket.

"Fox-two and -three, ETA five seconds!"

Vlada knew that if Ultra collapsed down onto its own legs as she hoped it would, rather than topple toward the storefront, her window of infiltrating that crater would be closed. She advanced, only for the spire's shockwave to take her legs out. The paralytic force seized her nerves and she cried out in pain.

Sixty yards across the way, Russo had eyes on her.

He moved, perilously navigating the shorter end of the crater, around where the Panera used to be, skirting scattered vehicles and crossing gaping fissures. Roback called after him, only to then transfer his words into actions, firing the machine gun up at Ultra—

The next two Hydra rockets hit their mark.

Twin fireballs erupted, one engulfing the bulk of Ultra's

skull, while the other struck closer to its neck. Flame and shrapnel devastated its hub of muscles there; strips of charred flesh fell to the pavement below, twenty feet left of Vlada. Rancid as it smelled, the sight was a small victory.

And the spire's hold on her had relinquished.

She moved to the edge of the crater, looking down. Although Ultra's shadow conquered the space, some wafts of early daylight illuminated a few spots. The earth wasn't completely untouched by civilization; waste pipes and underground wiring could be seen emerging from the sides of the cavity, but none were destroyed by Ultra's wake. Suggesting it had not dug itself here, as they had discussed and doubted.

Of Apophid presence, or any unusual signs of life, the cavern appeared empty.

Vlada felt a peculiar agony from being so wrong.

The continued gunfire to her far left, and Russo's voice in her ear, brought her out of this spell. Barley then declared that two more rockets had been dispatched by the Apache. She looked back, grateful for the new dim layer of light that had graced Cedar Plaza. Seeing Lloyd keeping that infrared laser directed at Ultra's head was another blessing; and De Horta doing his best to fend off flanking Drones.

Popov was even in the process of crossing Ultra's future path, and the fissured parking lot, to help De Horta. Arrington followed, knowing his borrowed Rattler was too compact to deliver anything with enough velocity to damage Ultra from below. This left just Roback in front of the enormous Behemoth, firing his RM338 in conservative bursts up at its charred neck and forelimb muscles.

"Sergeant Roback!" Barley snapped over comms. *"Three o'clock!"*

He spun to face a flanking force of two Drones and one Warrior. No more conservation with his ammo. He unleashed a volley of high-caliber rounds at the creatures. Vlada looked across the way, spotting the Apophids approaching him from the right side of Ultra. Its huge legs obstructed her full view of them, but it seemed that Roback was keeping them at bay.

Until his belt ran out.

"You good?" Russo asked, not over comms. He had reached her, standing to her left.

"Roback needs help," she said.

Russo looked, ready to move. But when his eyes returned to her, she was staring up at Ultra's underside, seemingly hypnotized.

"Coming to you, Pops," Roback radioed, leaving behind two dead Drones and a crippled but still mobile Warrior.

"He's rallying with Popov and the others," Roback said, looking at the side of her upturned face. He then glanced past her, noticing the wounded regular-sized Behemoth and a few other Apophids nearing the east end of the crater. "We should, too, V. Vlada!"

Finally, Russo followed her mesmerized gaze.

Just then, the next two Hydra rockets detonated around Ultra's head. It had been reduced to a standstill of irresolution, or possibly pain. These explosions tore away more than patches of charred muscle, though. Russo flinched from the blasts twenty-five feet above him, and to his left. He and Vlada watched as entire chunks of Ultra's skull and even damaged panoply fell to the parking lot, some landing on top of cars. Exposed tissue beneath the shards of biological armor was confirmation of serious wounding.

Still, somehow, Ultra remained afoot.

Vlada pressed her transmitter.

"Lloyd!" She practically shouted. "Aim the laser at its left side, near the belly!"

"You got it."

"Barley! I need a *Hellfire* on the lasered target. Now!"

"Negative! Friendlies are in the blast radius."

"This fucking thing is *pregnant*!" Vlada shouted, her voice nearly turning their comms into a burst of static, but her words got through. The last one sank a feeling of disgust and horror into everyone listening. Vlada regained her wits, looked at Russo, and mouthed "go." The look in her eyes was message enough, let alone her demand for a 180mm Hellfire missile so close to them. Russo gripped her alien shoulder in a heartfelt moment before turning to run toward the others. Vlada's hand remained on the transmitter, keeping Barley from contributing just yet. "Target will be clear of friendlies on impact. The laser stays. Tell Condor to deploy a Hellfire, or I'll run to the park and convince the pilot myself."

Knowing he was listening, Vlada added, with fervor: "Keign *needs this*, Captain."

She let go of her transmitter, and, still wielding the Warrior limbs in her hands like gladiator weapons, turned. She faced the east side of the lot, and ran.

"Condor-One, Hellfire inbound," Barley finally declared. *"Twelve seconds to impact."*

"Fall back!" Vlada radioed the operators. "Back to Yerkes! Cover Lloyd!"

Nobody in Cedar Plaza, even the acute Vlada, had noticed the condition of Ultra's underside until moments ago. The sun stopped being so lethargic, and against the heavy shadows still obscuring the space below the creature and between its three legs, she had seen. The belly of the beast, as it were; it sagged, slightly, and appeared deformed in parts, as if carrying multiple bulbous forms inside it. The underside of a Behemoth had never been properly studied, but this one exhibited tender striations between softer, leather-like hammocks of flesh.

Despite her mental connections to the Apophids, and what she had seen during her bonding process sixteen months ago, their reproductive methods remained a mystery. Even now, there were a myriad of questions left unanswered. It was a start, though. It was a heinous, apprehensive start.

Vlada swung the Warrior's arm at another as she ran through a throng of Apophids. The serrated exoskeleton caught a Warrior in the neck, gouging muscle and fracturing bone. She dislodged it in the same motion, simultaneously leaving the Drone's scythe gored through another's mouth. Forty yards behind her, the Hellfire missile struck its target. The explosion wasn't just flame, but shrapnel as well. Designed to penetrate reactive tank armor, the Hellfire's precursor warhead gave way to its main payload, and the huge blast rocked Ultra on its legs.

The Apophids around her shrieked and ignored her presence to rush to Ultra's aid. Their mother, Vlada presumed.

Chunks of partially charred and shrapnel-embedded flesh fell away from what would've been Ultra's left ribcage. If it was even remotely humanoid. But it wasn't, more resembling a scarab or rhinoceros beetle than anything.

"Target remains," Lloyd radioed, with fierce resolve. "Laser stands. Give us another Hellfire, ma'am. One more."

"If that thing falls onto the storefront…" Barley began, and scoffed.

The transmission opened.

"It won't," Vlada insisted. "Lloyd, lower the laser an inch or two. Focus on the upper legs. Ma'am? Take out its coxa, where the middle leg meets the body. Ultra will fall *toward* us, but we're in the clear. Nearby Apophids will be crushed."

Three long seconds passed.

Ultra and its concerned brood produced a cacophony of troubled shrieks. The innards of the giant Behemoth growled as if hungry, upset, or sick. If not all three.

"Hellfire two, ETA twelve seconds," Barley stated. *"Condor-One is circling west for a better angle on the head, but keeping its distance. No more Hellfires."*

"Copy. Thank you, ma'am. Lloyd?"

"Laser's solid. Rally to us. Popov is hurt, but no more threats."

All the Apophids in the region were focusing on Ultra, some of the Drones even climbing its legs, toward the deformed and squirming underbelly.

"I can't, not yet," Vlada said, her voice a strain of regret for not being able to group and possibly help Popov.

"Goddammit, V, fall back to—"

Vlada's surprisingly precise fingertips accessed the mute button on each of her earplugs. Then she looked to her right. The wounded Behemoth from earlier had returned with a vengeance. Selfishly, it fixated on Vlada. She wielded the Warrior's bladed appendage like a sword, two-handing the stubby exoskeletal base. She swung it at the tank of a creature, dwarfed by Ultra. The first two feet, from the rectangular tip, struck its face and lodged into the side of the skull. One of its eyeballs sprang from the socket, dangling by an intact optic nerve.

She wrenched the bladed arm free, just as the second Hellfire impacted Ultra behind her. She glanced, watching the massive fireball engulf the femur of Ultra's middle leg, which was bulkier than the others. Ultra uttered a loud, thunderous groan of pain. Simultaneously, multiple dead Drones fell to the asphalt below, others shorn by shrapnel.

Vlada wielded the serrated appendage like a knight's lance instead of a sword, thrusting it into the Behemoth's open mouth. The first half of it entered its throat, and with a twist she all but decapitated the creature. Instead of still using the Apophid limb as a weapon, she abandoned it, and leapt onto the dead Behemoth's carapace. She turned, in time to witness the collapse of Ultra. As she had predicted, its damaged upper leg and other faltered limbs gave way to its fall in Raven's direction. They were clear of its radius, but the scampering Apophids below it were not. Unlike the sluggish movement of the colossal creature when it was upright, it fell just as anything else would.

Quickly, and with its mass, a great impact.

Still touched by the reach of its rear end's shadow, Vlada was quick to dismount. *After* she had broken off the Behemoth's horn. She ran around the east end of the crater, just as Ultra landed with an immense sound and tremor. A few Drones had managed to escape its collapse, but Raven was quick to dispatch them.

Circling around to the storefront side of the fallen Ultra, she saw the new condition of its exposed underbelly. Many of the sagging, fleshy bands had broken apart. A miasma of indescribable stench billowed out from the beast's innards, visible clouds of yellowish vapors rising above it. Although part of the massive husk still moved, as did some of its other limbs, Ultra would not be getting up anytime soon.

Vlada heard the distinct beat of helicopter rotors as the

Apache navigated past the Labor District and toward Creek-moor for a better vantage point on its target.

"Hold your fire, Condor-One," Vlada radioed, unsure if she was within range of it or not. If the latter, Barley could relay. In the meantime, not waiting for confirmation, she ran toward the front of Ultra, minding its truck-sized jaws. She noticed its dull red eyes move in their sockets and appear to focus on her, despite their lack of pupils. She delighted in the sight of its damaged horn. The spire itself appeared intact, but where the base conformed to its skull was charred and gouged with shrapnel.

She even grinned, and approached the now horizontal spire of bone. She imagined some form of neural network snaked through the marrow, or possibly an extension of the Behemoth's brain composed its core. Also possible, a secondary extrasensory organ inhabited the spire. Whatever was the case, Vlada was thrilled to clutch it and twist the panoplied base off the Apophid's skull. Manual contact with the spire made her body tingle, but nothing more.

"You thought you could control *me*, conquer *us*?" Vlada snarled as she tore the horn away, one boot raised to press against what might be considered its nose. Ultra whimpered in pain and helplessness. She stood up straight, brandishing the nine-foot horn like a massive spear. "*I* am in control of myself, and we are perfectly capable of conquering each other…without your help."

She then spit on it, and the huge thing flinched.

"Now," she seethed, preparing to thrust the horn, "bleed for me."

Vlada sank four feet's worth of the spire into Ultra's left eye socket. She screamed as she exerted all her might into rotating the wider base and angling the spire up into the Behemoth's brain cavity. Then she stepped away, while still holding the base, her arms flexing. The horn broke halfway up, dislodging the sharpest and arguably strongest, neurologically speaking, piece inside Ultra's brain. Bloodied saliva and bile frothed at its jaws before its skull and limbs went limp.

"Fucking hell, I think you killed it, V," Russo said.

"Just about," she said, still holding the now broken five-foot horn like a victorious yet unimpressed gladiator. She whistled, loud and shrill, without the aid of her fingers, then pressed the transmitter with her free hand. "Roback, load a fresh belt and rally on me."

"You got it."

Zero hesitation. And more than a dash of brio.

"Barley," she radioed. "Area is clear for air support. Requesting immediate SAR."

"Lloyd here, ma'am. I second this. And request prioritization of the Labor District, many of those structures may be low-integrity."

"We read you, Raven. The Captain is making arrangements as we speak to get additional Little Birds to Keign and guarantee airspace security. A SAR exodus will take time, but before sundown we'll have begun."

Vlada remembered her promise to the civilians about not spending another night in this city. Not with it like this—supposing it would ever be the same again.

"I understand you not taking my word for it," Vlada said, and then saw Roback jog up to her—giving the visibly lifeless Ultra a wide berth nonetheless. "But I will happily accompany any SAR effort that welcomes my presence. Anything to expediate the safety and wellbeing of the people of Keign."

"Lima Charlie, Vlada." A pause. Then, Aleem's voice. *"Well fucking done, Raven. All of you."*

"Thank you, sir. We'll also need birds to help get our wounded and dead out."

She couldn't process the fury she would feel if an Apophid got a hold of Gaspar's body, or anyone else's, including the crew of Merlin-Three. It was awful enough, the fate of Keign's many citizens.

"Absolutely," Barley responded. Then her voice picked up a touch of distress. *"The Shadow is picking up movement from the south. Across the park. Maybe a dozen Apophids, mostly Drones."*

"Zealots," Vlada said, despicably. "Stragglers to be dealt

with."

"Condor-One is on it," Barley replied, and as she spoke the Apache rerouted toward the center of Keign. Seconds later, its M230 autocannon was punching out rounds at nearly three-thousand feet-per-second. Vlada wished she could be there to witness the effect of 30mm anti-tank rounds against Apophids. Then Barley redirected her attention. *"A U-Hawk is preparing to dispatch from Pegasus to retrieve you and your fallen. ETA eight minutes, Raven."*

This was great news for the rest of the MSOT, and their casualties. U-Hawks were Sikorsky's unmanned variants of the Black Hawk, ideal for troop transport. With Aleem still skeptical of Keign's airspace security, the U-Hawk was the next best thing.

Not that Vlada intended on leaving the city anytime soon. She didn't know how her superiors would respond to her stubbornness to remain, but if Ginley had any say, she knew he could convince them. She was simply far more fit to remain in the field for extended periods, even under duress, than others. The MSOT had planned to be in Keign for as many as two whole days, but with their losses they could at least use some respite outside the city.

She certainly wouldn't think any less of them for it.

"What've we got?" Roback asked her.

"That thing on auto?" she asked, side-eyeing the hefty machine gun.

He audibly toggled the fire selector.

"Is now."

Vlada nodded. "I still don't trust this thing, frankly." She gestured at Ultra's disgustingly malformed underbelly. Nearly forty yards across, and fifteen high. Its three legs hung from the right side of its body, but were easy to walk around. She raised the broken horn as a weapon, and drew the Taurus with her other hand.

"Well?" Roback said, eyebrows raised. He pointed forward, with his LMG. "Ladies first."

Smirking, head shaking, Vlada advanced.

Her face solemnified. She was grateful her olfactory senses weren't nearly as sensitive to the reek as Roback's, but she wasn't immune to it.

Almost within arm's reach of the underbelly, one huge band of flesh tore away from the main body. The flap landed on the asphalt with a wet sound, and to their relief nothing came barreling out at them. Instead, they were given—cursed with, almost—a better view inside the beast. Grotesque, teardrop-shaped sacs of dull pink flesh were suspended from the pulpy lining of Ultra's innards. In each appeared to be a fetal Drone, subtly twitching with life.

Vlada felt conflicting emotions.

In a way she was relieved to be wrong about the larviposition. But seeing this, now, elicited only disgust.

"The Doc's gonna have a field day with this, huh?" Roback said.

"What's left of it," Vlada said, hatred in her tone.

Before Roback could dissuade her, something along the lines of "preserving evidence," she impaled the nearest sac with Ultra's broken horn. It squirmed and squealed before spilling a vile fluid that preceded its death. Then she swung her other arm, which ended in the hand wielding her Taurus, and knocked down another band of leathery underbelly.

More of Ultra's innards was exposed.

Nearly a dozen of these fetal sacs. Through which some underdeveloped Warriors could be seen, twitching. Roback stopped caring about evidence, curiosity, or science. He aimed his weapon clear of Vlada and fired in six-round bursts, .338 Norma Magnum rounds decimating sacs and punching through sagging organs behind them.

Far left of Roback, and avoiding his arcs of gunfire, Vlada delivered one thrust after another, stabbing fetal Apophids to death. The fetor inside Ultra became intoxicating in a vile way. Dizzying, until she essentially had to be dragged out by Roback.

He began to, at least.

Then she got the message and stormed out on her own

accord. Roback followed, until they were both clear of the huge Behemoth's carcass. He quickly vomited off to the side and then raked in relatively fresh breaths.

"Appreciate your help, and discretion," Vlada told him.

"Anytime," he said, poorly suppressing another disorienting retch.

Lloyd had come around to them, and patted his comrade on the back as he finished vomiting his last rations. But Lloyd made eye contact with Vlada, who herself appeared almost nauseous, as she holstered her Taurus.

"Bet that *cockroach milk* is looking mighty delicious right about now," Lloyd said to her.

She failed to restrain a weak smirk, as well as a disgusted expression of pure humanity.

"That…That *what*?" Roback scowled, looking up at Lloyd.

"Don't worry about it, bud."

Vlada shook her head, and walked toward the rear end of the dead Ultra. The other two followed. She stopped, both hands on the already broken horn, and then cracked it in two more pieces across her knee. She looked into the center, noticing a sort of yellowish, spongy, organic material.

"Souvenirs," she said. "For Dr. Ginley."

"Pegasus will have their work cut out for them," Russo said, appearing around the narrower end of the crater, and Ultra's fallen body. Behind Russo, despite his own hand injury, Arrington helped a now-limping Popov with his other burly arm. De Horta followed, constantly looking around. She imagined he would intensely be more vigilant of his surroundings than he ever was before.

And of insects.

Had none of them experienced arachnophobia before Operation Malathion, this was ground zero.

Vlada lifted her chin, eyes scanning the sky. Dawn was still creeping over Keign, the sun shrugging off its quilt. She could hear helicopter rotors cut through the distance.

"That's your guys' ride," she said. "A U-Hawk, probably

to Pegasus, instead of Base. Better medical care and replenishment."

"Can't say I'm complaining," Roback groaned.

"Same," De Horta said, but then waved back in the direction of his fallen MV-75. "But I'm not leaving without Amir and Viv."

Merlin-Three and his copilot.

Vlada hated that she had never learned their names, or so many others. The casualties of Keign, from the original SFODs of Operation Downpour to the thousands of civilians that had perished over the last eight days. The bulk of deaths had probably occurred in the first few days, but having witnessed some herself, Vlada felt no better about it, wishing they had gone in sooner.

"We'll get 'em out, brother," Roback said, moving to join De Horta.

Part of Vlada suspected he just wanted to get as far from Ultra as possible. And all the dead Apophids littering the parking lot, those that had not been pancaked by Ultra's fallen husk. But she didn't blame him.

"Think they'll figure out how in the hell something this size wound up buried, with no signs of burrowing?" Arrington asked.

"Probably," she said, shrugging. "I have my own postulation, though."

The three operators looked at each other.

"Well, shit," Arrington said. "Postulate away."

"The meteor fragments. Little known fact not shared with the public: DNA used in Project Outreach was extracted from larvae that had burrowed into fungal-lined air pockets of the debris. These larvae vaguely resembled the grubs of Hercules beetles, which can be as big as five inches long and weigh more than a hundred grams. Each Apophid larva was *fourteen inches* long and nearly *two pounds*. But only three were on the fragments, and they never matured. One was DOA. Human intervention, despite HAZMAT measures and decontamination protocols, resulted in the desiccation and death of these larvae.

Of course…not before they mined all the genetic matter they could use for their own agendas."

Vlada scoffed before proceeding. She wanted to avoid a rant about the unaddressed villain. The proverbial elephant in the room—greed for scientific conquest, and power, among amoral men.

And that was just the tip of the iceberg.

"All it would've taken was one larva to find a drain in the area. And the day-one meteor shower made landfall less than a mile from here. Most grubs feed off decaying matter. A drainage pipe would've been a field day. While the others fed on anything from fibers, plants, dust, to dead tissue, and matured at an insane rate, Ultra here was swelling and nestling."

She heard the approach of the U-Hawk from the south, but was undistracted.

"For all we know, it *fed* off brainwaves using the spire. Absorbing neurons in a contactless way that we as humans can't even begin to understand. Who knows how many others in this area have suffered nightmares and seizures. Meanwhile, Ultra was channeling them into its gut…a uterine biome…and catalyzing an internal reproduction phase. One that seems like it was mere hours from its final stage."

The operators were dumbstruck.

Of course, this was all radical speculation. But coming from Vlada, and with such a passionate yet embittered tone, was quite convincing. After a few long and disturbing moments of silent reflection, Arrington posed a theory that he wished he hadn't. Especially if he hoped to sleep someday soon.

"It's possible, then, that whatever was *festering* in Ultra's gut was unlike anything we've seen. They could've even been part human, to some degree, or…"

He stopped himself. That was enough nightmare fuel for a century. Much less the rest of April.

The unmanned U-Hawk was wheels-down behind the Rite Aid, where Roback had been signaling. Whoever the helo's remote pilots were had a good eye, and some common sense—if not direct orders—to avoid going near the enormous fallen

Apophid.

"We need to gather the others," Vlada said. "Gaspar, Lebeau…Wilson, Fuller, Graves…"

Names she had come to know; lives she had never had the chance to.

The operators fanned out, although Vlada herself could easily carry two dead men over her shoulders. To maintain a sense of humanity and carry these slain operators by the shoulders and feet, she paired up with Lloyd. Arrington paired with Russo; despite his severely wounded hand, the sergeant could carry a man with his arms under their shoulders.

"What's next, for you?" Lloyd asked her.

They reached Cris Gaspar.

She hoped De Horta would forgive himself for this. How that minigun had cut down Gaspar so quickly, when Merlin-Three faltered. And Popov, for being where he was, when he was; for being saved.

"It'll be difficult to return to Pegasus, knowing what I do now," she said, squatting by Gaspar. With the same hand used to kill so many Apophids, she exerted meticulous and gentle care to close his eyelids. "But they weren't in the wrong, not really. Not to me."

"And the 'investors'? The higher-ups, responsible for the induced amnesia…the selection for Outreach…" Lloyd shrugged. "That's a crime that almost rivals, if not defeats, what the Apophids have done."

Vlada's brow furrowed. She nodded, looking down at Gaspar, and then to her far right, past an overturned vehicle, where Russo and Arrington hoisted Graves's body.

"You think?" she asked, still watching them.

"The Apophids are…organisms. They spread, kill, eat, propagate, and repeat. We're not terribly different, we just have opposable thumbs."

Vlada huffed and nodded.

Lloyd's voice was steady but grim throughout. When she looked back up at him, as he crouched by Gaspar's feet and slung his rifle, he seemed to look right into her. Not *at* her, and not *through* her, but…

He saw, and understood.

When he said what he proceeded to, she felt new cogs in her turning. Planning, not unlike she had for those three weeks after Axelsen's last crime. Only now she was cleansed of a lot of that torment.

"I'm not saying I don't want to kill them all—the Apophids. I do. And part of me will enjoy it, after what they've done to Keign. But those people…they *deliberated* what they did to you. They *slept* on it. And they *still* do." Lloyd shrugged. "That's just not something I think can be forgiven."

"And would you?" Vlada asked. "Kill them all?"

"The Apophids?"

She shook her head.

"I'd want to rip them limb from limb," he said, bluntly. Then he sighed, and shook his head. He raised his hands—his very human hands, and tried not to smile. The tiniest of smiles. "But I'm just a man."

She smiled…a slightly bigger smile.